THE MIGHTY WARRIORS

D1519744

EDITED BY ROBERT M PRICE

ULTHAR
PRESS

ISBN: 978-1718999138

Published by:
Ulthar Press
700 Metacom Ave.,
Warren, RI 02885
Www.ultharpress.com

ULTHAR
PRESS

CONTENTS

KNOW O PRINCE
AN INTRODUCTION

As I once told L. Sprague de Camp, I owed him my PhD (two, now) because it was his midwifing of the Lancer series of Conan paperbacks that turned me into The Incredible Reading Man. From the day I purchased a copy of *Conan the Warrior* in 1967, I was never the same again. I read voraciously, soaking up the fine vintages of Robert E. Howard, Lin Carter, de Camp himself, Lester Dent, Tolkien, Lovecraft, Edgar Rice Burroughs, and so very many more! In later years I supplemented these favorite authors with many others in various scholarly fields, especially Theology, Philosophy, Comparative Religion, and Biblical Studies. Finally I became friends with Sprague and with Lin Carter. Couldn't believe it! Still can't! Among all those wonderful books I treasure is a pair of Lancer Sword-&-Sorcery collections edited by Hans Stefan Santesson, *The Mighty Barbarians* (1969) and *The Mighty Swordsmen* (1970). Each offered tales old and new, sagas of Conan, Lin Carter's Thongor, Henry Kuttner's Elak of Atlantis, Michael Moorcock's Elric, and others. Each of these treasuries boasted a wonderful Jim Steranko cover. What's not to love?

I never had the pleasure of meeting editor Santesson, though I did, decades later, correspond with his friend and fellow Swede, Per Beskow, a New Testament scholar and author of *Strange Tales about Jesus* (1983). Santesson had departed for Valhalla by then. Still more years passed before I hatched the idea of putting together an homage anthology, a tribute to Santesson and his landmark collections. I loved his approach, combining pulp-era tales of heroic fantasy with new stories continuing the same tradition. The result is this book, *The Mighty Warriors*. I have not included the old stories of the old characters, since all that material is now readily available in many editions. Instead, I have elected to include a few tales starring some familiar heroes, but by new writers.

These avowed pastiches bring back Kuttner's Elak ("Spawn of the Sea God" by veteran fantasy and science fiction author Adrian Cole), Carter's Thongor of Lemuria, and Richard L. Tierney's Simon of Gitta, the most recent of these, but going back into the 1970s). Some will understandably object to my including my own work in an anthology I have compiled (I wrote both "Thongor in the Valley of Demons" and "The Secret of Nephren-Ka"), but please understand. There is indeed no reason for Price to be in this book, but there *is* good reason for Thongor and Simon to be here. So they are, care of me, in attendance.[1] I am Lin Carter's literary executor and have taken it upon myself to continue Thongor's epic with a number of new adventures, collected in my book *The Sword of Thongor*. Similarly, after Dick Tierney's decision to retire from writing, he has given me the blessing to carry on as Simon's chronicler.

These swashbuckling veterans are joined by several newer heroic adventurers whose creators have established a reputation and a troop of admirers in these later years. Charles R. Saunders's champion Imaro debuted in a book of the same name in 1981. David C. Smith's *Oron* appeared on the scene in 1978. Milton J. Davis's titan Changa came on stage a bit later, in *Changa's Safari* (2011). Innovative horror author Cody Goodfellow sets his fantasy tale in Clark Ashton Smith's future super-continent Zothique. Charles R. Rutledge's mighty character Kharrn travels not only around the world but through the ages as well. This story ("Kiss of the Succubus") finds him in the Elizabethan England of Dr. John Dee. Cliff Biggers's protagonist Gondar brings with him, by his very name, echoes of both Howard and Tolkien. In all of these stories, the contributory influences are as evident as the use made of them is innovative.

Japanese horror writer and anthologist Ken Asamatsu's "The Living Wind" further widens the cultural and geographical map in which tales of Sword-&-Sorcery play out. If Imaro and Changa adventured in a mythic Africa, Asamatsu's Ikkyu is a fighting Zen monk in Japan, while Paul McNamee's hero Lono is a Pacific Islander. There is no thought here of feeding the genre through a political grid of "diversity." No, it is simply that Sword-&-Sorcery's instinctive appeal has carried it far and wide. There is nothing tying it to any particular ethnic heritage.

Many of us love Sword-&-Sorcery fiction, not out of mere nostalgia but because the stories summon us back to a time in our lives

---

[1] What? No Conan? The mighty Cimmerian's publishing rights are tied up, and we are not interested in violating copyrights. However, my own Conan pastiche, *Temple of the Black One*, is available for free through Amazon.com.

when we knew that, though we probably resembled Bilbo Baggins more than Aragorn or Boromir, we were called to join a quest to realize our destiny, a goal of character development and the consolidation of virtues. "What if Conan was here today?" Well, he could be. He might be looking back at you from the mirror if you expect to see him there. Joseph Campbell says "the hero with a thousand faces" (Moorcock's Eternal Champion) is meant to model and to inspire the hearer to see that his life, mundane though it seems, is a quest from which, through many setbacks and challenges, he may emerge with the Grail in his grasp.

This is important in a still larger sense. We live in a day when a malaise chokes the land and its pitiful people. Americans and Europeans have succumbed to what Nietzsche called the slave morality, the slave mentality. We scorn heroes, binding them to the ground like the once-towering Gulliver because we do not want to be reminded that we, too, could tower, could rise, could bear the burden of greatness. Conan, Thongor, Elak, Imaro, and their fellows remind us of the heroic possibility.

Robert M. Price
June 7, 2017

SPAWN OF THE SEA GOD

An Elak of Atlantis story
by Adrian Cole

Chapter One: Madness by Moonlight

The huge mound of pillows and piled silken sheets heaved upwards and spilled across the edge of the bed in the brilliant moonlight. From deep within the mound came assorted grunts and groans, culminating in a belch that might have shaken the night watch beyond the sturdy bedroom doors. Something vast and seemingly many-limbed rolled over the bedding and thumped on to the carpet, where it uttered another groan. On the bed, something else snored sonorously, a bangled arm draped over the depression in the sheets left by the incumbent form now sprawled on the floor.

Lycon struggled to his knees, pulling a sheet around his not insubstantial waist. He glanced across at the sleeping Darruvia, who was evidently out for the night. He grinned ruefully. She was his favourite temple dancer – well, she was the only one capable of matching him tankard for tankard when it came to quaffing his preferred Atlantean wine. He'd lost count of the times they'd toasted each other into near oblivion and tumbled into the sheets. He grinned as the moonlight picked out several of her voluptuous curves. By the Nine Hells, it was nearing the time when he'd marry her. It would likely be courting disaster for two such restless spirits, but even so, it was time.

He waddled to the balcony, which opened out on to a view high over the city of Epharra, capital of Atlantis. Westward, across the Bay of Gold, the water shimmered in a reflected glow. Scores of ships, from war galleys to merchants, fishing boats to pleasure rafts, rode gently at anchor in the stillness of the hot night. The air was humid, though it cooled Lycon's skin as he leaned on the outer balustrade. Bel, but he would have to cut down on the wine! It was aging him too soon, and he knew that it was slowing him. He had always been agile for a big man, but these days his burgeoning frame was slowing him down.

He muttered something to himself about getting senile and

was about to go back inside, when he saw an unusual light a few buildings away to his right. He was in the royal palace, never far from the side of his master, the king of Atlantis: the building he studied now was a wing, where high ranking guests were housed when visiting.

Lycon frowned. The rooms where the light, a shimmering bright green iridescence, danced on inner walls, should have been in darkness at this hour. Ambassador Ormundal, lately returned from a mission to the north eastern islands, had delivered his reports to the king hours since and duly retired for the night, expressing his tiredness. Ormundal was not a young man, and his voyage had been exhausting, so his wish for an early night had been granted willingly by his sovereign. And yet his rooms were lit – by strange lights. Lycon's frown deepened.

No longer sluggish, he donned his robe and strapped on a sword. Outside, he slipped over the balcony and on to a flat stone roof beyond. His body protested at this nocturnal extravagance, but he ignored it and clambered across two more roofed areas, keeping to the shadows. He knew where the guards were and was careful not to let them see him. He nestled behind a tall statue, cloaked in shadow, and studied the nearest window of the ambassador's apartments, gasping at what he saw in the room.

Ormundal was in its centre, which had been cleared of furnishings - the ambassador was on his knees, his scrawny upper torso bared. The weird light emanated from three small braziers where the coals burned green - an unnatural, supernatural color. By that bizarre glow, Ormundal's skin seemed to writhe, its muscles twisting as the ambassador raised his arms and wove them like serpents in the smoky air, performing a ritual to who knew what dark god?

The islands from which he had lately come were clouded in mystery and it was to penetrate some of these that Ormundal had been dispatched. He had spoken of alien gods and sorcerers who exercised long lost sorcery in their worship. He'd brought back word of potential alliances with their northern tribes, but Lycon had sensed something sinister beneath the outwardly calm airs of the ambassador. And now, in this writhing green light, Lycon's deep unease grew.

He watched as Ormundal began a chant, using a deep-throated, unfamiliar voice, as though something else spoke through him, a creature of the deep night, not fully human. Around him, the light coalesced, thickening like fog, slowly wrapping round him until his entire shape was a misshapen mass, pulsing and glowing. Lycon cursed under his breath and slipped from the shadows, crossing to another balustrade and climbing over it. He stood just outside the chamber.

The stench of sorcery beyond was palpable, and Lycon felt the source of the power turned on him, licking out through the high window, eager to snare him. He made to thrust forward, but he was held in a clammy grip by invisible fingers, his body shuddering with revulsion at the touch of this living nightmare. He could only watch events unfolding in the chamber where Ormundal was now reacting to the terrible forces that worked on him.

Ormundal's body seemed to grow in size and begin an insane process of tearing at itself, claw-like hands ripping at his own flesh. To Lycon it was as if it boiled, abruptly bursting in several places to emit something – fat, slug-like creatures that flopped on to the stone floor, a score or more of them, dripping with slime that glowed with the same green pallor as the light from the braziers. Ormundal collapsed, drained, and the slug beasts congealed into a unified mass, slithering across the room – Lycon understood with horror it was coming for him.

He used every ounce of his strength to twist from the grip of the malefic forces that held him, then shouted for the guards. His stentorian voice echoed around the buildings of the palace as he broke free and swung his blade down at the globular, parasitic slug thing. It burst in a welter of skin and slime, becoming the component dozen smaller slugs again, quickly sluicing away into the darkness like fleas leaving a carcass. Lycon swept his blade to and fro in a frantic effort to destroy the horrors and it was only the loud hammering on the chamber doors that prevented the things from regrouping and pouring over him.

They swarmed like huge hornets, abruptly passing him, going out on to the balcony and sliding with terrible speed over the balustrade and down into the courtyard below, where the thick shadows smothered them. Lycon dropped his smeared blade and went to Ormundal just as the doors burst open, their bolt shattered by the combined strength of three imperial guards. As they rushed in, they saw Lycon leaning over the fallen Ambassador and assumed he was about to deliver a killer blow. As one they drew back their spears, their target completely at their mercy.

Chapter Two: In the Cold Light of Day

"Hold!" yelled the huge figure, limned in the braziers' light, now no more than a soft, natural glow, and it was only the power in Lycon's voice that prevented him from being skewered by the guards. Slowly they lowered their weapons, recognising him.

On the floor at Lycon's feet, Ormundal groaned, mopping at his brow. He tried to lever himself up and Lycon bent down and helped him to stand, albeit groggily. To Lycon's amazement there was no sign of physical damage to the Ambassador. His chest and abdomen, from where the slug things had burst, showed no sign of the grisly event. His skin was perfectly knitted. Even the clothes were no more than crumpled: there were no tears or evidence of what had transpired.

"Was it you who called us, sire?" one of the guards asked Lycon, his expression perplexed.

"Aye. The Ambassador was under attack."

Ormundal had regained his balance and was dusting himself down. "Attack?" he said. "Who's been attacked?"

"Those – creatures, sire," said Lycon. "I feared for your life." He stood back from Ormundal, who now seemed to be no more than a man roused from a deep sleep. There was nothing on him or in the chamber to suggest that the hellish slug things had been here.

"What creatures?" said the leading guard, immediately studying the room. The three braziers burned low, their eerie green glow dispersed. And the air had cleared of its unnatural stench of earlier. A cool sea breeze drifted in from the balcony.

Lycon went to the window and retrieved his sword. "I cut at least one of them down. Here's the proof –" But his words were cut short as he saw nothing smeared on the blade to support his statement. He looked around him. There were no stains, nothing to indicate what had happened.

Ormundal came to him and smiled indulgently. "Ah – I appreciate your concern for my well-being, Lycon, but I really don't think there's any need for this. A good night's sleep should be enough to settle all our nerves."

Lycon nodded, realising it was not going to be a good time to protest. He did not know the Ambassador well, though Ormundal was a man in whom the king invested his trust. If he was party to something sinister, it would need to be investigated discreetly.

At the door, a fourth soldier had appeared. Braxis, the sergeant of the watch, was glaring at Lycon as though in deep disapproval. It was no secret in court that the two men had little time for each other. Braxis, grizzled veteran though he was, made no secret of his ambitions to attain the higher ranks, but Lycon knew that Braxis resented his own unique relationship with Elak, the young king, and would have liked nothing more than to supplant him.

"What has happened here?" Braxis snapped.

"A little misunderstanding, that's all," said Ormundal reasonably. "Lycon seemed to think I was in some kind of danger and, good fellow that he is, sought to – ah, rescue me."

Braxis walked over to the open window. "You entered through here?" he said bluntly to Lycon.

Lycon stood beside him. "I heard sounds and saw something—"

"The celebrations in court were long and a little on the exuberant side, tonight," said Braxis quietly, his meaning clear. "Some of the revellers were notably – intoxicated – by the end of it."

Lycon glared at the man in fury. "By Ishtar! What are you suggesting? That I imagined the whole affair?"

"It's none of my business who the king choses to stand by his side, but if it were left to me, I'd be wary of putting my trust in someone whose love of the vine so obviously clouds his reason."

Lycon would have exploded with wrath, but he could see the Ambassador waiting patiently, watching them uncomfortably. There would be time to settle this insubordination later.

"I apologise for disturbing you, sire" Lycon said. "I'll let you sleep. I suggest, though, that you close and secure the window for the rest of the night. As a precaution."

"Of course," said Ormundal. "And thank you again for your concern."

Lycon left the chamber, with Braxis and his three guards close at his heels. Lycon paid them no further heed, turning away down another corridor, back to his own chambers. He could feel the eyes of the sergeant burning into his back. Sooner or later he was going to have to deal with the man.

In his bedchamber, Lycon set aside his weapon and disrobed. Darruvia was still happily snoring among the pillows, oblivious to all that had happened. As Lycon slid into bed beside her, he knew the accursed Braxis was partly right.

I do drink too much. I'm over my fortieth year and my body protests more frequently these days. And people know it. Yet I saw what I saw. Those creatures were as real as I am. There was sorcery at work. This business is not over yet.

His thoughts proved prophetic, as the next morning, shortly after Darruvia had slipped away in the dawn light, he received another visitor. Zerrahydris, a member of the city Council, entered the chambers, looking around in his supercilious manner, clearly disapproving of Lycon's loose life style.

"Word has come to me, Lycon, that there was something of an altercation last night. Ambassador Ormundal was concerned you might not have quite been yourself. He was being diplomatic. We all know about your propensity for –"

"I was not drunk, if that's what you're implying! Ishtar, I saw things –"

"That no one else saw, yes, I understand. Look, Lycon, you're favoured by the king, so we have to make allowances for you. But you go too far."

"Ormundal was in danger! I know sorcery when I see it. Something evil was at work in those chambers. And we haven't heard the last of it. Whatever it was, it's loose in the city. Ormundal may not realise it, but he brought something back with him from the northern isles -something that will work its deviltry on Atlantis."

Zerrahydris frowned, waiting for the angry flow of words to stem. "I see. Then we will be vigilant."

It was clear to Lycon that the Councillor didn't believe a word he'd said.

"I'll take a squad of guards and begin a search –" Lycon began, but Zerrahydris waved his words away.

"No, I think it would be better for the time being if you just waited things out, Lycon. Here in your chambers."

"The king will not be pleased."

"I don't see the need to disturb the king. He's enough business on his plate as it is. Ormundal will be with him today. They have much to discuss. By the gods, Lycon, you must understand that the situation with the northern isles is very delicate. If we are to negotiate with them, we need to exercise tact and diplomacy, not run amok with a sword, stabbing at every wine-induced shadow that raises its head!

"You're a liability. Leave politics to your betters. That's an order." Zerrahydris turned on his heel and left Lycon, mouth agape, as the doors closed and he heard the keys turn in the lock. He was to be a prisoner in his own chambers. And whatever was loose in the city would have a free reign.

Chapter Three: At the Sign of the Twisted Crab

Elak brooded. He sat in a small antechamber to the throne room where he occasionally met with his counsellors, ambassadors and advisors, of which there seemed to be far too many these days. Lycon had teased him about the burden of kingship, but there was no avoiding it. The young king – he had seen twenty eight summers - looked at the man opposite him, Zerrahydris, a strong supporter, but a man given to constant anxieties about protocol, procedures and diplomacy. He might not approve of the young king's tendency to take to the field and involve himself personally in affairs of state, but he was, to be fair to him, as staunchly loyal as any of Elak's politicians.

"I'm sorry, sire, but I have to speak my mind. I have no doubt at all that Lycon is worthy of your trust and would be the first to rush to your defence, but there comes a time when you simply cannot afford to take risks. His drinking –"

"Lycon could drink an inn dry before he compromised my safety."

"With respect, sire, the Council does not share that view."

Elak glared. "Lycon has saved my life on more than one occasion. Usually by putting his own in peril. He is like a brother to me."

"No one doubts his loyalty, his unswerving dedication to your causes. But last night's episode –"

"You say Ormundal slept, unmolested, only to be woken up by Lycon, who claimed to have seen supernatural forces? Yet you claim these were delusions, the result of too much wine. Lycon has over-imbibed before. It does not usually result in him seeing imaginary evils."

"He had a sword, sire. The guards feared for the Ambassador. In his drunken state, who knows what Lycon would have done?"

Elak growled his displeasure at the statement. "Well, we'll know soon enough. I've sent for Lycon. He will be here shortly. We will quiz him together." The king sat back. Doubtless Zerrahydris had acted in the best interests of the throne, but Lycon would be full of volcanic fury at having been virtually imprisoned in his chambers.

After a while there was a sharp knock on the door. Zerrahydris opened it and admitted two guards, one of whom was Braxis. Both men looked more than a little disturbed.

"Where's Lycon?" said Zerrahydris.

"Apologies, sires," said Braxis. "He was not in his chambers. We have searched the surrounding rooms, but we cannot find him. My men are widening the search."

Elak masked his amusement. "Bring Lycon to me as soon as you can. He will probably resist your efforts, but if you make it clear I want to see him, there'll be no need for excessive violence."

Braxis hid his own exasperation poorly, but bowed and left with his companion.

Zerrahydris turned back to the king. "This grows increasingly more unsatisfactory. Lycon will make fools of us all. I can't be responsible for the Council's views, sire. They won't allow things to continue as they are."

"I respect their *views*, Zerrahydris, but I believe my commands still hold sway here in Epharra."

"Of course, sire. Let us hope Lycon can be found."

They were interrupted by a second knock on the chamber doors. This time an escort ushered in Ormundal, who came before Elak and bowed. The king rose and took the Ambassador's hand.

"I gather you had a disturbed night. I am sorry to hear that."

Ormundal waved away Elak's apology. "Ah - it was nothing, sire. One of your retainers overdid the wine and imagined I was being assaulted by demons. Ironically, I think the demons were taunting him."

"What exactly did Lycon say?"

"Ah, he said there were creatures. He claimed he'd killed at least one. He went to the window to show me its corpse, but there was none. No blood on Lycon's sword."

"Where were you when this happened? Asleep in your bed?"

The Ambassador looked momentarily puzzled. "Well, I, ah – no, sire. I must have got out of bed. I had been asleep. I was praying."

"You got up in the middle of the night to pray? Had you been disturbed prior to Lycon's entry? Were you afraid of something?"

"I don't think so, sire. I don't quite recall. I may have had a nightmare. My visit to the northern isles was at times, unnerving. I confess I've not slept well since."

Elak had returned to his seat, but he stood coolly regarding the two men. "You slept unsoundly, got up and prayed. At that point, Lycon burst in. Did he, perhaps, see you praying and assume something was amiss?"

"My memory is very clouded, sire." Ormundal looked a little embarrassed.

"When Lycon is brought to us," said Elak, "we'll have a better understanding. If he cannot justify his actions, well, he'll have to take the consequences." The king knew he'd need to mollify the Council somehow, so Lycon would have to repent his actions if indeed they had been no more than a drunken lapse.

However, by midday, the city guard had still not been able to discover the whereabouts of the king's right hand man. It was unlikely now, Elak thought, they would find him. Taking two of his personal guards with him, Elak went to Lycon's quarters. The rooms were something of a mess, and a hint of perfume lingered in the air. Elak smiled grimly to himself. Lycon had never enjoyed being cosseted within the city walls. Elak, however, did find what he was looking for. A sign, meant for his eyes only.

There were a few small statuettes in the bedroom, one of which was a crude representation of Bel, and at her feet there were various creatures hewn out of onyx, including a small crab. It had been twisted to one side, almost off its base. Only Elak knew what it meant.

He returned to his quarters and waited until evening, calling two of his most trusted bodyguards to him. He explained what he wanted and donned a thick, hooded cloak, also strapping on his rapier. As darkness fell, the three men slipped away from the king's quarters. They made their way out into the citadel, the two guards smoothing their passage with other guards who halted them, maintaining Elak's anonymity, but saying they were on the king's business. In this way they entered the most insalubrious quarter of the city, a section of the docks where only the most disreputable and dubious of captains and crews set foot.

Along one small quay, its sides jammed with ships that bobbed on the evening tide, the three men came to a tavern, its leaning sign proclaiming it to be *The Twisted Crab*, and slipped inside. Although the two king's guards caused more than a few eyebrows to be raised, they were known to the packed company of freebooters and smugglers. Elak, still hooded, was taken to a small room overhead, his two guards posted at its door.

In the low-ceilinged room, Elak at last took off the heavy cloak. A stubby candle threw him into vague relief. He grinned at the solitary occupant of the room, who sat morosely at its table.

"Well," said the king. "You've really stirred up the hornet's this time, my friend."

Chapter Four: News from the Dark Island

"By the Nine Hells, it was no drunken dream!" Lycon said for the fourth time. "It may have been some sorcerer's work, but it had the feel of reality to it."

Elak sat opposite his friend, a restrained grin on his face.

16

"Well, I may be the only one who's taking you seriously. Rest assured that I am. These – creatures. Have you seen anything like them before?"

Lycon shook his head. "Not that size. Their color was sickly in that green light and they had the strangest mouths, full of writhing tongues, like a nest of worms. Nightmarish, I admit that."

"You say they burst *out of* the Ambassador?"

"As though he had been carrying them."

"And they disappeared out into the city? Do you think they'll infect others? Is that why they're here?"

"Aye," said Lycon. "Nothing from those northern islands is to be trusted. Ormundal may have been duped. He may be oblivious to what happened."

"I've not had reason to distrust him thus far. He's done good work for the kingdom, as his father did before him. A most loyal family."

There was a knock on the door. Lycon jerked upright, but Elak waved him back to his seat. The king inched the door open, spoke quietly and then admitted a lone soldier. The man saluted stiffly, a youth a few years younger than Elak.

"Thank you for coming, Jordis. Lycon, this is one of the crew of the ship that took Ormundal to the northern isles and brought him back. He was acting as my eyes."

Jordis bowed to Lycon and gave his report. "The principal island is Umaarsquu, and by far the largest of the group. Its central volcano rises high into the clouds, although it sleeps. It has a port and a citadel high up on the volcano's crags, difficult to reach. We saw strange creatures flying through the mists above its upper parapets. Ormundal was received, along with a small group of us, in the port."

"How long were you there?" said Elak.

"Three days and nights, sire. Ormundal had his own quarters. We were put in another chamber."

"You were present at the meetings with Kar-Kazool, the ruler? Party to the discussions?"

"Yes, sire. They were conducted politely and without argument. Kar-Kazool gave the impression that his people were willing to accept an alliance with the empire. We were expecting to see a show of strength, many arms. Yet we saw none. There were few retainers, all of them garbed simply and saying very little. It may have been a deception, but Kar-Kazool seemed to desire to show a peaceful attitude."

Lycon growled deep in his huge chest. "Indeed? A change of mood, given the aggression we're familiar with in those waters."

Elak was nodding thoughtfully. "You've seen action in the past, Jordis. Did this new approach from Kar-Kazool strike you as out of character?"

"I have to admit, sire, it did. It was not unlike visiting the lair of a serpent, only to find the beast dormant. Yet we were treated well and Kar-Kazool spoke only in friendly terms."

"What of the Ambassador? Did he seem in any way changed, especially after his nights apart from you? Speak truthfully."

Jordis frowned, looking a little awkward. "If anything, sire, he seemed almost too content. The Ambassador is not a stern man and enjoys conversation with his men. Not over-familiar, but he has a warmth. On the return voyage he was far more affable. One of the men joked that he may have been at the wine."

"Something had pleased him?" said Lycon. "You mean the negotiations?"

"Yes, he deemed the visit to Kar-Kazool a success, but it was more than that."

"Did you see anything else at the citadel, or in the waters in its bay that concerned you?"

Jordis gave a brief shudder. "The atmosphere there is uncomfortable. Something permeates it, sire. You'd have to experience it —"

"Sorcery?" said Lycon.

"Yes, sire. If I had to give it a name. The seas around the islands are dark and sluggish. They are full of repellent weed and the passage through it to Umaarsquu is fraught with peril. And the weed is alive. Things crawl over and through it. We all felt something much larger dwelt underneath us, and more than once the lookouts claimed to see humped shapes in the water. Not the sea beasts we are familiar with."

Lycon described the large slug-like things he had seen in Ormundal's chamber. "Did you see their like?"

18

Jordis nodded. "Yes! The weed in the harbour was thick with them, as though the inhabitants of the city's port farmed them, as we assumed. We saw a few in the main building itself —"

Lycon again growled. "Indeed! Where was this?"

"There were deep pools within the main area, where we met with Kar-Kazool and his retainers. The creatures dwelt in the pools. Not in great number. Where we have fish and other sea creatures in our palace pools to provide color and a restful atmosphere, Kar-Kazool's people have these."

"For viler reasons," said Elak. "It is becoming much clearer. These slug beasts are parasites, Lycon. And Ormundal, probably un-wittingly, brought home a host of them."

Jordis looked appalled. "Sire? We saw nothing of the creatures on our return."

"No," said Elak. "They were well hidden. And the last thing they wanted was to be discovered before they reached us. Jordis — go back into the city and have as many men as you can muster from the crew. Search everywhere for any word of these creatures. They're here and Ishtar alone knows what havoc they mean to wreak. Bring me a full report by sunset."

After Jordis had gone, Lycon was balling his fists in fury. "Kar-Kazool means to use these things to infect us and spy on us — or worse."

"Aye. I never trusted him."

"This is the worst possible time. I mean, with the coming wedding."

Elak cursed. "Of course! This is no coincidence. Kar-Kazool knows Epharra will be flooded with people from across all of Atlantis. By Ishtar, that's it! He means to infect as many as possible so that they'll take the parasites back with them. All Atlantis will be tainted."

"You're going ahead with the wedding, then?"

Elak looked glum. "Gods, but I'm torn, Lycon. My cousin Illyrin and I have been close friends since we were little more than babes, and I love her dearly. But more as a sister! And she feels the same as I do. It may well suit the empire to have our two families welded into an even stronger one. She confided to me she has a secret lover she'd rather have for a husband. She loves him as a wife should. I'm not ready to settle."

"You could postpone the wedding. It's not too late."

"I'll have to. You and I must visit Umaarsquu. With the mood of the Counsellors, it'll have to be a secret voyage."

Chapter Five: Death after Sunset

Zerrahydris frowned, his three closest colleagues shifting uncomfortably in their seats. "I cannot help but express my concern," said Zerrahydris. "Our king is a remarkable young man and I know full well how he cares for the empire. Yet this propensity for adventure compromises his safety and the stability of the throne. As for that wine-sodden companion of his, Lycon, well, he has far too much influence. I am sure he actually disapproves of the wedding. By the Nine Gods, it would be the one way we might expect Elak to settle down to the business of ruling!"

Later, Zerrahydris had his frustrations compounded as Elak sent for him. "I'm thinking of delaying my wedding until this business is concluded," said the king, his face set.

Zerrahydris was barely able to control his exasperation. He had toiled long and hard to finalise the preparations for the coming grand occasion and it was no secret at court that he was deeply frustrated by the king's apparent prevarication. Elak knew how much the Counsellor opposed what they called his escapades.

"Sire," said Zerrahydris, "surely the northern alliance can wait. It would be a pity to have Kar-Kazool think we consider him more important than a royal wedding. If we let him see that our affairs come first, it will set a powerful precedent."

Elak knew Zerrahydris had a valid point. However, there was no time to lose over this strange affair with the parasitic creatures. Elak had deliberately said nothing about it. He knew the Council would be horrified if they thought he was standing by Lycon. Elak's credibility would be compromised. This was no time to present enemies of the empire with any kind of advantage.

"I need time to think," said Elak. "A postponement may be unavoidable."

The Councillors left, clearly disappointed, muttering to themselves, barely avoiding outright rebellion. For the moment, they would respect the wishes of the king. Elak entered a private chamber and spoke to Dalan, the Druid, whose powers and advice he had often called on in difficult times.

"We must root out the parasites," said Elak. "Ishtar knows how they might spread."

"I will gather my acolytes," said Dalan. "There will be ways to find these creatures."

"Can your followers achieve it without you?" said the king.

Dalan's batrachian features screwed up in puzzlement. "I am a focal point for their powers —"

"Yes, but must you be here in the city? Can you not direct your sorcery from afar?"

"It would be less puissant, but it could be done."

"I intend to sail secretly for Umaarsquu before dawn, and I want you with me. We will pay Kar-Kazool an unexpected visit. It's a dangerous strategy, but I've had success with it in the past. There's sorcery at work in the north and we must fight fire with fire."

"I see. Very well. I'll make the arrangements."

Later, Elak returned incognito to *The Twisted Crab* where Lycon paced the small room above the inn like a caged beast, his nerves frayed, his patience shredding. Elak saw, to Lycon's credit, that the big man had not consoled himself with a flagon or two of wine. As the sun was setting, Jordis returned.

"We've had mixed success, sire," he said. "Several people have been detained and Dalan's acolytes have performed their cleansing rituals." Jordis looked uneasy, as though what he'd witnessed had been far more disturbing than he liked to admit. "The hunt continues. Dalan is certain that there are more of these - things - at large."

"Is the *Sea Skimmer* prepared for the ocean?" said Elak, referring to his favorite warship, the sleekest craft in his navy.

Jordis's face immediately brightened. "Of course, sire. Grondal is aboard. Should you wish to put to sea —"

"One hour. Have the crew fully armed, and have berths for three additional passengers."

Lycon, at last, was grinning.

The sun had slipped down into the west and the night heavens were rapidly losing their bruised, purple hues as Elak, Lycon and Dalan threaded their silent way through the narrow passages and alleys down to the quayside. Elak had deliberately had his ship moored at the far end of the naval docks, where it would be less conspicuous. There were evening revellers filling the various taverns along the main quay; otherwise few people moved through the darkness. Elak and his colleagues were not far from the *Sea Skimmer* when they found their way cut off by a sudden gathering - a dozen figures came sliding out of the shadows like phantoms.

Lycon spun round with a curse, pulling his sword free. Another dozen shapes were following.

Dalan lifted his staff, its runes glowing faintly as if it burned with an inner fire. "As for the remaining parasites," he said to Elak, "they have come to us."

In affirmation of his words, the figures closed in, now recognisable bizarrely as men and women of varying ages, a most unlikely mob of assailants. The first of them dropped to their knees, their chests and abdomens swelling obscenely before bursting to release the foul slug creatures that Lycon had seen in the palace. Scores of the things slithered across the stones of the alley, both ahead of and behind Elak and his companions. Dalan raised his staff high and brilliant white light fizzed from its globular tip, spearing outwards. Where it struck among the sea creatures, small eruptions of flame seared the darkness and scorched the flesh of the slugs, many of them bursting hideously. Lycon swung his blade to and fro like a scythe, relieved to be able to vent his pent up anger, carving several creatures apart in a welter of thick slime. Elak, too, was busily engaged with his rapier, cutting into the flesh of these stinking terrors. It seemed as though wave upon wave of the monsters must overcome the three fighting men, but Dalan's staff proved too much for them, its sorcerous fires incandescent and irresistible.

By the time the nearby ship's crew were alerted to the conflict by the strange light, and had come to assist, Elak was pulling his sword free of the last slaughtered creature. The alley stank of death, a twitching mound of the slug things steaming in the pale lamplight. The original hosts of the parasites were staggering to their feet, puzzled by their situation. Elak was relieved to see they were all unscathed, just as Ormundal had been when he'd been infected.

"With luck," said the Druid, "that's the last of them. You would have been their prime target, Elak. However, my acolytes will be watchful while we're away."

Grondal, the *Sea Skimmer's* captain, came forward, studying the king with relief. "You are unharmed, sire?"

Elak wiped his rapier clean of the thick blood of the fallen. "I am. Is the ship ready?"

Grondal nodded. Even in the dim light, he was scarcely able to conceal his pleasure, only too eager to be back at sea.

"Set a course for the northern isles," said Elak. "We leave immediately."

Chapter Six: The Island of Secrets

Elak, Lycon and Dalan studied the crude charts with Grondal up near the prow of the speeding war galley, its curved sail billowing in the fierce breeze. An hour after dawn they were far from Epharra, having slipped their moorings without anyone significant noticing. At the port's mouth they'd signalled the watch they were on patrol duties, and Elak knew it would be well into morning before he was missed in the city, where he'd left a message to say he was at sea on a vital mission.

"These charts are not entirely reliable, sire," said Grondal. "Though they show as much as is known about Umaarsquu and the waters around it."

"I take it you have a plan?" Dalan said to Elak.

Elak pointed to the map's north coastline of the island. "We must rely on stealth. And assume we will be met with hostility. This northern coast is the worst. Very high cliffs, their base not approachable by a craft of any size. In fact, the eastern and western cliffs are not much better. I can see why the place is a stronghold. Its only navigable entry point is easily defended, a perfect harbour."

"The skies above the island's peaks are rarely clear," said Grondal. "I have seen the place. Its volcano slumbers, but clouds cover it perpetually. It is unnatural. And there are sky beasts that dwell on the crags. They keep a constant watch, attacking anything that intrudes."

Elak grinned. "So we'd be unlikely to stumble into Kar-Kazool's guards up there."

Lycon was also smiling, but Dalan grimaced. "There are ways to deceive the watchers, but the use of sorcery would almost certainly alert Kar-Kazool."

"He'll concentrate on the seas," said Elak. "Particularly when we create a diversion. You, Grondal, will keep Kar-Kazool's people occupied while I take a small company up the cliffs and into the heart of the citadel."

"With what purpose, may I ask?" said Dalan.

"We'll abduct Kar-Kazool and bring him back with us."

"An excellent plan!" said Lycon. "One I'll happily drink to!"

Astonished, Dalan studied the young king for several moments. "A dangerous ploy. If we fail, either we'll be executed or Kar-Kazool will use us to bargain with Epharra, and with crippling effect."

"Why should we fail?" said Elak. "Our gods are with us. Our cause is just. And we are resolute." It was clear from his tone that he would brook no arguments.

Elak, Lycon and the captain studied the charts in more detail after that, while Dalan positioned himself at the prow of the boat, using his unique powers to test the winds, as though he could scent within them knowledge of whatever moved in the deep ocean around them. He knew it would be difficult to voyage to Umaarsquu unseen, certain that Kar-Kazool would have his own ships patrolling the restless waves. The *Sea Skimmer* must outrun them, but would have to be disguised.

As Dalan studied the waves and the horizon that rose and fell, he realised with a start that the ship was veering to the west of her goal. At this rate of progress, she would soon be far off her original course. He felt a presence behind him and turned to see Elak smiling almost mischievously.

"Yes, I've had Grondal change our course," said the king. "There's a small archipelago out to the west. Nothing but gulls and seals and the like. It's a pirate watering hole. Not known to many, but I have more than a few friends among them. Never mind how. The island will be the perfect place for us to prepare."

Dalan raised an eyebrow. "You plan to disguise us all as *pirates*?"

"Not quite. But the ship and the crew need to be cloaked as best they can. I'm sure I can leave the details to you, Dalan. We'll make the final approach to Umaarsquu's waters from the north, out of a thick fog. My small company can be landed before Kar-Kazool's people are any the wiser. Grondal will then take the *Sea Skimmer* around the island and draw their sting."

"I can easily organise that," said the Druid. "It will be the one part of this operation that'll be child's play."

"It might not be so easy to do from the top of the island."

Dalan scowled as understanding dawned. "You want me to go with your party?"

"Of course. You're the best weapon I have."

A week later the *Sea Skimmer* was cutting through the waves of the western ocean, wrapped in a persistent fog drawn around the sleek war galley by Dalan's craft. On the voyage the crew were aware of movement under them in the deeps, as well as shapes flitting across the skies, far too large to be gulls or even albatrosses. Finally the word came from the masthead that there was land ahead. They had reached the pirate archipelago. As far as they knew, they had come here unobserved by any of Kar-Kazool's spies.

The main island was flat, topped with rich jungle verdure, approached by treacherous sand banks. Dalan was obliged to assist the helmsman to steer through them, perilously twisting and winding. Had the ship snagged on any of them, it would have meant a disastrous, possibly fatal grounding. Slowly the *Sea Skimmer* was rowed through the last of the tortuous approaches and beached in a shallow lagoon, close to the mouth of a narrow river that slipped in from the heart of the island.

"We'll anchor for the night," said Elak. "Dalan, stay with the ship and keep prying eyes from us. I'll take a small party ashore."

Dalan scowled. "I can't protect you from the island –"

"You won't have to." Elak grinned. "The inhabitants are few, and they won't be hostile." He went among the crew, selecting those he would take with him.

Lycon could see the Druid's concerns. "If the Council knew half of the escapades the king has been up to these last few years, they'd wet themselves," he said.

"He's the king," said Dalan. "I know the gods seem to favour him – how else could he have survived this long? But this is a reckless quest, Lycon. This island is not safe. I sense something deeply evil here."

"Maybe. Yet Elak has forged many alliances on his travels, not least with the pirates. No one else could have done it. It's taken his nerve, his courage, to face them personally, to fight alongside them at times. They respect him. Soon, I think, most of them will be a part of the empire."

"They are here?"

"A few. We go to meet them."

Shortly afterwards, the Druid watched as Elak and Lycon led their small party out on to the sand flats along the riverside. As the king slipped into the evening shadows, Dalan suppressed a shudder. It was true. Elak had carved a reputation for himself out among the scattered lands and islands of empire. The Council at home, who would have had Lycon thrown out, were men who'd never tasted the heady wine of battle, or its terrors. A wine, Dalan thought, that Elak's moody spirit seemed to need, more so since he had become king. Of late, something troubled him, something unspoken. There was a shadow behind his ready smiles.

Chapter Seven: Island of Terror

Deep into the night the strangely silent jungle disgorged a small party of figures. Dalan had kept watch himself, fretting over the safety of the king – the longer they were on this island, the more Dalan's deep unease grew. It was as much as he could do to maintain the invisible barrier he had erected, the sorcery taxing his powers.

It was Lycon who headed the company, hailing the *Sea Skimmer* in a voice that was almost smothered by the thick night. Moments later Elak and his men had clambered aboard, bringing with them a solitary figure. Dalan knew the young man immediately for a pirate. He had the neutral clothes and deep tan of one of the ocean's scavengers, although he favoured the Druid with a dazzling smile.

"This is Vorganis," said Elak. "One of Queen Shiveeri's captains."

Dalan knew the pirate queen had promised fealty to the Atlantean throne, thanks to another of Elak's wild adventures. Elak had a way of speaking her name that made Dalan smile.

"I am charged by my queen to provide you with anything I know," said the pirate and he sounded convincing. "You are seeking Umaarsquu."

"Vorganis tells me," said Elak, "that our plan to scale the northern cliffs is doomed to fail."

Dalan grunted. "We know well enough the cliffs and their defenders will be daunting."

"However," said Elak, his spirits not in the least curbed, "Vorganis knows of an alternative way into the island."

"Aye," said the pirate. "There's a place along the northern coast where the cliffs have been riven by ancient volcanic activity. Invisible from the sea, the huge gash cuts deep into Umaarsquu and at certain tides it is possible to enter and use the path. It is very dangerous – the waters drag and there may be other guardians, set there by the islanders."

"You've seen it?" said Dalan.

Vorganis beamed. "Aye, sire. And wound my way into the guts of the mountain. Once past the sea's clutches, it's possible to climb high up, under the very brow of the citadel. I've not been there, but I've seen its walls."

"He'll point the way," said Elak, clapping Vorganis on the shoulder.

"I'll do better, sire. I'll lead you in!"

Lycon laughed. "I think we should get this man a tankard or two of ale."

Dalan was about to remind Lycon that the *Sea Skimmer* did not carry ale, wine or any other potent drink, but realised that he was in all likelihood mistaken.

Shortly after dawn the galley again manoeuvred through the convoluted sand banks and out into open water. Dalan, who for once had slept deeply, reinstated the fog that clung to the vessel as she swung round to the north east and set a heading for the deep waters north of Umaarsquu.

It took several more days for the war galley to reach a point where it could turn southwards and approach the island with the least possibility of being discovered. Dalan still felt the unseen presences both below the ship and in the fog-snarled heavens, but there had been no attacks, no skirmishes. At length, still wrapped within the moonlight-drenched fog, the *Sea Skimmer* was within a few miles of the immense northern cliffs of Kar-Kazool's island.

They could hear the roar of the ocean as it flung itself incessantly at those cliffs, clouds of thick mist and spray cloaking everything in blurred detail, the waters at the base of the cliffs foaming, swirling viciously and flinging high columns of spume upwards. Vorganis guided the ship to within two miles of the place where he insisted they would find the high crevice, but for now a combination of wild seas and darkness completely obscured the passage from view.

Dalan watched the skies. There were more of the invisible aerial creatures diving and circling up there, and it taxed him to screen the ship from their eyes. He knew they plunged into the ocean to feed and perhaps it would be enough to satisfy them. The cliffs, however, were slick with their droppings, the nests covering huge areas of rock, an avian citadel that would have been impossible to cross. Vorganis's way in was indeed the only hope.

Three hours after dawn, the pirate came to Elak and Lycon. "The tide is receding," he said. "It is still high and the channel will be treacherous. In a few days it will be a little safer –"

Elak shook his head. "If we are found, Kar-Kazool will snare us for certain. We have to act now, while we can still surprise him."

Vorganis grinned. "Very well. Ready your small boats."

Elak's selected company was comprised of two dozen warriors, with Lycon and Dalan included. Three small craft rowed out from the *Sea Skimmer*, watched by its captain, Grondal, who grumbled for a while at not being able to accompany the king. However, he soon had his hands full keeping the ship from being run aground on the merciless rocks of the coast. Elak had told him to make all speed back to Atlantis if the company had not returned in two days. The Empire would have to be told of events, in preparation for what would follow, almost certainly war.

Vorganis stood in the dipping prow of the small boat as the warriors rowed it through the first of the churning seas at the base of the cliffs. The craft swung high and dipped low, sheets of spray drenching its occupants as it made inexorably for the tall cleft which only now had become visible. It was only a matter of yards across and steering the three boats into it was a terrifying process, all of them within inches of being smashed to pulp on the rock fangs. The tide surged and one by one each craft broke through into the opening, still buffeted by the waves, trapped like fish between the jaws of the defile.

The path, carved by ceaseless waves over the centuries from a horizontal fault in the rocks, was slick with weed, exposed only at low tide, and was as treacherous a way into the chasm as by water. Vorganis chose a place where he made a leap upward, gripped the rock and swung like an ape on to the path, holding the mooring rope in desperation. He shouted back to Elak, and the king urged his boats further in, where the sunlight overhead dimmed and threatened to disappear as they pushed on below the jutting overhang. Other warriors joined Vorganis on the path, barely able to make their way along it. Deep inside the cleft there was a shallow beach, heaped pebbles pulverised by the waves. Vorganis had told Elak that the boats could be secured here for a short time, a matter of hours before the tide turned and raced in once more, like a giant fist. They had to be away before that happened.

There was another path, a natural defile in the chasm, and Vorganis, still grinning as though he had never been more content, ushered Elak and his bedraggled company upward. As they climbed, they heard the roar of the ocean far below, snarling like a frustrated beast.

Chapter Eight: Citadel on the Edge

They wormed their way through the labyrinthine veins of the volcano, along dead, tubular passages where lava had long since ceased to flow. Vorganis amazed the company by knowing each twist and turn, despite the vague filter of light that found its way down from above. Elak grinned – it was a pirate gift. Once they found a treasure cache, they never forgot its whereabouts. The hours drifted by until Vorganis paused, listening, as if he could hear the rocks grinding out messages.

"Kar-Kazool's port is at the south of the island," he said.

Jordis, the warrior who had escorted Ambassador Ormundal on his visit, was nodding. "Aye. We were taken there." ·

"Beyond the city," Vorganis went on, "high on the upper crags of the volcano's rim is another citadel. It is Kar-Kazool's retreat. If you are to surprise him with an attack, it is that citadel you will have to enter. No man other than his servants has ever been inside it. It hangs like an eagle's nest on its vertical pinnacle. The only way to reach it is from the air."

Dalan's face clouded like the threat of thunder. "We have come this far to learn this?" he growled.

Vorganis was grinning. "However," he went on, unmoved by the Druid's glare, "there is a narrow crack in the stone. It will permit an agile man to climb."

"Where does it breach the citadel?" said Elak.

"Not sure," said Vorganis. "We'll have to trust to the gods."

Dalan's temper teetered on the brink of explosion, and Lycon looked similarly appalled. Elak, however, was laughing softly. It was the sort of challenge he relished.

Vorganis appeared to be only too glad to lead on.

It was not a large island and by nightfall the company had reached the southern rim of the volcano. They were able to exit from the tunnels and camp under the curving walls that rose up to the volcano's lip. High overhead, in the dying rays of the sun, they could see the ancient stones of Kar-Kazool's citadel. Its architecture was strange, as though its builders had been other than human, its spires and curved walls mocking the eye, the entire structure apparently defying gravity as it hung there like some outrageous alien craft. The lights that shimmered in its long, slitted windows were baleful, unwelcoming.

Several times in the night, shapes flapped across the misty upper air of the crater, huge creatures that called to each other in raucous voices, the beating of their wings lost in the night as they flew to and fro across the gaping maw of the volcano, while up from below the plumes of smoke curled and twisted like the last exhalations of a vast campfire. Elak studied the sky beasts for a while before sleep claimed him. In his dreams he saw again the flying creatures, and upon their broad backs there were hunched figures, dark and demonic, crying their alarms in the wind.

Once dawn had established its new light, the party again took to the tunnels, Vorganis searching several low vents for the one he promised would take them up into the citadel. As they moved upwards, they were all aware of a foetid stench, the pungent smell of rotting meat and offal. There were wider chambers off the passage where daylight played on grisly scenes – the sky creatures brought their prey here and fed, casting aside what they had not eaten. Here, too, were endless mounds of excrement, the detritus of years, its fumes assailing the company so the men fought to avoid choking. They knew if they were discovered by the beasts, they would be eaten alive.

Eventually Vorganis brought them to an almost vertical flue. It disappeared up into the high darkness, suggesting an endless ascent.

"That's easy enough for a pirate monkey to climb," said Lycon.

"It's either that," Vorganis replied with his usual insouciance, "or you can grapple with one of those sky beasts and have it carry you aloft."

Elak pointed upward. "Go, Vorganis. The sides of the chimney are rough. There should be enough handholds."

The pirate proved to be as agile as any monkey, as Lycon had suggested, and made his way with surprising speed up the flue. The rest of the party followed, and although Lycon found progress almost exhausting, he managed to wedge himself across the narrow span, pausing to rest before moving on. Slowly, like spiders, the men rose up from the lower levels to the upper reaches of the chimney, the light a distant blur as the sun reached its zenith and began a slow wane.

Vorganis went on ahead, to find out where the chimney ended.

Elak whispered to Lycon and Dalan. "We may have to act swiftly. If we wait until darkness to enter the citadel, we risk a long delay in getting back to the ship. If Grondal sails before we get to him, we'll be marooned."

"*If* the gods see fit to return us to Atlantis," grumbled Dalan,

"I trust you will settle down to the business of ruling and forget about these accursed adventures, Elak. I'm beginning to think the Counsellors are right. And my powers are limited - my bones are wearing thin."

Mercifully Vorganis was not long in returning. His sweating face beamed down at them from above. "All is well, sire. The flue ends in a place where we can easily clamber into the citadel. It appears to be a garden, or possibly a shrine. There are but a few people about. The last thing they are expecting will be visitors from below!"

Elak sent word back down the chimney to his warriors to be prepared. With a final glance at Lycon, he followed Vorganis as they clambered up towards brighter light, the heat increasing almost unbearably. The pirate paused at a metal grille, waiting briefly before pushing it up. He emerged among ferns and other plants, wriggling through them on his belly before slipping behind a boulder. Elak followed as, one by one, the company came up from the chimney.

Elak studied his brighter surroundings. This was an inner court, partially roofed with a high, crystal dome, no doubt the reason for the oppressiveness of the cloying heat. He had emerged into its rear section, close to a sheer wall. There was a fountain in the centre of the courtyard and beyond it a wide balcony with an open view of clear skies, cloudless and free of the flying creatures within the volcano's pit.

Numerous rocks studded the garden, the whole area screened off from the main part of the court, and Elak's company quietly secreted themselves among the plants, swords drawn. Vorganis indicated to Elak there was movement out on the edge of the balcony and sure enough, two robed figures came out of the light and stood conferring in whispers by the fountain.

Elak and Lycon slipped from cover and came up behind them like ghosts. They each put a hand over the mouth of the hooded beings, a sword to their necks.

"Where is Kar-Kazool?" demanded Elak.

"In the lower citadel," hissed the robed figure. "He will not return until the moon is high."

Elak mentally cursed. More time lost. The reunion with the *Sea Skimmer* would undoubtedly be compromised.

32

Chapter Nine: Claws of the Sea God

A muffled cry behind Elak made him turn, still gripping the hooded figure, but he almost lost his grip as he saw a group of his warriors backing out of the garden. They were followed by a strange, lizard-like creature, its head raised, teeth gleaming as it hissed threateningly at them. Dalan also broke cover, directing his staff at the creature as it unfurled a pair of short, membranous wings.

"By the Nine Hells!" exclaimed Lycon. "It's a nest! This heat — for incubation."

The being Elak gripped twisted away and the hood fell back to reveal its head. It was human, but unlike anyone Elak had seen before. There was no neck, the wide head a continuation of the shoulders, the eyes more reptile than man, and a long tongue flicked in and out of the mouth as it spoke, its voice a low hiss.

"You must not harm the children of the Royal Wing," it said, rows of tiny serrated teeth gleaming in the brilliant sunlight.

Dalan's staff evidently emanated enough power to repulse the winged lizard. It backed into the grasses of the nest as all of Elak's men emerged. There were several winged lizards visible, but they held their ground.

"They grow into the sky creatures," said Dalan. "And serve Kar-Kazool."

Before Elak could comment, the being he had been holding rushed across the balcony and flung itself out into the vault. Elak raced after it, leaning over the dizzy drop. He saw the creature falling, but then a huge shape flew beneath it and with unexpected dexterity the tumbling creature had swung up on to the shoulders of the flying lizard and was guiding it down towards the city.

Elak turned and saw Lycon still had the other figure tightly gripped.

Its eyes bulged, teeth barred like a beast's cage. "You will pay for your intrusion!" it snarled. "Kar-Kazool will fall upon you all and feed you to the Royal Wing."

Elak faced the creature, his rapier point flicking out to touch the skin at its throat. "How soon will your ruler come?"

"You have no time!" the creature said, with what passed for a bark of laughter.

Elak called his men to him. "Bind him to one of the columns. And gag him. If he struggles, kill him."

Lycon and Dalan stood beside him, gazing down at the city far below. They could see the sweep of the dock area, where the tide had receded, leaving huge expanses of dark green weed. Even from this distance, it seemed to writhe and pulsate, seething with outrageous life. Sunlight gleamed on the wide mud flats and as he studied them, Dalan gasped with understanding.

"By the gods, it's a pathway, Elak! They've opened a pathway, out into the ocean. They mean to summon something up from the deeps and bring it to the city."

"Aye, their sea god," said Elak. "Ormundal said they worship some deep sea dweller."

"To spearhead an invasion," said Lycon. "Those sea slugs went to Epharra to prepare the way."

They did not have long to wait before there was movement down in the city, where several aerial shapes rose up from the long, flat roofs and swiftly assembled into what could only be a host of the flying creatures. As they spiralled upwards to the heights, their size became clear, as did the riders on their backs. Elak and his men made ready, knowing they would soon be under attack. They had lost the element of surprise, and possibly all hope of abducting Kar-Kazool.

Soon the first group of sky lizards circled the upper citadel and hovered beyond the balcony. Three of the huge creatures dived downward and alighted on its edge. A handful of Kar-Kazool's servants leapt from them and raised their long swords, eager to engage. Elak waited as a dozen of them formed a line. From their midst, a taller, cloaked being stepped forward, his body dressed in light armour, his head encased in a steel helm. Only his eyes were visible as they gazed in anger at Elak and his warriors.

"So, it is the very king of Atlantis who violates the sanctity of the children," said Kar-Kazool, lifting a curved sword in evident menace. "You have spared me the trouble of snaring you in your city. You have hastened its subjugation."

"Your treachery is no secret to the people of Epharra," said Elak. "Already they are preparing your overthrow. You'd do better to submit before the fleet surrounds your island."

Kar-Kazool's scarlet eyes widened. "Is that so? And why are you here, so poorly manned?"

Elak would have retorted, but an abrupt movement behind him made him turn – to see Vorganis on his knees, his face twisted in sudden pain. The pirate's chest and abdomen rippled and moments later parted wetly as a fat slug-like creature emerged and dropped on to the paved floor. Vorganis clutched at his chest, but already his body was repairing itself.

Kar-Kazool's laugh was a snarl. "You should be more careful who you trust, Atlantean," he said.

Vorganis was shaking himself as if waking from a drugged sleep. "What is happening?"

Lycon bent and used his blade to slice the slug creature in two, though its disgusting business was concluded.

"By now, half of your city will be infected," said Kar-Kazool. "Soon, your entire island!"

Dalan raised his staff in anger. "Not so, traitor. My acolytes will sear the last of your verminous servants. You'll find the empire more than ready for your assault."

Kar-Kazool waved his swordsmen forward. "Kill them all, save the king! I want him in chains, at my feet!"

Chaos ensued as the two bodies of warriors engaged in a frantic struggle, swords clashing, showering the combatants in sparks. Elak and Lycon fought side by side as they had often done, barely able to repel the furious onslaught of their opponents, who clearly drew on greater physical strength. Dalan smote with his staff, but three blades reached for him, pushing him ever backwards towards the nest area. Beyond the lip of the balcony, yet more lizard-borne warriors massed in a cloud. Each of the huge winged beasts was capable of carrying several swordsmen.

Elak realised, for all the heroics of his company, they were outnumbered and it would not be long before Kar-Kazool would have his victory. He knew also that none of his men would surrender. They would rather die here, to a man.

A high pitched shriek rose above the din of steel on steel and for a moment there was a lull. Elak realised that one of the young lizards, disturbed by the battle, had emerged from the nest and attacked an Atlantean. The man had defended himself, cutting into the neck of the creature, which had emitted the shriek before falling, lifeless, to the stone, its thick blood running from the fatal gash.

Kar-Kazool screamed orders to his swordsmen and as one, they pulled back.

Dalan directed his staff at the nest. "Perhaps we should wipe out all of these vermin," he said.

The horror in Kar-Kazool's eyes was easy to read.

Lycon grinned at Elak. "I think the tide of this battle has just turned."

Chapter 10: Wings over the Sea

"What do you say, Kar-Kazool?" said Elak. "What will you give me if I spare your creatures? Their survival is evidently paramount to you. Perhaps they are the seeds of their next generation. Irreplaceable."

Dalan spoke up behind him. "Aye, sire. Perhaps the existing parents mate rarely and can only produce after several of our lifetimes."

Kar-Kazool's fury, barely repressed, testified to the accuracy of both Elak's and Dalan's words.

"Send your swordsmen back out into the city," said Elak. "All of them! You stay, and you alone."

Kar-Kazool waved his men back. "If I obey you," he said to Elak, "you must give me your word – the word of the king of Atlantis – no harm will come to the children of the Royal Wing."

"By Ishtar, I swear it," said Elak, though both Dalan and Lycon looked deeply uneasy.

Kar-Kazool barked a sequence of curt orders and, whether his swordsmen approved of their instructions or not, as one they pulled back and again took to the skies. Elak had their ruler drive them back down towards the city.

"Throw down your sword," he told Kar-Kazool, who obeyed.

"We have reached an impasse," said the latter.

"No," said Elak. "I came here to make you my prisoner. I'll take you back to Epharra to face its justice for your treason." He called one of the warriors to him. "Chain his hands behind him, Jord-is."

Kar-Kazool stood rigidly while the young warrior did as bidden, using a small-linked but strong chain and locking it tightly so Kar-Kazool's hands were almost immovable.

"As for our return to the ship," said Elak, "I propose a swifter, safer journey than the exhausting climb that got us here."

Lycon looked at him dubiously. "There is no other way down, unless —"

Elak was grinning. "The sky lizards will carry us. Bring them!" he told Kar-Kazool, and one by one the creatures were made to land on the balcony and load up three of the Atlanteans behind a single rider, who was forced to obey the commands of Elak's men. When the entire raiding party had taken to the air, Elak had Kar-Kazool mount his own beast and sat behind him, with his own warrior, Jord-is, behind him.

The sun blazed from an unusually cloudless vault as the winged creatures rose upward on the air thermals and flew north-ward across Umaarsquu, above the deep bowl of the silent volcano. The company flew in an eerie, unsettling silence, and Elak's warriors were watchful for any sign of treachery. With Kar-Kazool so tightly bound, however, none of his swordsman dared attempt anything foolish.

Beyond the northern shore, high above its daunting cliffs, the sky lizards slowly spiralled down towards the clouds of mist and spume rising from the constant pulse of the strong tide as it battered the towering ramparts of stone. Eventually the *Sea Skimmer* was sighted, two miles from shore. Elak had given whispered instructions to all his men before they had climbed onto their mounts, and they followed them now.

Each of the lizard creatures was made to drop down to sea level, where the warriors dived into the waters, close to the war galley, taking their pilot with them. The sea lizards were then free to glide skywards, where they hovered, riderless and unaggressive. All of them discharged their riders. As Elak had the last creature drop to the sea, most of his men, including Dalan and Lycon were back aboard the *Sea Skimmer*.

Elak's sword touched the neck of his prisoner. "I trust your men will not attempt to pull you free," he told Kar-Kazool. "My archers will kill every one of them who swims close to us. And I'll have you killed before I let you escape."

Kar-Kazool had said nothing since the flight from the city. He burned with fury, Elak knew that, but understood his position was impossible. As the sea creature flew closer to the surface, Elak felt sea spray and the sting of its salt. Abruptly, directly ahead of him, the waters erupted in a white wave of foam, from which the huge head of a sea reptile emerged, mouth gaping, rows of serrated teeth flashing as the beast snatched at the passing sky lizard. It closed those frightful jaws on a wing and tore the sky lizard down.

Elak, Jordis and Kar-Kazool were all flung sideways, immediately plunging into the sea. The sea reptile gripped the flailing lizard and shook it violently, its victim's blood pumping from numerous wounds, before diving deep down. Elak knew that he and the others were now beyond the discarded swordsmen of Kar-Kazool, who were between Elak and the *Sea Skimmer*. He felt something thump into his back and moments later Kar-Kazool had his chained hands around his neck. He had worked them free, enough to effect a stranglehold.

"You reckoned without my sea servants," said Kar-Kazool and Elak realised he meant the huge sea reptile. His powers were far more dangerous than he'd known. What else could he conjure up from the deeps?

In desperation Elak attempted to break Kar-Kazool's hold, but it was impossible and he felt the darkness closing in. His captor snarled something to the skies and almost immediately another of the sky lizards was swooping down, obedient to the command. It glided across the surface and landed a few yards away. Kar-Kazool forced the almost inert Elak towards it, intent on reversing their recent roles. The last thing Elak saw before he passed out was the neck and shoulders of the sky beast as it ducked to receive him.

Kar-Kazool swung Elak up across the shoulders of the sky lizard and started to position himself up behind him. As he did so, a figure appeared in the swirling sea. Jordis had swum alongside and as he, too, swung up on to the creature, he jabbed his sword into Kar-Kazool's side, between the metal plates of his armour. The armoured warrior swung round in pain and fury and lashed out with his chained hands, but Jordis had been expecting the attack and rammed the hilt of his blade into Kar-Kazool's chest. It could not penetrate but skidded off the metal, the force of the blow sending Kar-Kazool tumbling backwards.

As Kar-Kazool's snarling form again fell into the sea, Jordis dug his heels into the flanks of the sky lizard and prodded its flesh, shouting at it in an attempt to get it airborne. The pain must have jolted the creature into action, for it flapped its wings and took to the sky. Below it, Kar-Kazool's helmeted head broke the surface, looking around to locate the sky lizard. It was gliding above his fallen swordsmen, who shouted at it, though they did no more than confuse it. Kar-Kazool screamed instructions, but in the chaos, the sky lizard ignored them.

Jordis saw the *Sea Skimmer* below and chose his moment. He sheathed his sword and gripped the unconscious king. Together they tumbled from the back of the rising creature, plunging deep into the sea. Jordis felt the air almost bludgeoned from his body, but he clung on to Elak desperately until at last his head broke the surface and he was able to drag air into his lungs. He could see a number of Kar-Kazool's warriors swimming swiftly towards him and knew that he had no strength left to fight them off. His own consciousness was slipping away.

***

When he came to, Jordis was looking up into the face of the king.

"You're alive," said Elak, a wide grin splitting his features. Behind him the Druid, Dalan, nodded in silent approval. "And I owe you my life," Elak added, helping Jordis to sit. He was on the bare deck of the war galley.

"Kar-Kazool-"

"Far behind us," said Elak. "It's over – for now. You'll recover soon enough. And I'll reward you - with anything you desire."

Jordis's face clouded. "I am grateful, sire, but the one thing I wish for can never be mine."

"If it's within my power to bestow it, it will be done," insisted Elak. "What would you have? Come, you saved my life! All Atlantis is in your debt."

"The one who has my heart," Jordis breathed.

"Well, if she loves you, then she will be yours. I would not agree to a marriage if it were not so."

"Aye, sire, I confess we are lovers."

"Then you will have the finest ceremony Atlantis has seen for many a long year! Who is she?"

Jordis's face clouded and he seemed to find words difficult. "Forgive me, sire, but she is your cousin, Illyrin." He slid his sword from its sheath and Elak had no time to draw back, gaping for a moment, hoping that Dalan had not heard. If Jordis intended to plunge that blade home, Elak realised he was powerless.

However, the youth handed him the sword. "I am your servant in all things, King of Atlantis."

Elak put his hand on Jordis's shoulder. "I vowed I'd grant your wish. A king does not go back on his word."

"Your own wedding plans –"

Elak shook his head. "The gods have their own plans for me, it seems. I see their hand in this. So – be blessed! What better way can I reward you than by bringing you into my family!" He helped Jordis to his feet.

"We may have let our prize slip," Lycon remarked to Dalan, "but when we return to Epharra, I think we should toast our king heartily. And the young warrior."

Dalan nodded thoughtfully. For some reason, he saw, Elak's mood was one of suppressed elation. Evidently this had not been a defeat. Perhaps the king's dark mood was turning. Well, that was a blessing from Mider, the Druid's god. They would all need to be strong, with war now certain.

THE CORPSE'S CRUSADE

By Cody Goodfellow

In all of Zothique, no memorial fane or idol looms higher or shines brighter than the golden statue that stands like a radiant funereal obelisk upon the grave of the empire of Istanam. The gleaming figure mocks the sun and drowns in shadow the minarets and broken domes of the once-proud capitol of Avandra, which lies in ruins half-engulfed in scarlet sand, as if mortally exhausted by its erection. Cracked, blistered and distorted with the strain of its casting, its features distorted and obscured by the hands of vandals and the teeth of time, its colossal arm, held high in triumph or defiance, brandishes what appears to be the hilt of a broken sword. For a few coins or a skin of untainted water, the flagellants who gather at its feet will tell the curious traveler that the hero immortalized in gold was Thrascus of Xylac, who never sought glory.

The songs of his exploits are the only tales still told by the people of Avandra, who can remember little else of their faded epic history. That such a monolithic honor would be heaped upon a commoner and a barbaric northern foreigner would speak to both the extraordinary virtue of the subject and the eternal gratitude of Avandra's populace. But few monuments are consecrated to the truth, and the celebrated campaign that made a legend of the humble warrior only began with his death.

Though renowned throughout Zothique for his ruthless courage as a freebooting warlord, Thrascus cared only for gold. King Vukrota summoned the mercenary to a private audience in the Hall of Blind Spiders and plied him with black orchid wine and the promise of the pick of his harem, if he would but entertain a simple proposition.

For reasons known only to himself, the regally obese ruler of Istanam cast his restless gaze all about as he spoke, roving from the tarnished armor carapaces to dusty tapestries to his own extravagantly stained garments and the primitive yet majestic lapis-inlaid engravings in his ancestral throne, rather than meet the shrewdly hooded gray eyes of the barbaric commoner clad in a rude frontier tunic of wyvern-leather.

The steppes south of Avandra were sorely plagued by rapacious raiders out of the Myrkasian Mountains whose insatiable hunger had driven them to pillage the caravans from Yoros and the fertile fields of Zhel… not for their merchandise or livestock, but for their human produce. The brigands were, he reluctantly admitted, a rogue tribe of anthropophagi. Beyond the incredible lies spread by cowardly rustics in Zhel, little was known about the reavers, for they left only gnawed bones, when they deigned to leave any remains at all.

King Vukrota made a clean breast of his grievance as he made his proposal, but he held his fortune a bit too dearly in his negotiations, or the northern mercenary held his courage too lightly, or secretly valued his pride more even than blood-money. Thrascus gave no reply, but after the taciturn manner of barbaric Xylac, simply dropped the paltry purse of gold coins at the king's feet, and took his leave.

Here, there yet hung a pregnant moment when all that would transpire could have been unmade, had either man succumbed to the softening of forbearance. King Vukrota well knew that the coffers of Istanam were the deepest and most densely packed in all of Zothique. Indeed, the capitol was founded upon the site by a renegade general who discovered in nameless ruins a forgotten treasure-hoard too large for his army to move, and his yellow-eyed descendents had added to it with all the power of the ledger and the sword. Well could he have buried a much larger army in gold and orichalcum for its service, and never felt the slightest bite of want.

For his part, Thrascus of Xylac had shown little sign of cowardice or hauteur in his storied career. Alone, had he not slaughtered the nine Lamiae of Iribos to win a drunken tavern wager? Did he and his motley band not behead the lich-king Olvolvulus Yx, and use its undying gorgon gaze to render the army of Chaon-Gacca into pillars of glass on the dunes of Tasuun? And did he not also hunt and cut down even the least of the scores of scattered scions of the profligate king Hraddomun of Ummaos, so that no pretenders could claim the throne of Xylac? No feat of arms was too daring or too debased, but that Thrascus would see it through for the right price.

42

But neither man would yield; out of the unknowable, adamantine ore of the hearts of such men are carved the unlovely tablets of fate.

Only a coward turns his unarmored back on the enemy, but only a fool turns his back on a king. Vukrota was too craven to lead his own army into battle, but more than equal to the task of yellow murder. Chasing after the retreating mercenary on gout-raddled feet as if to beg his indulgence, the wheezing king drove his long, crooked poniard up to its ruby-riddled hilt between the blades of the mighty warlord's broad shoulders. Though hitherto only employed for the torment of impudent harlots and anything else that bored him, the royal dagger yet sank into its new sheath with sickly aplomb. Without fanfare or glory or even a gurgled epitaph, Thrascus of Xylac silently died.

The spirit of Thrascus was too weak for the bold commission of King Vukrota, but under the ministrations of his royal magi, his vacant flesh proved willing enough. Spirited away to the mildew-ravaged catacombs of the Hall of Sharp Shadows, the cooling cadaver lay upon a slab encircled by geomantic rings daubed in demons' blood as fell cantrips and incantations were chanted, drawing forth the wrathful spirit of Thrascus from its cold cage and binding it to the king's service.

In the case of the crass mercenary, they thought themselves quite clever to trap the barbarian's soul in a fetish which had been his prime motivator in life. By their lights, the cold echoes of greed in the cold carrion of the slain mercenary would serve as the motive spark of its reanimation. Thus did King Vukrota secure the haughty brigand's services for a single gold coin.

Walking the coin stamped with the king's saturnine profile across his acromegalic knuckles over the dead man's head and heart, venerable Uqbor Yuril, the eldest and most powerful necromancer in all Istanam, blew a luminous cobalt powder into the still chimneys of mouth and nose, then commanded the vacant vessel of Thrascus to rise from the slab.

With much mummery and whispered warnings, Uqbor Yuril entrusted King Vukrota with the ensorcelled coin. For so long as coin and corpse existed, the servant would retain its grotesque semblance of life and dogged loyalty to the possessor. For his part, King Vukrota had already all but forgotten his abortive transaction with the upstart barbarian in the press of fresh concubines and aged vintages, and so he carelessly left it to be added to the royal coffers.

One and all, the sword-thralls of Thrascus awakened from drunken slumber to find their missing chieftain returned to them a taciturn and ashen effigy, but as he seemed no less afflicted than the least indulgent of his underlings, they had little cause to suspect treachery, and because he mutely led the way to carnage and plunder, they had no reason to question his command.

Out from the gates of Avandra galloped the wolf-legion of Thrascus of Xylac, out into the rubicund dust of dawn. Its grim, gray-faced leader sat stiffly astride his horse like a masterwork of taxidermy, but even the crowds who cheered the myrmidons' exodus from the capitol with no little relief took note of the stoic rigor with which he rode out to face almost certain death. All the soothsayers of Istanam had agreed that no man living could hope to prevail over the rapacious raiders, and yet here was their champion.

Through Ymorth and Zhel the dread company marched, looting and burning all they met to whet their appetite for battle, but the road to Yoros was beset by threats even more fearsome than themselves.

As the company rode into a deep serpentine vale, they came upon a caravan of wagons abandoned with all its baggage left suspiciously intact. The brigands wasted no time appropriating the sundries and scarce valuables, and were so engaged in dispute over the choicest prizes when they were ambushed and overrun by those whom they had come to slay.

Full well, yet too late, did the thralls of Thrascus learn why the reavers of the Myrkasian wilderness struck such terror into the heart of the red empire. For the ferocious horde that dismembered their column and dragged them down from their wild-eyed mounts were no mere human savages, but a feral band of jackal-headed Ghorii.

Perhaps driven to such desperations by the famine upon the fallow necropolises of the land, from which the last mummified remains were harvested out of all unliving memory. Maybe, in these last days of the spoiled red sun, the living had become so steeped in poisons and fatigue as to become indistinguishable in sapidity from the dead. Whatever their cause, the Ghorii needed no weapons but claws and ravening, slavering jaws to reduce the proud warrior band to so much rude, raw provender.

Though lethal as ever on the battlefield, the reanimated Thrascus proved a less than agile commander. Laying about him with his sword and dirk like a thresher at high harvest, he trampled cracked canine skulls like cobblestones, but gave no tactical commands to rally his men, who were swarmed and slaughtered even as they stood and fought in a haphazard phalanx.

When the last living swordsman had fallen, Thrascus stood alone, oblivious to all about him unless some enemy strayed within sword's reach, as the battlefield became a banquet. If any pang of anguish stirred his cold, putrid heart, he masked it behind the stoicism of the tomb.

Gore-glutted and blood-drunk, the Ghorii decided against risking their leprous hides in laying to rest the intractable cadaver, but still sought to convey the lethal curiosity intact to their stronghold as a walking trophy, a distracting plaything for their terrible mistress.

Leashed with leather thongs from his horse's reins, Thrascus docilely followed where his captors led—into a winding, camouflaged crevasse of black-red granite, through caverns narrow and vast, until at last they came to their citadel, a crumbling cathedral hewn from the bones of a behemoth overlooking a sunless gulf, and the court of their queen.

With much bowing and whined endearments, the tomb-hounds presented their grim offering to the veiled figure reclining upon her fossil throne, and for once, they did not disappoint her.

Few who lived in that age knew the ancient legends of the enchantress Qariona, and the unspeakable means by which she had preserved her perverse beauty while men and nations withered and fell around her, dancing and slaying and begging for her pleasure. But though she had thwarted death and no mortal man could resist her, yet none could quench her necrophilous lusts, which could only be sated by the unyielding rigidity of the grave.

The excellent cadaver of Thrascus of Xylac betrayed no slightest symptom of arousal as she parted her diaphanous shroud and revealed her voluptuous, marmoreal nakedness. Even the whip-shy Ghorii courtiers slavered and stifled howls as she inspected their gift, but Thrascus stood unmoved, gazing through her with clouded, unseeing eyes. For the first time in numberless centuries, Qariona the deathless seducer was mutely, morbidly seduced by death.

With feminine wiles and blackest sorcery, Qariona warped the empty vessel Thrascus to her lascivious will. Without knowing his true name, she could not hope to possess him utterly, but yet she could cloud his dread purpose and turn him into a coldly amorous puppet.

But no grimoire or scroll could detail the subtle enchantment by which the chill touch of the dead barbarian worked upon her cold heart, and so kindled in it the banked embers of a most vital and life-like passion.

Revived to old appetites, Qariona commanded her jackal pack to bring her a parade of live human specimens, which she squandered in ecstatic orgies of torture and defilement that left them unfit even for ghoulish consumption. Refreshed with each exquisite expiration, Qariona only grew more cruelly beautiful, but her efforts seemed only to drive her to greater extremes of frustration, for though she admitted it not to herself, yet she hungered to arouse some spark of reciprocal passion from the incarnation of death that shared her bed.

When her debaucheries offended even the sanguine sensibilities of the corpse-eating Ghorii, Thrascus repelled her would-be usurpers with a swift and tireless headsman's axe, and by slow turns, as only an ensorcelled corpse could, he won Qariona's heart.

While Qariona languished in the throes of morbid loveplay with her mechanical plaything, her Ghorii subjects connived and schemed. And in the careless murmuring of Queen Qariona's bedchamber, they found what they sought. As the ghoul-queen uttered the spell that renewed the binding of her undead paramour, so did Wyruxtos the shaman transcribe and twist the forgotten syllables for his own fell ends.

With blackest invocations to Mordiggian the maggot-headed charnel-god, the treasonous priest learned the true name of Qariona's beloved, and with it he negated the queen's enchantment, and cut the arcane reins that stayed his geas-damned hand.

Like a mirror-mad succubus, Qariona tirelessly rode her saprogenic bedmate, showering his lipless rictus with searing kisses and caressing his unyielding flesh, but found no respite from her burgeoning carnal appetites. It exhausted and distracted her to have to impel his every slightest gesture, and though the touch of the unexpired was more repellent than ever, yet she hungered for Death to take her of Its own volition and quell her insatiable lust with Its morbific kiss.

Perhaps at last she felt some final surge of release, when her puppet stirred at last and rose up of its own volition to trap her in rigor-stiff arms, shivering as if with some atavistic echo of bygone consummation. But if she knew any pleasure at the fulfillment her dreadful obsessions, it fled as quickly as it found her, when Thrascus took hold of her lovestruck head and her supple white neck, and deftly separated them.

Even in death, Thrascus was unexcelled in every task set before him. But now, he took no pain or pleasure from his work, knew neither fear nor remorse. He had become a perfect soldier.

Holding aloft the beguiling lantern of Qariona's severed head trailing dripping vertebrae upon silken shrouds, Thrascus remained oblivious to either triumph at his victory or anguish at his loss. He loomed like a gruesome statue, waiting, perhaps, to be paid.

But when it came time for his reward, his erstwhile master proved as treacherous as the old one. While he stood at attention, Wyruxtos crept up behind the triumphant cadaver and with a single great stroke of a uranium mace, dashed out the fermented curds of his brain.

His use at an end, the Ghorii refrained from tasting his venenose flesh, and cast their spoiled instrument into the abyss beneath their citadel. Down through lightless fathoms he plummeted, to fall at last into the racing subterranean headwaters of the mighty River Voum.

Churning, frigid currents dashed him against boulders like gnashing molars, and roaring whirlpools bludgeoned him with the cold stone throat of the riverbed. For three days and nights, the river Voum had its brutal way with Thrascus, dealing him a score of mortal wounds; but eventually, bloated and buoyant with zymotic gases, he floated to the surface and came to rest on a stygian shore deep within the moribund earth.

Scarcely had Thrascus emerged from his riverine sojourn, when the battered carcass was discovered by some others who felt no repulsion at his degraded condition, but only a calculated clockwork joy at his discovery.

With nearly every bone of him fractured, almost every organ punctured or pulverized, and with a shattered dome for a skull, yet the automatons of Diur Siluxis quivered with eagerness as they carried his remains from the river with the reverence of acolytes bearing a holy relic.

For though life was fled far from Thrascus, his usefulness was far from over.

For centuries beyond counting, the automatons of Diur Siluxis had labored to extract the crystalline embryos of unborn god-spawn of the Unbegotten Source from the once-molten mantle of the earth. Programmed to serve eons-dead masters who madly hoped to renew the senescent land with fresh pantheons of new deities, the automatons had finally discovered a rich vein of fossilized fetuses encased in the cold metamorphic magma, and over centuries, they had painstakingly mined and cached them in a mammoth cell within the hollow heart of a vast diamond. They lacked only a sturdy human host to carry the divine larva into the world.

The broken soldier's shell was more than adequate to the task. Its crushed skull only made it easier for the automatons to decant the cosmic embryo directly into its new home.

The humble gearwork servants expected no reward for their service, and got none. Immediately, the twice-reanimated corpse arose from the workbench, crackling with fuliginous waves of negative cosmic energy. At its glancing touch, lead and steel machinery melted like cheese in a furnace. The automatons trembled with joy as one by one, the newborn avatar caressed their pitted, featureless heads and snuffed out their mechanical lives.

Out into the wide, weary world, the apotheosis of Thrascus of Xylac bore the black-lit mantle of the larval god. Through Zhel and Ymorth he rampaged, converting or consuming all he met upon the road with the mad abandon of an aborted first child of the Earth. The crepuscular glory of his radiant gaze left his new devotees blind but forever faithful, his image burned indelibly into sightless eyes. Those who stood aloof from his majesty were devoured and added to his galvanized flesh until his footfalls shook the rusty road and his negative halo eclipsed the feeble wine-dark light of the sun.

Eyeless, half-headed Thrascus now beheld the world from a

boiling mass of diabolical eyes, which filled the smoking crater of his skull. Vast, razor-feathered wings fanned out from the column of his spine, wafting scorching, radioactive winds over the plains as he strode with a lurching, smoldering gait towards Istanam.

Did he come to exact his revenge, or to collect the coin that stole his soul? Such mortal concerns were far beneath the awesome monstrosity that Thrascus had become. To bring new miracles and revelations to the decadent last sons of mankind? None can say why he retraced the route of his fateful campaign, but at last he came to a city in need of new faith... the decadent city of Avandra.

The looming silhouette of the approaching godling spurred the decadent city to panic. The armies rallied and marched out to meet the invader, but pyroclastic clouds of ebony fire from its wings steamed them in their armor until meat fell roasted from bones. Like a child at play, the leviathan plunged its colossal claws into the earth and rendered the sandy crimson battlefield into a sea of molten red glass.

The royal magi gathered on the uppermost balconies of the palace towers and cast spells and summoned demons to disenchant or divert the unstoppable abomination, but working blindfolded, they could only hope to beg their diabolical superiors for mercy. They found none. Even Thasaidon, patron demon lord of the city, did not deign to intercede on their behalf.

From his vantage point at the summit of the palace, Vukrota was among the first to behold the advancing avatar as it trampled the imposing city walls. He had scarcely credited the wild rumors of the effect of the monster's gaze, and believed himself immune to the frailties of mere mortals. Only when he met the terrible basilisk stare of the titanic godling and was struck instantly blind, did the addled royal wits seize upon some telling detail in the ghastly ultraviolet image seared into his brain. Too late did he learn the identity of his unstoppable usurper.

Only in the reflective refuge of total amaurosis could King Vukrota see that the mercenary, whom he had purchased so cheaply to serve his ill-conceived whims, was the city's new master. If he had only heeded his wizards and secured the ensorcelled coin, then he could have struck the terrible revenant down in its tracks...

But King Vukrota had carelessly left the coin to be collected and deposited in the royal treasury. While the battle raged outside, a legion of courtiers searched frantically for it. But the vaults and galleries that contained all of Istanam's wealth had never been mapped, let alone inventoried, and every coin of Istanam was stamped with the king's profile, and so there was no other solution but to destroy them all.

A massive cauldron was erected atop a blazing pyre inside the central tower of the palace. As crews of women and children fed the flames, brigades of slaves with buckets relayed the precious wealth of Istanam's thousand years of tribute and plunder into the glowing cauldron, where it was rendered unto a luminous golden soup. On the hemorrhagic horizon, unmistakably drawn to the offering, Thrascus approached, carelessly breaching the last glimmering thaumaturgical barriers the magi had desperately thrown in its path.

No altar to any god of humankind ever groaned under a greater sacrifice than the mountain of golden oblation the court of Avandra fed to the great cauldron. And no god was ever less heedful to a prayer. Crashing through the palace curtain wall, the towering avatar fell curiously still and pressed its ear to the tower as if seeking the heartbeat of the king, or the silent scream of its human soul trapped in a misplaced coin.

Storms of flaming arrows, catapulted boulders and burning oil only lit up the monstrous homunculus as it punched a hole in the tower. Its gigantic fist emerged from the opposite wall, clutching a bloody fistful of soldiers and magicians. Withdrawing its fist, it rooted around in the halls and courtyards of the palace as if through the paper chambers of a hornets' nest, heedless of the hundreds of trivial stings dealt to his undead, indomitable flesh.

Perhaps at the last, King Vukrota sought to save his kingdom by flinging himself into the grasp of the crushing, questing hand. The venerable brotherhood of magi forbids any suggestion that Uqbor Yuril, eldest and shrewdest of their number, might have shoved the blind monarch into the path of the questing hand to save himself. Thus it must be accepted that at the last, King Vukrota leapt bravely into the clutches of the soldier he sent to die a hundred deaths for a single gold coin.

Now, Thrascus fumblingly sought the cauldron, perhaps intent upon adding the king to his boiling fortune. But with the curious synchronicity of cruel destiny, the fateful coin was cast into the cauldron just as the giant hand upset the pyre and tipped it over.

If King Vukrota's fondest wish was never to be parted from his wealth, then to be drowned in gold might've seemed like paradise. Even as the wave of molten metal cascaded down over the gargantuan avatar, its mighty limbs stiffened and petrified with the dissolution of Thrascus's reanimation. The ebony aura evanesced in a feeble glow through its cooling shell of pure gold and slowly died out as the embryonic godling within withdrew to hibernate in its shining cocoon.

And so ended the reign of King Vukrota, and the rule of Avandra over Istanam. The gutted city drained of all who hoped to rebuild a life elsewhere, leaving the armies of the blind and the mad to wander the ruins, flagellants and dervishes singing songs of appeasement to the man who left the city a corpse, but returned as a god. The palace collapsed around the skyscraping golden statue of the giant holding the semblance of a broken sword hilt. Only from the vantage of crows is the object revealed as the tiny xanthic idol of vain King Vukrota.

And so the mortal husk of Thrascus of Xylac, who never sought glory, became the proudest monument to the city that bought him for the price of a meal. And yet travelers in proceeding ages remarked that any city that so loved their heroes must have been a brave and faithful one...

THONGOR IN THE VALLEY OF DEMONS

By Robert M. Price

I. Hall of Heroes

The royal dining hall of Patanga might have been compared to an earthly Valhalla and might possibly have served as the model for the Norse myth. From the high-vaulted ceiling hung the banners of the city-states that composed Thongor's Empire of the West: Patanga, Shembis, Thurdis, and the rest. This night, as the fires roared in the gigantic hearth, the Emperor roared with laughter, sitting at the head of the long banqueting table. The merriment was shared with his nobles: Prince Dru, slender and foppish; Lord Mael whose lined and grizzled visage cracked with hilarity despite himself; Barand Thon, and others, who had joined Thongor and Sumia his queen for this special occasion. Thongor was celebrating the visit of his old comrade Shangoth, chieftain of the towering, blue-skinned Rmoahal nomads. One figure, though easily ignored and forgotten, sat unmoving, benignly watching the others like a father observing his children at play. This was Eumonius Eld, hierophant of the Nineteen Gods. One had the feeling that he enjoyed the proceedings but felt it improper to let on, preferring to maintain a pose of superior detachment. As he sat, clad in golden robes, a vermilion skull cap surmounting his hairless head, he imbibed the occasional sip of *sarn* wine and let go a small grin at the occasional ribald jest.

Shangoth sat at Thongor's left, Sumia at his right as, inevitably, the two warrior kings traded, and embellished, favorite war stories. Thongor, never keen on civilized protocols, had laid his crown aside, parking it next to his huge wine goblet. Sumia dreaded the moment Thongor would reach for the wrong one, in the process spilling wine on the ancient diadem of her ancestors. She was relieved when it finally happened and was over.

His advisors had given up trying to shape Thongor, a barbarian from the snowy peaks of Valkarth, into a polished royal exemplar. It wasn't going to work, and Thongor's subjects would never have forgiven them if it had. He was a man of the people. Behind his high-backed chair hung two banners, one featuring the flame design of Patanga, the other emblazoned with the black lizard-hawk of Thongor's own tribe. Casting state decorum to the wind, the Valkarthan pounded the table with his mace-like fist and clapped his visitor's shoulder, though he had to reach high up to do so. His black mane shivered like a curtain in the wind as he shook his head in mirth or exclamation. The fire illumined his high, broad cheek bones and surprisingly white teeth. But even in ordinary sunlight his skin was bronzed, his eyes maelstroms of gold dust. His clean-shaven jaw bore a minor scar or two, reminders of battles past. He wore no ermine robes but only a tunic of common design, though cut from finely woven cloth. Sumia wore traditional royal attire, as did all the other nobles present—except for Shangoth, who was more scantily clothed than his friend the Emperor, clad mainly in a loincloth and a cloak made of exotic feathers of fantastic hues. His earlobes bore rubies set in electrum, his massive throat circled with gold and silver pendants and amulets, some carved with miniature effigies of his tribal idols. It was only with difficulty that he squeezed into the specially constructed chair that struggled and creaked to accommodate his stature.

The raucous feasting declined to a dull roar as a guard stepped up to his sovereign's side with news. The other diners paused, knowing something serious must be afoot to justify interrupting the king's festivities. Thongor's demeanor changed abruptly as he listened gravely, then gestured at a second guardsman to come forward. This the young soldier did, his weapons sheathed, as he half-carried a staggering figure into the royal presence. Seeing the poor wretch's condition, Thongor rose from his seat and helped the broken, bleeding figure to take his place. In that moment, Sumia saw crystallized the difference between Thongor and other kings: they stood on ceremony and pompous pretense to maintain their royal dignity, whereas her beloved earned respect and honor by acts of selfless concern.

"Tell me, my man, what has happened to you?" The old fellow had suffered multiple injuries, strangely varied in character. There were burns of some severity, a broken arm, numerous bruises, and just as many crudely treated flesh wounds.

"My Lord, Hell has broken loose upon my village. It has fallen, and I alone have escaped to tell you."

Withal, he expired. Thongor looked up at the guards, then around at the faces of those at table. All had heard the brief exchange, and the face of each was identically blank with puzzlement, as if the dead man had spoken in some language unknown to them.

Thongor picked up the body and carefully handed it over to the guards with orders to provide an honorable burial. Taking his seat once more, he motioned for the rest to sit as well. Pensive for a few moments, the king looked up at the waiting faces and said, "We must assume the old fellow's village was upheaved by a great earthquake. We all felt tremors but a few days ago. I received no reports of serious damage till now. I shall send men to investigate. But what have the rest of you to say? I value your wisdom, as I think you know."

The high priest spoke up. "Majesty, if you will indulge me," he said with a slight bow, "I cannot help thinking that, as awful a misfortune as this is, there is something even larger and more sinister at work here. I would suggest that whatever has transpired, it merits direct inspection by your Majesty or his appointed agents—and myself. If there is a greater danger, who knows but that it might endanger all of Lemuria if not checked right away. Call me an old fool, but..."

"Not at all, your Holiness! You are of course very wise. Tonight I shall question my guards as to the location of the disaster. On the morrow I shall depart. Any of you are welcome to join me."

II. Exiles from Tartarus

At dawn a small party of palace guards accompanied Thongor, Shangoth, and Eumonius Eld to investigate the destruction of the small city, as it turned out, of Teloth. Prince Dru and the others, present at the feast the previous night, volunteered to join the expedition, but Thongor decided they would be of more value busy at their regular duties. After a few days ride they began noticing strange omens and collapsed structures. Corpses were scattered, the more thickly the closer to Teloth they came. Dismounting their reptilian *kroters*, Thongor and his men stooped down to examine several of the bodies and found the same odd mixture of wounds, bruises, and

54

burns they had seen on that first refugee. Reaching the site of Teloth, they first thought they had gone astray, then realized the city had been completely obliterated. There was a huge, gaping rift in the ground from which mephitic vapors rose.

Eumonius Eld spoke. "This is no mere quaking of the earth, not even a terrible one."

Mighty Shangoth replied, his tone respectful. "Wise hierophant, remember that there had been tremors, and the manner of the damage here is surely that of an earthquake, is it not?"

"It is that—and more, my friend. The upheaval was of itself a mindless convulsion of the earth, true, but I fear it has by chance led to something much worse, *released* something much worse."

"And what is that, O priest?" Thongor asked.

"My Lord Thongor, would you not agree that a disturbance of the earth would not by itself produce all the injuries we have observed on the bodies of these poor victims?"

"It is true. The burns remain unaccounted for. And the bruises, the wounds. They are more naturally the result of attack by weapons. I suppose wandering marauders might have taken the earthquake as an opportunity to despoil the survivors. Still..."

"And," Shangoth said, his blue, bald pate mirroring the noontide sky, "consider the distance at which we found the outlying bodies. With such wounds, could they have made it so far? And if they fell where attacked, why would marauders have pursued them there? Those fleeing for their lives could not have carried much to interest thieves."

Thongor readily accepted logic when he heard it. And he had no longer a recourse to purely naturalistic explanations. "So what, good Eumonius Eld, are we likely to be facing?" As he spoke, Thongor instinctively began to draw his sword, Sarkozan, from its scabbard.

The priest met his king's inquiring gaze, then looked off into the distance of contemplation.

"I believe, my friends, that we stand upon the verge, not only of a crevasse in the earth, but of a rift between heaven and hell. Some even among my priests think it a legend or a holy allegory, but I have always believed the old epic of a war between the Devas and the Asuras, the angels and the devils. These demons anciently defied the Nineteen Gods and were imprisoned deep in a subterranean cavern, some in their solid flesh, others incorporeal."

"Aye," Shangoth added, as if to second the priest's speculation, "We tell a similar story among the Jegga Horde. I, too, believe it!"

"Now an opportune earthquake has freed them," the priest continued. "And as the *Xanthu Tablets* foretold, the day has come when they will challenge the Gods anew. They have emerged from the pit of imprisonment energized by long-simmering hatred. It was they, I venture, who hunted down the inhabitants of Teloth, wielding adamantine clubs and swords and spears flaring with infernal fires."

Thongor's golden, lion-like eyes scanned the horizon. "Where are they now? We must be ready in case they return. There are too few of us to stand against a sudden assault. We shall spread out and climb these hills to get a better view of the land surrounding us. Then, if the way is clear, we must hasten back to Patanga to prepare for battle—military and spiritual."

Thongor took the priest with him to one of the hilltops. From there they saw nothing. But it was not long before danger appeared, though not from the anticipated direction. The ground began to shake, and the king and the priest braced themselves. Thongor dropped to the earth and motioned for Eumonius Eld to do the same. The former was clad in warrior's harness, the latter in hieratic robes, though less heavy and elaborate than usual. The dirtying of his splendid vestments struck the hierophant, with an inkling of irony, as emblematic of the crisis now upon them. Every vestige of a carefully crafted world might well be swept away in a brimstone avalanche. For now a demonic horde of Asuras was pouring forth from the newly made ravine.

III. Hostages to Hell

Eumonius Eld, not a young man by any standard, struggled to his knees, then to his feet with Thongor's help. Without complaint, but with a quiet, involuntary groan, the priest made to descend the hill by his sovereign's side, but Thongor prevented him.

"Hold there, father! You know the difference between valor and suicide! You will serve best by staying here and watching. If the Gods have decreed this to be my last day," withal he looked down into the valley, "and it looks like they *have*, I will need someone to return to Patanga with a report. Now wish me luck!"

Thongor saw the rest of his men descending another of the hills and ran to reconnoiter with them. Shoulder to shoulder they would make a last stand against the charge of the demon host! Night was falling, and when Thongor greeted his fellows it was with a fatalistic shout of *esprit de corps*.

He expected the tidal wave of infernal warriors to break upon the shore of their upraised swords and shields in scant seconds, but instead, the demon horde, indistinct in the twilight, had halted many yards away, waiting silently on their shadow-shrouded mounts. Thongor, utterly puzzled, looked back to address his silent men. At once he saw their eyes glowing fiery red in the deepening dark. They had been possessed! Shangoth, his pigment now turned purple, wordlessly felled him with a single blow.

All this Eumonius Eld viewed with astonished horror. He returned to his knees, then to the ground, hoping to become as inconspicuous as possible. The last thing he saw was the parting of the Asura ranks to let Thongor's possessed troops pass, carrying his supine form between them, seemingly with the care and respect to which their king had been accustomed. It did not take long for the whole silent company, silhouetted in glowing furnace smoke, to return into the unseen cavity within the rift.

The priest remained on the deserted hilltop, sleeping a bit, until the sun god's chariot rounded the horizon. The valley below appeared to be empty, too. So the lone Patangan ventured down the hill. A look around revealed two welcome sights. One was his waiting *kroter*, contentedly grazing. That was a considerable relief. The other was an equally great surprise: *Sarkozan*, the sword of Thongor, forged by magic from a white-hot meteorite! The blade flashed with crimson dawn light, but the great jewel set in the pommel glowed with an inner radiance of its own. Eumonius Eld walked over to it, stooped down, and gingerly reached to pick it up.

He wrapped the sword, missing its scabbard, in a yard of cloth torn from his cloak, then secured it in the harness of his *kroter*. He wanted neither to damage the sword nor to hurt the animal. When he had, with arthritic difficulty, made it into the saddle, he noticed his pouch of provisions was missing. It was going to be a difficult journey home. And what would become of Thongor in the meantime he feared to guess.

IV. Priestly Prayers

Some days later, the council of Thongor's trusted advisers met in grave deliberation. Thongor's seat was occupied by his queen, Sumia. She knew the affairs of the Empire as well as her husband did. Thongor had swiftly learned to respect his queen's intelligence and judgment and often asked her advice. Conversely, over the years of their marriage, Thongor had spent what time he could training her in combat skills. She had many times shown a natural bravery, and her voluptuous beauty promised lithe strength. She would soon be putting that strength and skill to the test.

Sarkozan lay on the table amid those assembled and, though they paid due attention to whomever was speaking, their eyes were drawn again and again to the broadsword as if all deep down sensed that, even in their monarch's absence, the weapon held their answer—if answer there were. But just now, His Holiness Eumonius Eld held the floor, explaining the nature of the foe they faced.

"You must bear in mind, my friends, that these Asuras have no interest in the prospect of conquest or empire. Not being short-lived mortals, they feel no urgency to feign godhood by ruling as many men, as much territory, as they can. They seek not to rule but simply to destroy. The Asuras command powers we cannot hope to match. The sword Sarkozan has great power, as its very presence here attests. The devils dared not touch it. There is, in its pommel gem, some occult virtue the nature of which I cannot yet fathom. But it is only a single weapon. My studies lead me to believe that our real hope lies in a different direction. The might of our army notwithstanding, we will need powerful allies."

Lord Mael raised a hand and interjected, "We have sent word to the Blue Nomads of Shangoth's... abduction. A contingent of their best fighters should be here quite soon."

"That is good, my son. Still, the apparent ease with which Shangoth himself was turned to the cause of the Devas is a daunting sign."

Barand Thon protested. "You make him a traitor, priest!"

Karm Karvus and Prince Dru fumed with indignation as well. But Eumonius Eld sought to smooth their feathers.

"Nay, my sons! Just the opposite! Shangoth would never yield to evil! He was not beguiled or persuaded, but *possessed*. He had neither choice in the matter nor any means to resist. If even so mighty and loyal a hero could so helplessly fall victim to the evil threatening us, what chance have *we*? Or the eight-foot giants who serve him? Do not underestimate our foe for fear of selling our own valor short! In such an hour we require wisdom as well as courage."

"You paint a grim picture, holy father! What is this hope you speak of? Whence cometh our help?" asked Lord Mael, speaking for the rest.

"Our deliverance lies with Armageddon, our salvation in Ragnarok. I see you are puzzled. As I believe you are aware, we are seeing ancient myth coming alive before us. Thus I have gone to the sources to study that myth more closely. The fullest account of the primordial struggle of the Devas against the Asuras is to be found in the *Upa Puranas*. And in that version I have found a very important detail. The relevant passage, as in other versions, describes the long conflict between the holy Devas and the wicked Asuras. Where it differs is in its treatment of the beginning of that war. We learn that the earliest men were tested by the Nineteen Gods (though in those days, there were an even Twenty) who feared they had made men's earthly sojourn too easy. They resolved to subject our first ancestors to a bitter trial to prove whether men were worthy to reign over the earth. The Gods had many times had to suppress the evil Asuras but, in their compassion, they disliked to destroy them. So they set them free to plague infant humanity."

It was the queen who interrupted this time. "But how is that a test? From what you have told us, the defenseless human race could have been no match for them!"

"Indeed they were not! Even as *we* are not. But that was not the test. By sending upon them the scourge of the demons, the Gods sought to determine whether men were wise enough to admit it when outmatched and to acknowledge their need by seeking aid where it might be found. Men did as the Gods hoped, and the Gods rejoiced to help their children by ordering the company of the Devas into battle on their behalf. And thus began the epic contest."

Prince Dru had followed this recital with eager ears, but suddenly he felt he must have nodded and missed some crucial point. "And what, may I ask, is in this for us?"

"Simply this, O Prince. We require the intervention of the Gods, and we will not get it until we ask for it."

The faces around the long table seemed uniformly unimpressed.

"So that's your plan? We should just *pray*?" So said Lord Mael. "I must say, I have never had much luck with that!"

"Nor I!"

"Nor I."

"I am not surprised, my children. We cannot expect the Gods in their holy Transcendence to concern themselves with the trivial troubles of mere mortals, much less on a daily basis. Only major crises gain their notice. And this is why we have priests like myself. I serve as an ambassador to the Nineteen Gods. I may bring important matters before them, though only rarely, lest they tire of my pestering. But this is surely one of those occasions. I shall now enter the Temple and offer the customary sacrifices. I shall chant the traditional psalms of supplication. And then I shall retire to my apartment to fast and pray without ceasing and hope the Nineteen Gods will hear. The rest will be up to you. May the Gods observe your valor and judge us deserving of their aid!"

With that Eumonius Eld left the chamber, head bowed.

Queen Sumia had till this moment sat covered with a curtain-like cloak of black silk embroidered in gold thread with stylized flame designs. Now she rose to her feet, allowing the cloak to drop from her shoulders. Those present locked eyes on her, now revealed as clad in battle armor. Her arms and midriff were covered with silvered steel mail. Her proud breasts were contained in steel cups, each tipped with a purple sapphire. With one gauntleted hand she retrieved from under the table a helmet crowned with the sculpted Flame Phoenix, the emblem of Patanga, City of Fire. Setting it on her head, black hair spilling out beneath it to both shoulders, Sumia inclined forward to seize the hilt of Sarkozan and hefted it toward the ceiling.

"We shall be away within the hour! Onward for Thongor and all Lemuria!" And all shouted the same.

V. Attack of the Damned

Sumia led a small war party in the direction of ruined Teloth. Karm Karvus and Ald Turmis led two more, spreading out to determine how far the horror from the rift might have expanded. The bulk of the standing army remained in Patanga in readiness for any possible assault. The streets there were deserted as all sought shelter, fearing the worst.

As the Patangans passed through the countryside, they were troubled at the signs of devastation everywhere. Houses and barns lay in wreckage. Burnt and mutilated bodies littered the ground and swayed in the stinking wind as they hung from charred trees. Relief rivaled puzzlement, though, as the queen and her riders began to notice a peculiar disparity: there did not seem to be *enough* corpses to account for the necessary populace of the towns. They met no refugees dragging themselves along the roads. Where might they have fled?

The answer appeared abruptly as the company had dismounted beside a stream to refresh themselves with the modest provisions they had brought. One and then another of the companions looked up, brows knitting in concern. A ragtag group of villagers raced toward them, beginning to shout in almost bestial voice and to brandish hoes, shovels, clubs, and an occasional knife or sword. They varied in age and physical condition, some looking like they should hardly be able to walk, much less to rush headlong. The queen's men wordlessly sprang to their feet and drew their weapons, confused at the strange spectacle. To join battle with such a mob would be cruel butchery, but one must defend oneself in any case. All looked to Sumia who appeared equally nonplussed but shrugged and settled her helmet on her head.

As their motley attackers came within striking distance, a thing even stranger became apparent. Proximity, added to the closing sunset, allowed it to be seen that the eyes of the villagers glowed eerily *red*. They were possessed, their very bodies having become the clothing, the vehicles, for alien spirits! As such, they constituted a genuine threat. Regretting the necessity of slaying these poor people, but knowing they had already been fatally victimized, Sumia and her men laid to with superior weaponry. The demoniac mob outmatched them in savagery but could not equal the soldiers' prowess. Slaughtering them proved surprisingly easy work. But the brief moments the victors took to catch their breath were only the calm before the storm.

One by one, the decimated bodies of the slain began to quiver, then to convulse. Some of the Patangans shuddered with superstitious fright. All stared in amazement at the sudden agitation of the dead. But the awful motion soon ceased, at least among the corpses. At once it resumed among the same number of Sumia's soldiers, who commenced to jerk and pitch, limbs going momentarily rigid, before retrieving their weapons and turning upon each other and their former comrades who had not become possessed. The transformed men were of course far more formidable than their predecessors, but their frenzied attack was every bit as futile since every man turned on his fellow, making no distinction between demonized friend and still-sane foe.

The pile of dead bodies was shortly twice as high. Only Sumia and a handful of others survived to set fire to the heap, quietly lamenting the loss of their heroic comrades who had perished in so bizarre and pointless a fashion.

All this Thongor witnessed with rage and horror.

VI. Sword of Exorcism

"There is nothing to be done save to press on to the grave of Teloth, to the valley of the demons," quoth Sumia. "Courage may not save our lives, but it will guarantee a glorious death!"

The pyre of the dead illumined the night sky behind them as the Patangan riders continued their way to Teloth. There were no further attacks, but the company did now and then catch sight of winged figures or in some cases manlike forms riding on the backs of winged mounts, probably *graaks*, the lizard-hawks of primordial Lemuria, cousins of the pterodactyls known to modern science. They could be seen against the stars because of a sulfurous glow they emitted.

***

The hierophant of the Nineteen Great Gods of Lemuria rose from his posture of abject supplication before the altar of Father Gorm. He had already offered the precious sacrifice of a *Vandar*, the great black lion of the Kovian jungles. He had intoned not one but several psalms of petition. One thing remained: a sacrifice dearer even than a Vandar. To win the favor he sought from the Gods, a *human* sacrifice was mandated. By tradition, it ought to be the son of the reigning king, in this case Prince Thar. But Eumonius Eld could not brook that. He took the sacrificial blade from his sash and walked to the edge of the altar with its bowl for collecting the blood of the sacrifice. With a final word of prayer, he proceeded to plunge the ritual dagger into his own abdomen. As he fell forward onto the sacred table his body knocked over the great bowl, now overflowing with his own blood and bowels, which splattered on the gorgeously tiled floor. The offering was admittedly not quite orthodox, but he died with a light heart.

***

The other two parties of Thongor's men had departed the city an hour or so after Queen Sumia's vanguard. One was commanded by the king's trusted comrade Ald Turmis, the other led by another of Thongor's stalwarts from earlier days, Karm Karvus. Inspecting their men's armaments and administering encouragement in the face of unknown danger, Ald Turmis suddenly had an inspiration and told Karm Karvus to delay things for just a moment while he sped off to the Temple. It was not the high priest he sought, but rather a couple of the trinket merchants who maintained stalls just inside the entrance. Today there were few pilgrims examining the paste amulets and scapulars devoted to the various deities and divine heroes. The merchants flinched guiltily at the approach of the warrior prince, thinking they were about to be arrested for any of several likely offenses. They were greatly relieved when Ald Turmis made his real intention known. It turned out, in fact, to be a rather profitable night for them.

***

Sumia's few remaining soldiers sat their restless *kroters* and waited outside the rift of the liberated Asuras. They felt a pressure as of two great invisible walls, one of destiny, one of danger, pressing in on them.

The equilibrium was broken by the sound of hoof beats beyond the circles of their campfires. They clutched their weapons more tightly and sat up straighter in their saddles, ready at any moment to charge into battle.

But they wouldn't have to—not yet, anyway, for from either side came the war parties of Karm Karvus and Ald Turmis. Relief gave way to rejoicing as comrades greeted and embraced one another. But even this could not dispel the abiding fog of foreboding. Somewhat distracted by looking over their shoulders, the reunited Patangans shared provisions and reports.

"Ald Turmis, Karm Karvus! Thank Gorm your numbers are undiminished. Then you were not set upon by gangs of the possessed, as we were?"

Both men started to answer, then made to defer to one another.

Laughing, their queen decided the issue: "Ald Turmis, you start!"

"Gladly, your Majesty! Though my friend here can supplement my account. Well, we did indeed have occasion to cross swords with groups of demonized villagers, poor wretches! They were easily dealt with, I'm happy to say, though we all bemoaned having to do so. They were hostages, not really enemies."

Karm Karvus nodded, having nothing to add. Sumia was surprised at what she did *not* hear.

"But why did not the possessing spirits flee the bodies of those you slew and turn your own men against one another, as they did with us?"

As one, the two captains and several of the nearest soldiers reached beneath their mail shirts to reveal pendants, protective charms depicting the scowling face of Shadrazur, the Lord of Warriors.

"I had thought it superstition" Ald Turmis confessed, "but I thought it worth a try."

"We must welcome help from any and all quarters, my friends!" the queen exclaimed. "And this is a hopeful sign! Ald Turmis and Karm Karvus have proven that the Gods are not indifferent to our

64

plight!"

From this, Thongor, too, gained new hope.

The Patangans waited and watched, and finally made camp for the night. The great, golden moon of Lemuria sailed slowly above them, drifting in a sea of deceptive calm. But instead of its usual color, it shone scarlet as its beams were filtered through the red mists rising from the rift, now a veritable chasm, that cleft the ground where lost Teloth once flourished. Those on watch in the camp found the sight of the Valley of Demons a hypnotic magnet for their eyes and were thus in little danger of careless vigilance. They watched also for the arrival of the promised warriors of the Jegga Horde, though it looked more and more likely that events would not wait for them.

Few could sleep deeply for anxiety over what the dawn might bring. They wanted it over with, and most everyone was awake and ready when it came. First there was a rumble, the sound of a great host advancing from deep within the earth.

All at once, like a tidal wave of magma, a mighty company of red-eyed berserkers erupted from the earth. They appeared to be possessed humans, no doubt drawn from surrounding villages, now enslaved by the devilish Asuras. This was by no means unexpected; the real surprise that took away the breath of Sumia and many others, was the sight of the mounted warrior spearheading the assault: it was Thongor! His eyes, like the other possessed, flamed red. Sparks seemed to scatter from his face and the ends of his whipping mane. His features were easily recognizable but no longer handsome because of the snarling mask of pure hatred that distorted them. Sumia had never seen such a countenance, even when she'd seen him close -up in the course of battle. For a moment she felt relief for the fact that her beloved was still alive, but it passed in seconds in light of what he had become!

Sumia's Patangans quickly suffered some losses, but the men led by Ald Turmis and Karm Karvus seemed invulnerable, irresistible. The talismans they wore proved to be amazingly effective, shielding them from possession by the demons fleeing their slain, borrowed bodies. The demoniac fighters faced additional disadvantages. Their steeds were ordinary horses, and these struggled with their infernal riders, their sulfur stench, the baking heat they radiated, and the universal sense of alarm animals feel in the presence of diabolical evil.

The possessed fought with bestial fury. They were fierce predators but knew little of combat skills. All told, the battle was not going badly, but Sumia knew it was only the preliminary phase. Things had plenty of room to grow much worse.

She knew her target had to be the demoniacal Thongor. She could not bear the sight of him like this. And she knew he was the lynchpin of the enemy force of attack. If she had to kill him, and if she could, Sumia knew Thongor would command her to do it. She did not know whether she could maneuver her mount close enough to her husband's, but as she scanned the clashing hosts between them, looking for a path of access, she saw Thongor was saving her the trouble. He was making his way, sword swinging, directly for her. The bloody blade he wielded had belonged to some one of the possessed soldiers or from one of the slain Patangans, but he wielded it with lethal skill. Sumia had neither seen nor heard of a swordsman who could match her husband's skill. But even so, she thought her chances more than even. For she wielded mighty Sarkozan!

As the two closed in combat, Sumia found herself able to evade some of Thongor's blows and to parry others. She felt almost as if another hand guided hers. But she knew she could not maintain this level of prowess for long. And at that moment she saw an opening and heard a distinct voice inside her head: *Kill me! Slay me, Sumia --now!*

Without a thought, she drove the sword home, right into the heart of her beloved enemy. The mighty form went blank-eyed and slumped over, the borrowed sword dropping from his nerveless hand. His body remained on his steed only because the straps and stirrups held him in place.

Several warriors clustered around the battling couple paused in startlement, while tears rushed unbidden to Sumia's eyes. But then she very nearly flew from her saddle as the great jewel set into the pommel of Sarkozan flashed like a miniature sun, unleashing a tangible concussion impact. The radiance focused like a lightning bolt following the exact path Sarkozan had taken but a moment before. Thongor's arms and head flew back like a puppet's. His eyes, gold-flaked again, were no longer vacant. For an instant his hair stood on end. His chest wound was gone, as if welded shut. As Sumia recoiled from the shock blast, her gloved fingers involuntarily released the sword. Sarkozan arced end over end until Thongor's enormous hand plucked it out of the air.

VII. War in Heaven

Thongor, his soul glorying in its restoration to its accustomed habitat, laid about him in the thick of the possessed host. Back to back with his heroic mate, the mighty Valkarthan thrilled to the joy of battle as a *Vandar* thrills to the hunt. Soon the demoniac army, small to begin with, though outnumbering the Patangans, was decimated. But through the bloody mists rising from the steaming piles of gore, Thongor beheld the unmistakable outline of the man-mountain Shangoth. It was he, Thongor's beloved battle companion, who had, in his possessed state, struck him a traitorous blow days earlier. Housing a demon, Shangoth's Rmoahal hide had gone from bright blue to purple.

The king of Patanga squinted to discern his old friend's hue, for he hoped he would not have to fight the gigantic figure. But before he could determine the color, the point became moot: the fabled spear of Shangoth, larger than a weaver's beam, shot like an arrow straight at Thongor's head. The barbarian ducked down, simultaneously bringing Sarkozan into play, chopping the shaft asunder. The purple colossus leaped at Thongor like another arrow from the same bow. The two crashed to the ground. Several of Thongor's men immediately rushed to their king's assistance, but he waved them away. He never relished the prospect of being rescued by another.

Thongor disengaged himself from the *Poa*-like constriction of the nomad giant's steely thews. He wanted to do as little permanent damage as possible to his bewitched friend, so he did not strike with the sword, though Sarkozan might have settled the matter quick enough. As for Shangoth, he shook off blows that might have decapitated any lesser man. Thongor quickly realized the only way to defeat his possessed foe was to kill him, and that he refused to do.

An inspiration struck him, and he got the attention of Ald Turmis, motioning him over. When the man drew near enough, Thongor reached out and yanked the talisman from around the other's neck. Clutching it in his fist, Thongor evaded another lunge and leaped onto Shangoth's broad back as the latter charged past him. He put a choke hold on the blue throat with one arm, then fastened the amulet's thong around the giant's bull neck with the other. Amazingly, it was just big enough.

Shangoth raised himself onto one knee and started to reach for the pendant, but he stopped in mid-gesture. Blinking, he looked up at Thongor, then at his own hand, which had now become blue again.

The two men, no longer surrounded by knots of struggling combatants, were about to embrace in friendship, but in another instant all eyes were riveted to a new stream of demonic troops pouring out of the crevice like wasps from a disturbed nest. These were no mere men indwelt by demon spirits. These were the Wrathful Deities themselves, the very Asuras, lusting to even the score and gain revenge on the heavenly Devas who had once banished and imprisoned them. The beings were horrible in appearance, bristling with fangs and tusks, asymmetrical faces sprouting goggle-eyes that moved randomly, nostrils and jaws breathing flames. Their hides were scaly and mottled. Some flew with their own membranous wings, while others took to the sky on dragon-like steeds.

The Asuras ignored the mortals, passing over them to join combat with rival host now making itself known from *above*. The celestial vault was brilliant with the pure light of the angels who serve the Nineteen Gods. They were hard for mortal men to look upon but seemed to approximate the forms of winged men brandishing javelins and swords. Or such was all the sense the human mind could make of them. The conflict now joined was echoing with crashing weapons. Sumia could not help thinking of the stories she had heard as a child explaining the rumbling of the thunder as the sound of angels and devils brawling. She now realized it was not far from the truth.

She stood by her husband's side, marveling at what was transpiring above their heads. The queen whispered in awe, "The real hero of this day may prove to be Eumonius Eld, for it was he who summoned the Devas to take up their ancient struggle against the Asuras." Of course she did not yet know the extent of the priest's ultimate sacrifice.

"A good man indeed! And a true hero, as you say. But the day is not yet done, is it? Now excuse me, my love." Withal did

Thongor find and mount one of the lizard-hawks that had lost its rider and urged it on into the sky where he intended to enlist on the side of the Devas. For he, too, had a score to settle.

***

The rejoicing over the defeat of the Asura hosts was tempered with mourning for innocent villagers as well as valiant heroes who perished in the nightmare conflict. There were many funerals, and Thongor attended as many as he could. Just now, he sat, dressed for once in the traditional finery of the ancient kings, with his queen and his nobles in the front row of seats in the Temple of the Flame, the holiest shrine in Patanga. The place was filled with those gathered to honor the sacrifice of the priest Eumonius Eld, whose self-immolation, of which the Sark and Sarkaja learned upon their return to the capital, had turned the tide of battle. The hierophant of Lemuria was now seen to be the greatest champion of the conflict. Thongor was the last in a series of dignitaries eulogizing their friend and mentor. Or so it seemed until a surprise visitor mounted the dais.

The whole company gasped in astonishment and fear as the one whose sacrifice they celebrated removed his hood and commenced to speak.

"My children, I shall at once return whence I came so long ago. All your lives you have prayed to the Nineteen Gods of Lemuria and no doubt puzzled over the saying that once there had been a Twentieth God, unremembered by name, honored in neither myth nor hymn. *But I am he!* The memories of my former life returned when I cast off the veil of stupefying flesh.

"We Gods met in council long ages ago, planning against the day when the demon horde should trespass into man's domain. I alone foresaw the means to turn back that tide. On that day I volunteered myself as the sacrifice required to vanquish the enemies of the Gods, and so I took on mortal flesh in the fullness of time. As a man, yes, I am dead. But weep not for me, for now I return to the glory of the Twenty Gods!"

Withal did the luminous form of him who had been Eumonius Eld dissolve into a golden mist, to the great rejoicing of all present.

THE SHADOW OF DIA SUST

by David C. Smith

For Retired U.S. Army SFC Robert Price, Sr.

1. The Outlander

> We bargain for the graves we lie in.
> James Russell Lowell
> *The Vision of Sir Launfal*

Bodor moved quickly, faster than Oron had anticipated, and Oron paid for his slowness: Bodor's bleeding knuckles hit the younger man hard on the left side of the face and scraped painfully along his ear. Still, Oron managed to twist away as Bodor reached for the young man's long hair. Bodor missed—and leaned off balance.

Oron moved in. He punched Bodor's bare skin powerfully at the ribs. Bones cracked, and Bodor winced. He stepped away with his mouth open.

Around them, at the fires that circled the open yard in the middle of the war camp, laughter and cheers came from two hundred brutal men—fighters and killers, all of them. For this company, two angry men throwing down in blood sport was a diversion subordinate only to open combat on the red field itself.

A diversion, and a chance for winnings. They called to one another from fire to fire, warning each other to be prepared to be shamed.

"The boy's going to put him down!"

"Get your money ready, pig! And your sister! I'm taking both!"

"Can I change my bet? Bodor's going to break this pup in half!"

Beyond the hot campfires, seated in a tall wooden chair that had accompanied him on half a lifetime of murderous campaigns, crouched Maton, their war captain and chief. With the experience of many years, he watched these naked brutes, Bodor and Oron, each without armor, without weapons, covered only in animal skins wrapped tightly below their belts—Bodor, able to push out the eyes and tear away the throat of anyone in bare-handed combat, and this young dog who had come into camp only weeks before, alone, an outlander, clearly a fighter, but from a distant land and of a heritage legendary to Maton and his easterners, and with a history that the war chief reckoned to be lies and exaggerations.

For no one could have achieved in a lifetime what Oron the Nevgan claimed to have done in only a few years. Leading men into battle and fighting sorcerers and important chiefs both. Measuring himself against the love of proud women and winning their strong hearts. Witnessing remarkable transformations of reality within the lodge huts of mystics, shamans, and other lost souls. Spending count-less nights alone under the cold stars, tracking whatever he could find alive to eat raw and squirming. Killing his own father.

His own father.

Performing an act that even renegades such as these in this camp, murderers and cutthroats every one of them, regarded as evil, direct evil.

More howls came as Bodor began circling to his right, keeping watch on Oron. He was a head taller than the outlander and thicker in the chest as well as the waist, but the young Nevgan was quicker by far with his lunges and hits and feints. Bodor had marks on him to demonstrate this: welts on his shoulders and upper arms, bleeding scratches on his chest and back, even a bite mark on his right forearm earned from an attempt to cuff Oron across the mouth.

Oron himself had not accepted as many hurts. He was bruised on the left ear and sore on his chest and jaw where Bodor had gotten inside with punches, but he had kept his ribs intact.

And he was smiling, whereas Bodor, not at all pleased that he had failed so far to take down this cub, was grimace and frown.

And taunt. "Dog," he said to Oron. "Outlander. I've killed so many like you, I've lost count."

Oron answered by spitting at him.

Bodor sneered, and he continued to move to his right, trying to back Oron against a nearby tree. "You're a Nevgan pig. Do all of you pigs kill your own fathers?"

Oron lost his smile.

"Or did *you* do it just so you could stick it inside your own mother?"

Oron moved. Ran at Bodor. Leaned right as though intending to punch the broken ribs—

Bodor pulled back.

—then crouched forward as he ran, ducking his head.

Whoops from the campfires.

Oron rolled onto his shoulders and back. Lifted his legs. Pushed them forward so that the heels of his feet struck Bodor full on the chest.

Howls, all around.

Bodor, off balance and gasping, tripped away.

Oron got to his feet and jumped forward. He pushed Bodor in the chest. Bodor lost his balance and fell backward, crashing hard.

Oron jumped and straddled him, seating himself on the bigger man's chest.

Bodor lifted his arms in an attempt at defense. Oron caught the wrists and held them.

Out of breath, Bodor stared up at the Nevgan.

Oron squeezed his legs together; Bodor groaned as pain oozed from his broken ribs. Oron twisted the bigger man's wrists until the snapping bones gave way in both. Then he took Bodor's head between his hands.

Bodor tried to speak.

Oron lifted Bodor's head, then pushed it back down quickly, hard against the earth. He did it again. And again. Did this many times. Finally he wrapped his bleeding hands in Bodor's hair, twisted the long hair until he had a secure grip, and stretched the head back and up until more bones broke. Oron pushed until the head could be moved no farther on the contorted neck.

If Bodor still could see from so ridiculous an angle, then his sight rested on the hot stones of a campfire somewhere above the top of his head.

But likely he saw nothing; his skull had been separated from his spine.

Oron stood, panting, and spat at Bodor again, directly onto the side of the dead man's face. He said to the corpse, "Son of a

72

whore. We kill our fathers and *anyone else* we want to. Stick it in *your* mother! *And* your father. In *Hell*."

Men at the campfires hurrahed and pushed forward to clap the young man on the back, rub his hair, or punch him on the shoulders in their excitement.

"He did it!"

"I'm rich! Pay me, Butt-face!"

"I knew he could do it!"

The losers grumbled and paid their bets, then returned to their tents or bunk rolls or stumbled off into the deeper woods to urinate the beer they had drunk, as though doing that could help relieve their disappointment.

Then came a loud voice from behind the happy company of killers. "Make way! Step aside! *Move!*" Maton himself, taller and heavier than Bodor, even, pushed through the mob.

His black beard was stained with food and drink, and his long hair was oily and braided where it fell over the leather-and-bronze cuirass he wore. The chain loosely draped around his protected waist was woven with spikes and metal thorns, and it was weighted on one end with a heavy ball, also studded with spikes; fools had died, bleeding from opened throats, when Maton swung that weapon overhead like a wheel and then savaged those unguarded necks. And in swordplay, he was better than nearly every man in camp; few had ever challenged him, and none of those had lived.

Maton came straight at Oron and stopped an arm's length away from him.

And did not smile.

"You killed my best man."

"Some men need killing."

"Which of you provoked this?"

"He took my food and called me a dog. Told me I didn't deserve to eat the food that men eat."

One of those near Maton, a bald, lean veteran named Agol, told the chief, "It's true, Captain. It's the truth."

Maton glanced at him, then asked Oron, "Who's going to lead these bastards into the field tomorrow?"

"Not Bodor, unless he finds a way back from Hell tonight."

Men laughed until Maton glared at them. When he looked at

Oron again, he demanded, "Who am I going to get? You?"

"Pay me what you paid Bodor, and I'll give it some thought."

More laughter and a few whoops. "Do it, son!" came a voice from the back.

"You can lead these men?" Maton said. "I doubt it."

"I've fought animals better than Dasagak, and I've met him before."

"Where?"

"South of here. I'll stick him like a pig if you give me the chance."

"Why didn't you stick him like a pig when you were south of here?"

"Because he's a cowardly pig. He ran away. He lets other men do his fighting for him." Oron said it as he looked Maton in the eyes.

Maton smiled. "Then you lead the men. I want you out there front and center. And I want to see you do whatever you need to do to stick your pig."

"You'll see it. Now can I have something to drink? Killing pigs makes me thirsty."

Maton chuckled and lifted a hand. Someone behind him produced a wine flagon, and he handed it to Oron. He asked him then, "Where did you learn that trick, jumping like that?"

"I didn't learn it." Oron unstoppered the flagon and lifted it to his mouth. "I thought of it. I did it because I needed to."

"You're full of surprises, Nevgan."

Oron nodded as he guzzled.

"You'll find that I'm full of surprises, too. Tomorrow," Maton told him, "you lead the way."

Oron slurped wine and wiped his mouth with the back of a hand. "You just be ready with something sharp to stick his head on. I'll bring you a trophy, and I'll get myself some honor back."

Maton turned away, pushing past his men to go to his horsehide tent.

While half the dogs in his company once more encircled Oron and congratulated him with laughter and more hard slaps on the back.

*** *

"Could you even have hoped for such luck?" Damu asked as Maton settled into a camp chair in his tent.

"I see no luck," the captain complained.

His bodyguard sniffed with amusement. Damu had served as Maton's shadow for years, since losing the use of his left leg, which remained attached to his hip but was no better than a wooden prop, the meat of it dead and the muscles, weak. Maton had saved Damu's life the day that leg had been cut nearly free by men with quick swords, killing the attackers and pulling Damu to safety as the mangled leg rolled in the dust. In gratitude for that gesture, Damu had sworn ever to assist his chief. And since earning that wound, Damu had killed many men; he was superb with a knife and able to drop birds from high in the air when he threw his daggers. And in swordplay, he was equal to nearly every man in camp, perhaps second only to Maton himself.

Now, as Maton brooded over what Oron had done to his champion, Damu said to the war chief, "It is evident to me that letting this pup lead the way tomorrow gives us the advantage of delivering him to his old enemy."

Maton considered it, and he realized the good that could come of it. "Let that dog have Oron," he grinned, "while we lay aside our steel?"

"Do it," Damu urged his chief. "We pay in this way for safe passage through Dasagak's lands. We can return to fight him another day, and on that day, we will not be outnumbered five to one."

"I do not fear the numbers."

"Nor do I. Nor do your wolves. But why risk losing some of these fighters when you can risk fewer of them when we return next spring?"

Maton weighed this in his mind. "Hire more men over the winter. Match Dasagak sword for sword, come spring. Pile the heads high, and increase our armory. And raid these lands at our leisure the summer long."

"And at what price?" Damu reminded his lord. "The head of an outlander boy whose sole gift, clearly, is that he wanders into war camps where he's more trouble than he's worth."

Maton laughed. "Send a rider into the chief's camp with our pledge to let him take Oron in the morning as we stand by."

"I'll do it now."

"If Oron tells the truth," Maton said, "then Dasagak will agree to this. We'll have our safe passage and our winter's spell, and then all the plunder we wish next spring. If Oron lies, then he dies first in the morning. A man that kills his own father is no man at all, and he deserves no better than to be killed like a dog."

***

The wind heard those words, as did the shadows outside Maton's horsehide tent, as did a spirit waiting within those shadows.

The spirit held still, listening, then drifted on as heat might from a campfire, as a breath might when carried on the night air. The drifting spirit returned to its body hidden in a cave in the high stones of the low mountains that crouched west of Maton's camp, west of Dasagak's camp, west of the wide field that tomorrow was to be a blood field.

A groan, as spirit moved inside flesh and as a woman, middle-aged but weary, strong but exhausted from years of effort and change, shuddered with the return of her secret sight. There was a young woman seated in the shadows beside the sorceress, a girl of perhaps twelve years who was no more than a stick, a malnourished thing with full hair and dark eyes, dressed in someone else's cast-off clothes. This young one touched the sorceress as she shuddered, making sure that her mistress was well enough after her challenge. The woman of spirit strength took in long breaths to awaken fully. Both then looked into the small campfire before them, the only light in this deep cave.

"Is it he?" the young woman asked.

"It is."

"A man that kills his own father is no man at all. . . ."

This is what the sorceress had heard. This is why she had followed the signs in the stars, followed the indications shown her when she read the smoke and had the young woman cast colored bones. The signs and indications had led her here, far from her original home, so that she could complete the destiny she had devised for herself.

She could not complete that task alone, the stars had told

her, and her bones and her visions.

She would need assistance.

And this man who had killed his own father offered precisely the assistance that was needed.

2. Betrayal

I wish only that my fury would
drive me to hack your meat away
and eat it raw for the things you
have done to me.
> Homer, *Iliad*
> Book XXII, 408-410

Before dawn, as the earliest sunlight fell through the heavy mists on the wide field, Oron sat his horse and watched as Dasagak's one thousand aligned themselves in the distance, facing him. Beside the Nevgan wolf, to his right and left, sat six others ordered to advance with him—one of them the old, tough Agol, the others, younger fighters chosen personally by Maton and Damu.

And behind the seven of them, waiting upon the grassy slope of the valley wall to the south, were Maton and his hundreds.

At a signal from Oron, these hundreds would advance.

The morning brightened. The gray mists lifted. Birds called from the outcroppings, the rocks and deep forests on either side of the flat plain.

Now the infantry at Dasagak's front line pounded their weapons against their heavy shields, and they let out high sounds to intimidate and challenge—roars, howls, animal cries. When they had worked themselves into a fighting rage and dropped to silence at last, a loud voice lifted from behind them, calling across the field.

Agol leaned close to Oron. "What does he say? I don't understand him."

"It is Dasagak, the Man Eater," Oron told him. "He knows I'm here. He says he'll have my head before the morning is gone."

"Then take his head instead."

"That I'll do. But how does he know that I am with this company?"

Horn sounds lifted behind Oron, from Maton's lines—and an arrow flew over Oron's head.

Startled, he reined his horse around, pulling hard.

And as he did, a man farther to the left of him, not Agol but one of the young retainers, coughed as a second arrow caught him in the chest and pushed him from his horse.

The horse bolted.

"What have you done?" another of the retainers roared at Oron—Kess, a man as young as Oron himself.

They heard the snap of more bows, a hundred of them, and the bright sky darkened.

Oron, Agol, all of them lifted their shields over their heads.

As arrow tips bit into their bucklers, another of the young men went down. His horse caught an arrow and fell onto its side. The warrior, thrown free, took two quick arrows in the side of his head, both of them entering above the left ear. The force of them pushed his eyeballs from their orbits; the wet eyes hung on his cheeks like teardrops.

Now the five dismounted and slapped their horses to be gone.

As the mounts ran free, galloping toward the far outcroppings, Oron ordered Agol to crouch beside him and the other three to put their backs against theirs.

"Why?" Kess asked again.

"They mean to trap us here," Agol growled.

"But I've done nothing!" Kess complained. From under his shield, he looked at Dasagak's restless thousand at the far end of the field.

Another round of arrows lifted and came down. They punched into the field to form a small forest of feathers between them and Maton's lines.

A horn sounded from Maton's formation, and then Maton yelled loudly across the wide plain, "Dasagak! He is yours! Take the wolf cub!"

Oron grunted. Crouched under his shield, he looked at Agol. "Because I killed Bodor?"

Agol sniffed. "You're a threat to him, son, that's all. Don't you know that? The first thing you do is kill strong men who can challenge you. That's what leaders do."

"I kept such men at my side."

"Then you're a better man than Maton."

"But you and these men have no reason to be killed."

"An old man and a few pups? We don't mean anything to anyone."

Oron took in a deep breath, then told the four still alive with him, "Run for that mountain." He meant the outcropping to the west—sufficiently far that they all could die trying to reach it, but surely offering a better chance at life than being caught by Dasagak's swords.

Agol nodded and spat onto the grass.

Another round of arrows made wide sounds in the air above them and joined the forest already planted.

"But you can't take Dasagak this way," Agol said to Oron.

"We'll see," Oron told him. "He won't kill me here. He wants to do it face to face. I'll not die here. Now go. Stay under—"

Gas erupted from one of the dead boys near them, the one with the arrows through his head—an abrupt sound.

Oron ordered them, "Go! Now!"

But Agol said, "Wait. Look," and pointed toward the arrows that had landed in the earth. They were difficult to see.

Steam was lifting from the tall grass.

Oron leaned forward.

Not steam. Mist. It was green, and not rising from the grass but coming across the field from the west and filling the ground around them like a carpet.

"What is it?" Oron asked Agol.

The old man had no answer.

Oron waved at the mist with his sword; it did not disperse quickly. There was no smell to it, but it grew thicker, and very soon, within heartbeats, it had covered the men completely and cut off the sky, cut off their view of everything except one another.

Oron heard Dasagak yell across the field, "What sorcery is this, Maton?"

If Maton answered, Oron did not hear him because, from within the mist, just as Dasagak's voice ended, Oron saw a snake move toward him, a large snake, fat and longer than—

He tried to back away.

Not a snake.

A tentacle of some kind, a vine—

It caught Oron by his legs, and when he turned to strike at it with his sword, a second vine came through the mist above his head and wrapped around his arm, preventing him from moving.

And now he was lifted into the air, into the green mist, lifted three man lengths toward the sky.

Agol called out, "Oron!" and ran toward him as Oron was pulled toward the west. Quickly.

Agol followed him.

Kess called, "Wait!" as he, too, followed, stumbling through the dense mist.

And the other two came after him.

Across the field, horns blew sharply, and the drums beat from Dasagak's army. "What treachery is this, Maton? You lie! Your man lied to us!"

Oron, still being carried by those vines, and the men running beside him heard the powerful thunder of warriors taking the field.

Dasagak's thousand were a storm bringing their anger to the unprepared two hundred—unprepared because Maton, in his pride, had told his sword men to keep their edges sheathed and their armor unbuckled, for this morning's battle would be short.

Indeed, he had assured his men, there would, in fact, be no battle at all.

**

"*Where is he?*" Agol called, scuttling up a stony path as quickly as he could.

Kess and the other two were ahead of him, and the great green mist already was going, blowing east and lifting into the bright sky.

The tendrils or vines, whatever they were—nowhere to be seen.

Neither was Oron.

Until Kess, pushing through some thin trees rooted in the

tough soil of the outcropping, said strongly, "Here!"

They all heard his voice, then—Oron's growl of rage—and as Agol came up behind the younger men, he saw the Nevgan on his feet, sword out, roaring at something not to be seen.

There was movement there—a shadow, or the last piece of a vine moving away, pulling itself between small trees—and an angry Oron jumped at the movement, prepared to swipe at it with his sword.

But the movement was gone.

Oron looked over his shoulder and saw Kess, Agol, and the other two, but he said nothing. He ducked his head and prowled forward, moving past the trees, and walked up a grassy incline that led deeper into a copse.

Agol moved past the others to follow, but Kess put a gloved hand on the old man's shoulder to arrest him. He asked, "What does it mean?"

"I don't know."

"This makes me cold. What kind of man is this, him and this sorcery?"

The two younger men were watching them, listening as though for clues to help them decide what to do next. Follow Oron? Go back down into the valley? What would be the purpose of that?

"It's not *his* sorcery," Agol said, and moved past Kess to follow the Nevgan.

"And Maton?" Kess asked.

Agol paused and looked behind, stared down into what he and the other three could see of the battlefield far below, through the bending branches with their leaves and past the tall rocks and stones at this height.

"He is routed," was Agol's opinion. "I'll wager Maton's head is on a stick as soon as this." He sneered. "I fought with him and those dogs for many years. Damn him for doing this to me. Him and that right hand of his."

"Damu?" asked one of the young men. "I never trusted him."

"His mother slept with shadows," Agol said, and spat a wet stream onto some nearby leaves. "He's what came of it." He looked at the younger man. "Nadul? Am I right?"

"Yes."

"And you?" Agol asked the other.

"Borin. It was my grandfather's name."

"Stay close," Agol advised them. "I trust the Nevgan, and this trick is not his doing. It was done *to* him. And by Damu or Maton or someone else—" He looked up the grassy path. "Stay close."

"You don't need to tell me," Nadul said. He was without one eye—he wore a leather patch over it—and otherwise betrayed numerous hurts for a man so young, scars and two missing fingers, and an ear that had healed awkwardly and was out of shape. Not the best of fighters, those wounds told Agol.

The other one, Borin, taller by half a head and heftier than Nadul, showed less damage and was brighter in the eyes. He could face death well, Agol reckoned—if not fearlessly, then with pride. He was a man to have with one.

Maton must have considered him a fighter of potential, perhaps a born leader.

And so to be sacrificed.

The weak ever send the strong and young to their deaths. It is how the weak keep their power.

***

The path led Oron into a place of tall boulders and overhanging trees with man-sized roots dug into the stones, and past those boulders was an opening, the black, cold mouth of an antre or cave, some delve.

Poking his sword before him at the shadows, he moved in, sniffing and listening.

The odor of this place was rich with the rush of damp earth and damp leaves, of roots and moss and the underearth, moist, ripeness feeding all of the growing things around. The great stones that Oron moved past were wet, almost slick with moisture, and furry with moss.

He heard a sound then but could see little ahead of him in the cave.

He moved his blade back and forth in front of him, ready for whatever might be there.

"Stop, please"—a woman's voice.

Oron stopped. He squinted, trying to see who this was.

Shuffling—boots on the earth floor of the cave—and a face came into view, the dark-skinned, worn face of a young woman, and then the deerskin vest and skirt that she wore, and crude jewelry about her neck and waist—ropes of bone, carved and painted. Magical.

He said to the young woman, "Who are you? And why did you take me that way?"

"Warrior, I am not the one to give you answers. Swear by your mother that you will not raise that weapon against me or against my mistress."

"Who is your mistress? Did she do this?"

"She did."

"Then she is a witch or a sorceress, up from hell. Better that I kill her now so that she can't hurt me further."

"She wishes to help you if you will help her."

Oron heard further boot steps behind him and looked over his shoulder at Agol and the young men at the mouth of the cave.

"This is for your ears alone," the young woman told him. "Bid your companions stay."

Agol asked Oron, "Who is she, son?"

"A witch. Or her mistress is."

"Her name is Dia-Sust," said the woman in deer skins. "I am Sen-Odit."

"Southern names," Agol said to her. "Many a way from here. Why come this far north?"

"For vengeance," Sen-Odit replied. "And this man can assist my mistress in doing it."

"How?" Oron asked her.

"Because of what you are." She looked at Agol. "You are old. You have heard much in your years?"

"Aye." Agol nodded.

"You know that this man killed his own blood-father."

"I do."

"Do you fear him because of that?"

"I fear no one."

"Him you should fear," said Sen-Odit. "This is the warrior my mistress requires." She looked at Oron. "Will you come freely, to

83

hear what she says, and sheathe your sword?"

From behind, Kess said, "Kill them now, Wolf. I don't trust witches."

Sen-Odit regarded Kess darkly but asked Oron once more, "Will you come? You know that you are unlike other fighters. You have been told this."

"I *have* been told this." Oron lifted his sword and dropped it into its scabbard. "How does Dia-Sust know it?"

"It is her way. She works with spirits. Please tell your companions to wait here."

Oron turned to Agol. "Do it. Keep *them* on a leash." He meant the other three.

"Are you sure?"

"I am. We'll talk, Agol, when I am back."

"Just so you *do* come back, Wolf."

Oron smiled at him, and his eyes brightened, for he had been down such paths before, and in other caves such as this.

***

Dia-Sust must have been, once, as dark skinned as Sen-Odit, and attractive—dark eyed, full lipped, strong of limb—but she was no longer. The skin of her face now was green, a heavy green. She reclined under a thin blanket on a pallet of sticks and woven grass alongside a fire that was more hot coals than flames. A few objects were nearby—more jewelry, as well as items that Oron judged were for witch work: bowls, sticks and wands, many pieces of bone, two rolled parchments.

The knowledge that such people kept in their charmed objects and their powerful, marked stones was as strong as the ability Oron had mastered with sword work and fighting and hunting.

Sen-Odit held back as Oron came forward. He looked at the frail witch, old beyond her years, and nodded to her. "My weapon is covered," he told her.

"Will you sit?"

Oron moved to position himself cross-legged on the ground after the manner of all tribal people at a fire.

"I sense no fear in you," the witch said to him. "Only curiosi-

84

ty."

"I have learned when fear is proper and when it is not need-ed," Oron told her.

"Good. You are the man I am looking for."

"Because I killed my father?" Oron asked.

The spirit woman told him, "This is the sign that you are a new man. This is why I brought you here."

Oron grunted. "The vines. The ropes. I've waited long enough to ask you about them."

Dia-Sust smiled, showing sharp teeth. Oron realized that she had done that to herself, filed her teeth into points, as necessary for her magic—to bite and chew living things and so take their spirits as they died.

"The vines are me, Oron," she said to him, and lifted her blan-ket.

She lifted it high, and Oron saw that Dia-Sust had no arms but only vines, green ropes extending from her, at least ten of them, and all without hands. Her body itself had become as tuberous and shiny as a green young plant. She was wrapped in coils of these green vines. She had no legs or feet—she was a large plant with many vines and tubers growing from her. Those not wrapped around her stretched out on the floor beside her like undone netting.

"I have achieved this for myself," Dia-Sust told Oron, "to ac-complish what I must. Just as you killed your own father to accom-plish what you must."

Oron stared in wonder at her. "Erith and Corech . . ." he whis-pered, naming his gods.

"Are you prepared to listen to me now?"

Oron nodded. "I am."

The spirit woman looked at her servant. "Sen-Odit."

Oron heard her boot steps grow quiet as the young woman went away.

3. The Spirit Woman

> For of the soul the body form doth take:
> For soul is form, and doth the body make.
> Edmund Spenser

"Damu is dead," Oron told Dia-Sust as he sat by her fire. "None of them could have lived past the attack by Dasagak. I know Dasagak. He murders everything."

"Only what is within his reach," the witch corrected him. "Damu lives. As does Maton. Others, as well. They escaped when they had the chance, to fight another day. But I made certain for my-self that Damu and Maton survived."

"How? And how do I know that this is true?"

"My mist, barbarian. The mist that I sent into that field. It serves as my eyes and ears. It senses everything. It hid those two for me, and it knows now where Maton and Damu and the survivors are. They are hurrying on horses that they will beat to death."

"If they live, then my sword wants them. I will drink their blood."

"You will drink Maton's blood. Damu is mine."

"Why?" And then Oron, understanding, said, "This is why I am here."

The plant-woman, the witch, regarded him with her slow green eyes. "A thousand ghosts surround you, barbarian. These are the ghosts of old heroes. I see lights around you like so many camp-fires in the night. They are like stars, like dust in the sky. These mem-ories from old times are with you. They guide you. They pull you to-ward a destiny."

"I have been told I have a destiny."

"You have many paths to choose, but if you persevere, you may yet find these ghosts and lights fighting with you against a great evil."

"And why do you wish to drink Damu's blood?"

She smiled at him, baring those teeth. "Damu came with more swords than there are trees on these hills. He and his killers de-stroyed my people. Our wizards used magic to fight them, and many of the killers died screaming like children, but at last we were over-come, and Damu and many of those with him escaped with cattle and gold and with those of us he could sell as slaves. This was ten years ago. So my people are gone. My heart is broken. Only I remain, and this one who assists me. The father of my people bade me es-cape and avenge our name on this man. He said that he would protect me in the next world if I do what is necessary in this one to destroy Damu. You yourself, Nevgan, have survived such cruelty and loss. The shadows that follow me, the ghosts of my beloved people, tell me this. Are they not correct?"

Oron grunted. "My people, too, were killed by a powerful sorcerer in my home far from here."

"And you avenged your people."

"I killed this sorcerer."

"And then what did you have? No people. No father. You are the No-Tribe Man."

"This is true."

"Nevgan, what we do echoes in the earth and is guided by the stars. We are one with all that is. Now you, without a people, with your history gone—you are free. You have no father; you are your own father now. You must create yourself. Do you understand?"

"Yes."

"We are human. What is a human being? Here is knowledge: before we were human, we were animals. And before we were animals, we were plants. Have you heard of this?"

"No. Not even the shamans of my people claimed this."

"Your people worshipped animal totems. But the human soul is far older than that. I know that Damu protects himself with men who are no better than animals, but he cannot protect himself from the things that were us before we became us. Look at the stars; plants observe them, as we do. Plants speak. Plants grow angry. Life abounds, and life, abounding, fights to live, whether it is plant or animal or human.

"Warrior, if I abandoned you to the plants, could you live? If the plants rose in anger and came for you, could you survive? If plants tore at you and pulled you apart the way you pull apart flowers and trees—could you continue to live as a man the way that plants would continue to live as plants? They do not speak; they listen. They do not tear and swallow; they strangle and rend. They do not stop growing. They live forever. One plant is every other plant, and all plants are the same plant. They fill the world, they stretch above us, they surround us—and you will say that they are merely plants. Can we do these things? We have paid a great price in becoming human. We are no longer plants.

"Now, Damu and his fighters will say that what surrounds them is merely plant life. Will they say that these things are merely plants when the plants suffocate them, and creep inside them, and rip the skin from their muscles and the tendons from their bones? Men will scream, and the plants will continue to tear and pull. They are plants, as I am."

Oron sat by the fire, listening to this, watching the green woman.

"I have saved your life, Nevgan. In return," the witch said to him, "assist me in my vengeance. I ask for a bargain. I seek a balance and wish to redress an evil done me. You, of anyone, will under-stand."

"I do understand, yes."

"I am dying. I am becoming a plant, and I am dying. I had hoped to defeat Damu by now, but I have not, and my people watch, their ghosts watch and pray for me. I sought you out, and now, here you are. Will you assist me?"

Oron told her, "I fear being touched by your sorcery if I agree to this. It can act like a powerful poison. I have seen magickers and witches die in agony with powers they could not control."

"This is where we will assist each other. I will not harm you. Promise that you will not let others harm me. Nevgan . . . we that are human cast many shadows, in this world and in the next. We all have many shadows. I do. You do. Your shadow touches spirits in places beyond this one, just as your life touches lives beyond those only in this world. We are connected by shadows. Have you been told this?"

"No."

"It is an ancient truth. It is shared with only a few. You are my shadow, Oron. Here is where our shadows touch. Are our lives acci-dental, or is there a purpose to them?"

"I have been told that there is a purpose to life."

"And you, a new man, free to create yourself, free to make yourself into whatever you wish, born to confront evil—you have walked with shadows and are at home in the night as well as the day. Your dreams are deep. Your passions, deep. Am I not correct?"

"You are correct."

"Your path to greatness lay on this path to my cave, Oron. If you leave now, your path is a changed one. Have I not saved your life

88

and brought you here?"

"You have."

"Have I not looked into your heart and seen you there, in truth?"

"You have."

"Assist me, and you will be assured a path to great deeds. This is how the shadows join the future, and join the world to come."

Oron nodded.

Dia-Sust said then, "The father of my people is pleased. I sense this. Your people, too, understand this new man who was born among them. We have spoken, Oron, and shared our hearts. We are each other's shadow, and our destinies assist each other. May we both awaken now from this."

Oron took in a breath, shook his head, and swallowed, although his throat was dry. "I have been away, and have just returned," he said. "What did you do to me?"

"We spoke of deep matters, Nevgan. Do you remember?"

"We are here to assist each other. I am a man to make his own destiny. I have no past. I make my own past. I make my own future. I make myself."

Dia-Sust nodded.

"I saw hints of the future," he admitted. "A princess, or a queen. A monster. Not like Mosutha, the *izhuk* I killed. More powerful. Like a dragon. A darkness over the lands."

"This is your destiny, as you are the new man of the world, yourself, and no one else's man."

"This is my path."

"Yes. Assist me now, as I have asked, for I have given you this insight as a gift, as a gesture, in return for your aid."

Oron stood. He was weary and thirsty, and his body ached, not only from the punishing fight of the night before with Bodor but also because, sitting here with this witch, his spirit had been drained, and he was made tired.

"Go," Dia-Sust told him. "Sen-Odit has food. Dried fish. Berries. Small animals we have caught. And the water in these hills is cold and refreshing."

But as Oron turned to go, he heard a scream from the front of the tunnel, a woman's voice—Sen-Odit—and the men there yelling.

He hurried.

***

As he reached the opening of the cave, Oron stopped running. Before him, under a group of thin, tall trees, lay Sen-Odit, dead, cut through the belly. Above her stood Kess, his sword still held above the girl's body and her blood along the length of it.

Kess was angry, and that anger was in his eyes as he looked at Oron.

The Wolf regarded Agol, to his right, and then the other two, Nadul and Borin, where they stood by a great rock.

"Why?" Oron asked Kess.

"She threatened me!"

Oron grinned. There was no humor to the grin. "A threat? This one? How?"

"She's a witch, Nevgan! I hate things like her!"

Oron looked at Agol again. "Why did he kill her?"

"No reason," the old man told him. "He wanted her. She's a child. We told him to stay away from her. But he killed her to spite us."

"Dog!" Kess spat at Agol.

"You *killed* her," Borin said to Kess, "because you could. You have no honor."

"Show me *your* honor!" Kess yelled back at him, and stepped over Sen-Odit's red body. "Face me!"

But Oron drew out his own sword and with his left hand warned Borin to stay where he was. "You face *me*," Oron said to Kess. "You face *me*. And I will kill *you*. *Because I can*."

Kess grunted and jumped, his sword raised, intending to take advantage by speed.

But Oron met his downstroke and pushed Kess back with quick moves, step by step, with hard blows, with steel that was everywhere at the same time.

Kess lost the anger in his eyes.

Oron now saw fear there.

Kess moved to one side, then the other, and finally made a lunge to surprise the Wolf. But Oron was there, blocking him. Pushing

90

his sword back. Pushing Kess back.

Oron brought his blade down and around and up, so that the end of it caught the wrist of Kess's sword arm and severed it. The gloved hand, still holding the sword, dropped heavily to the ground. Oron's blade continued upward and took Kess's other hand through the forearm, so that the left hand, too, and the bone and muscle above it, nearly to the elbow, slipped away from Kess and landed against a tree.

Kess roared. With no hands, no hands, with only parts of both arms, he jumped at Oron, trying to stab him with the sharp bone protruding from the end of his left arm.

Oron stepped aside, lifted his sword and brought it down through Kess's tough neck, the heavy muscle there. The body fell forward, and the sharp bone of the left arm pushed into the earth, while Kess's head dropped near Agol's feet.

The eyes were open, and the mouth. A hiss came from the mouth, a sigh, the noise of air.

Agol kicked the head into shrubs and green things some distance away.

Oron knelt next to Kess's body as the blood was coming from the open neck and going into the ground. Oron cut free a length of the dead man's woolen trousers to use to clean his sword. As he stood and wiped his steel clean of blood and gristle, he looked at the other men there.

"The first thing you do is kill strong men who can challenge you. That's what leaders do."

Agol told him, "You had the right, Wolf."

Oron looked at Nadul and Borin.

"Aye," Nadul agreed. "The choice was yours."

Borin said, "He had no reason to hurt the child."

Oron sheathed his sword, but as the steel settled in its scabbard, a noise came from the cave mouth behind him, so that he bared his weapon again as he turned, kneeling in a defensive posture.

Dia-Sust was there. Not all of her, but four of her tendrils or vines, her arms.

Agol asked Oron, "What is *in* there, Wolf?"

Oron sheathed his sword again, understanding what was

needed. "Wisdom," he told the old man. "Wisdom, of a kind." He approached Sen-Odit's corpse, knelt and lifted her, and carried the body to the opening of the cave.

The tendrils rose, the ends of them touching the body.

Oron held the corpse out, and tendrils wrapped around it, took the body from him, and carried it back with them into the darkness of the cave.

There was silence. All of them there let their blood calm, let their anger and fear settle.

The tendrils returned, six of them, reaching out of the dark cave and almost touching Oron's chest.

He understood and backed away until he was at Kess's corpse. He removed the man's boots, then dragged the headless body toward the tentacles.

None of the other three said anything.

The tentacles came down, scraping on the grass and stones, and wrapped around Kess's body and lifted it back into the darkness.

Oron retrieved Kess's head; holding it by its hair, he lobbed it into the cave. It landed with a noise and rolled farther into the shadows.

Soon enough, from within those deep shadows, other sounds came to the four of them—moist sounds, sucking noises, something being eaten, and something doing the eating.

It was Dia-Sust doing what she must, Oron knew, eating Sen-Odit's body and Kess's, or draining them to stay alive. Doing what was necessary.

Agol shook his head. "Wisdom?" he asked Oron.

Oron didn't answer; he shrugged. Then he moved toward the small trees around them to collect matter to build a fire.

Nadul retrieved Kess's boots. They fit him well and so replaced his old, worn pair, which had been giving him blisters.

4. The Search

> I have no other image of the world ex-
> cept those of evanescence and brutality,
> vanity and rage, nothingness, useless

hatred...vain and sordid fury, cries suddenly stifled by silence, shadows en-
gulfed forever in the night.
Eugene Ionesco
"Lorsque j'écris...."

Just inside the cave, Oron and the others made a small fire, and there they sat, eating berries and some of the meat that the witch and her friend had caught. Initially, Agol and Borin and Nadul were uncertain about eating the witch's food—who knew what kind of meat it was, in fact, or what it might do to them? But Oron, as hungry as he was, put away many swallows and came to no visible hurt, and finally their own hunger made the others join him.

They gathered water from a cold stream that Borin found down one side of the height where they were, and every one of them filled his skin. They were silent as they ate and drank until their bellies were full. Agol burped; that brought a laugh from Borin, and his grinning eased the tension among the four of them so that, at last, Nadul asked Oron, "What is in there? The thing with the vines?"

He told them about Dia-Sust, what had happened to her and what she had become, made herself into. He told them that she had, by a magical kind of sight, discovered Oron and sensed that, because he himself had endured the same loss—his people being destroyed by a powerful evil man—and because he had managed to destroy that man, a sorcerer, in revenge, Oron could help her, as well. This is why she had saved him on the field. She had kept Damu and Maton alive, as well. Tonight, they were still running away with other men of their company who had survived with them. Dia-Sust wished to kill Damu; Oron was free to confront Maton. However, she was not a true woman any longer. She had used sorcery to change herself into something more plant than woman.

"You, Nadul and Borin, and you, Agol . . . this is not your matter if you don't wish to continue. But I'm convinced that my path is designed to join this woman's. Kess killing her servant settled it for me. And she has kept me alive to kill Maton and to meet Dasagak, my enemy, on another day. So my path is set. But you may do what you will. I don't expect you to fight my fight with me."

Agol said nothing; he stood and placed a hand on Oron's shoulder as a father or uncle will do to a young man, reassuring him, then went outside to sit under the clouded stars.

Nadul and Borin spoke between themselves, and Oron listened as they made their decision.

"We would have been dead on the field, either by Maton's arrows or by perhaps by Dasagak's killers," Borin said. "One left us to die, the other wished only to kill us and take what we own. Now, here we are with you and this witch who has kept you alive. Our chance is better with you, Oron, and with this strange woman. We feel that you are a man of honor, and honest, and I think you are a good leader, as well."

Oron smiled at them both; anyone used to hardship and a lonely life spent on the edge of things would have agreed with them. Some of us know no other way. Oron thanked them and assured them that they could sleep safely here at the mouth of Dia-Sust's cave. Surely she, too, now knew that these hardened young men would assist her, as well.

Then Oron went outside. While the younger men sat by the fire, then stretched out to rest, Oron talked in a low voice with the veteran of many conflicts and a veteran, as well, of much that life accords us.

After an agreeable moment looking at the stars and enjoying the sight of the forest at night, quiet and full of life as it was, Oron said, "Her gifts are powerful."

"They are," Agol confirmed.

"Nadul and Borin will come with me. And you?"

"Of course," Agol said. "They have made a wise decision. I'll keep my eye on them. They want women and money. They have nothing else in life. This will educate them."

Oron told the old man, "She says, Agol, that before we were men, we were animals, and before even that, we were plants, which is the source of her magic. Have you ever heard of this?"

"No. But the world is full of those who sense deep things and talk to the gods. It's not my way. But surely the powerful earth is full of such mysteries, and she has communicated with some of them."

"I was also told by her that I have a destiny."

"That may be. I have tried all my life to understand the sense and order in what the gods do. It is beyond me, Wolf. They play with us, but it is serious play. And they never quite tell us enough for us to know what they are about."

Oron agreed with that. "But," he admitted, "I don't feel it in me."

"Still," Agol told him, "inside every god is a mortal man. Is this not said? And inside every man is a god. If your destiny is planned, they'll give you signs."

"This witch is such a sign. I trust her, Agol. And by doing this, I will one day take Dasagak's head, as well."

"No doubt."

Oron confided to Agol then, "She says I am to fight a great evil one day."

"Not Maton?" Agol asked. "Not Dasagak? They're only men."

"Something else. I sensed it but could not name it. She says that I am a new kind of man because I killed my father. It marks me. But in the eyes of the gods, it is not a crime. It is something else."

Agol asked him, "Why did you do it? I've never heard of such a thing before."

"He was drunk, and he wished to take the woman I was with. I didn't set out to kill him, but he forced it."

"You could have walked away."

"But I didn't."

"Perhaps the evil you'll fight is also something you can't walk away from," Agol said. "It would be a proud destiny, to fight a great evil."

"She says we are each other's shadows. I help her, and she helps me."

"Our shadows and spirits can have lives of their own. It is of the gods, and beyond me, as I say. But I have not known any other young man like you, Wolf. If anyone has a destiny, then you are the man."

"I won't lead you into death if I can prevent it, Agol."

"I know that. That's why I'm here. Fortune—or destiny—is with you."

Oron said, "Right now, I wish only to have Maton's head. And the witch will need me, now that the girl is dead." He stood then. "I'll sleep by the fire with Nadul and Borin."

"I'll be there shortly. I like to look at the stars."

Oron asked him, "Do you think our destiny is in the stars? Many say that."

"I think our destiny is in our own hearts. But the stars watch. And we amuse the gods."

Oron went back toward the cave and the fire.

***

In the morning, when Oron awoke and stepped away from the others sleeping at the cave mouth to relieve himself in the under-growth nearby, he heard horses whinnying. He didn't wait until he had urinated to investigate. With a full bladder, he moved toward the sounds and saw, on the other side of some lean trees near where he had killed Kess, five horses, those he and the others had released the morning before when they were under Maton's arrows.

Surely Dia-Sust had managed to bring them here.

Once he had emptied himself, Oron returned to the others, who were now awakening, and went past them into the cave. He called out to the witch so that she would know that he was the in-truder (although surely she could sense it) and asked her about the animals.

"I followed them, yes," she told the Wolf. "I created breezes to urge them here for you. And for me, Oron. You must create a bed to carry me on. Attach it behind one of them."

"I understand. We'll do it now."

"I will give you the directions. Begin by returning down this mountain and across the battlefield."

He looked at her eyes, the glow of them in the shadows of the cave, then returned outside, where the others were eating what they had not put down the night before, and also gathering some berries, and drinking water.

Oron with his sword began cutting away saplings and strip-ping them of their branches. When he had two long poles, he lashed them together at one end by securing them with strips of bark and lengths of tough grass. Then he used a third pole to hold the opposite ends apart, wide enough to accommodate the spirit woman.

As the others finished their meals, they assisted in tearing strips of bark from trees and weaving lengths of grass into netting that they stretched across the wide, triangular end of their construction. When they were finished, they had a small frame or sled that could easily be pulled by one of the horses down the outcropping and onto the field.

This done, Oron went into the cave and shortly returned carrying Dia-Sust. Only her head and face were visible; the remainder of her was covered in her old blanket. She was no larger than an adolescent, but the swelling of her beneath her covering gave her the appearance of being a great, swollen bladder with a human head, a green human head.

There was no need to secure her to the sled with strips of bark or grass. The woman's own tendrils wrapped through the netting and around the poles to keep her comfortably in place.

The four mounted their horses and began moving in a single file down the mountainside toward the low valley. Oron led the way, with Agol behind him, then Dia-Sust, her horse led by Agol, followed by Nadul and Borin.

Borin, watching the sled and its passenger as it bounced over stones and large roots, said, "I notice that the horses are not frightened."

Dia-Sust twisted her head to look up at him. She did this without effort, although it would have strained or injured anyone else attempting it. She asked Borin, "Does this frighten *you*?"

He told her, "I'm not afraid yet. But I wonder that the animals are not concerned."

"I am no threat to them," Dia-Sust told him. "I am a plant. I am vegetation. What reason do the horses have to fear vegetation?"

***

On the field, tens of bodies were scattered, singly or in lonely groups, fallen where arrows, spears, and sharp edges had cut them down. The younger men moved their horses in wide paths to see whether any good pickings remained on the corpses, although their mounts were shy in the presence of so much death.

Agol, leading Dia-Sust's horse, and Oron moved toward the southern edge of the field, where the bodies were more numerous. It was clear that Maton's hundreds had broken in this direction, chased by Dasagak's army, and had been taken in great numbers, for the dead were in piles, and the crows and wild dogs were still busy picking at whatever remained exposed.

Oron slowed his horse and held still until Agol and the witch were alongside him. He asked Dia-Sust, "We continue south?"

"Yes. They are not far ahead of us. They see to their wounds."

Agol leaned back in his saddle and told her, "We came this way. There is a lake ahead, and trees and water. A falls."

"I saw these things," Dia-Sust said. "It is where they are."

Agol looked at Oron, and they nodded to each other, both of them of the same mind, to circle west, keeping in the forest that was there, and taking a path that led upward as the land steepened, so that they would be near the height of the waterfall, which would give them an advantage. And the sound of the dropping waters would obscure the noise they made as they approached.

When Nadul and Borin reached them, Oron told them of his plan. The two had found nothing of value left on the bodies of their dead companions; Dasagak's army had taken anything worth having or trading.

The sun was climbing in the morning sky, behind clouds that might bring rain later on, as the five moved into the rocks and trees to the west. And as they entered the cool forest, as the clouds were hidden beyond the height of tall trees, and as Oron listened to the horses' hooves moving over earth and roots and to the sound of the witch's sled as it was pulled across the flesh of this land, he regarded everything around him with new senses. He knew that the world is a living thing, but Dia-Sust's comments had enriched his measure of that.

He watched the shadows around them, the deepness of the forest, the waving of leaves, and the soft moss on fallen trunks, the cool dew on spiders' webs and animal nests tucked away in silent corners, and he began to have the sense of an awakening, as though the new man within him, or the god within him, shared more of this world than he had previously realized.

What must life contain, all of life, if a poor woman from a broken tribe could magic herself into a plant, another kind of living thing, and see with mist and smoke as though with eyes? What must life be if an important event awaited Oron himself one day, a destiny to fight great evil, to confront a monster empowered by the earth and stars to challenge the Wolf himself? Where was this evil now? Resting? Sleeping? Forming? Growing into its evil as Dia-Sust was growing into a plant?

What must life contain, all of life, and what must life be, if such things as these filled out the world beyond people and their limited sensations and hungers?

Your people worshipped animal totems. But the human soul is far older than that. We have paid a great price in becoming human.

***

When the sun was nearly as high as it reached at midday, the four men dismounted and tethered their horses by a cool stream that came down from rocks above them, surely an arm of the same waterfall they were approaching. Dia-Sust rested with closed eyes in her hammock while the others took out what food remained in their belts, filled their skins once more with good water, and searched nearby for nuts or berries or roots to add to the dried meat they had.

Oron was seated beside the witch and was about to say something to her when, looking at her, he saw her open her eyes in fright and warn him, "Oron!"

The warning was not for him. Just as she said his name, the leaves behind Borin made a sound, and then Borin groaned, lunged forward from where he had been sitting, and kneeled on the ground.

An arrow point extruded from the meat of his left shoulder, with the shaft of the arrow standing out from his back.

Immediately Oron was up, his sword out, and charging toward the bushes behind Borin.

But Agol, who had been seated closer to Nadul and Borin than the Wolf, was the first to move, crouching, into that wild green growth, steel out, eyes alert for whatever was there.

Just as Oron was approaching behind him, Agol raised his sword and brought it down. The edge cut through branches and leaves and brought up a man's cry. Agol leaned into the brush, grabbed hold of something, swore mightily, and pulled out the intruder.

He was one of the younger rogues of what had been Maton's company. His quiver was still slung on his back, but he had dropped his bow and had not even moved his sword from his side. Agol's steel had caught him along the right elbow and forearm, and the blood was dripping quickly.

As the young man stumbled forward, Agol pushed him onto the ground in the middle of the small campsite.

Holding his wounded arm, the youth rolled onto his back, spat at Agol—and then saw the witch close by him.

"Gods!" He moved away with terror in his eyes as Dia-Sust lifted her cover with two snaky green arms and held the ends toward him.

Oron walked over to him, placed a boot on his chest, and pushed the frightened youth again onto his back. "You're one of Maton's," he said. "Where is he?"

"Far away."

"Not so far. Are they by the river?"

"Go to hell, Wolf."

Oron lifted his boot from the chest and brought it down hard on the wounded arm.

The young man growled and moaned.

Oron asked him, "How many with him? How many left?"

"Ten and eight. No more than that."

"By the river?"

"Yes."

"Not by the waterfall?"

He shook his head and looked at Dia-Sust. "What is that? What have you done?"

Oron did not answer him. Instead, he asked, "Why attack us?"

"To take what you have."

"Alone?"

"I can kill four men."

"You can't even kill one man." Oron swiveled to look at Borin, who was standing now with Nadul beside him.

Borin told Nadul, "Now, yes."

Nadul broke the shaft as closely as he could to the skin, held tightly onto the ends of the arrow with his hands, and quickly pulled them out of Borin's shoulder.

"Clean," he said, meaning that the point had not severed one of the arteries there. Borin would not bleed to death.

Agol was waiting with strips of cloth he carried under his shirt; the years had taught him to ride with many different tools available for just such reasons as this. Now he bound Borin's wounded shoulder, covering it first with leaves he found that he knew would help ease the pain, then wrapping them with the cloth.

When he was done, Oron asked Borin, "Do you want the kill?"

Borin nodded and stepped forward, pulling out his sword.

As he stood above his attacker, the youth asked him, "What is that?"—meaning Dia-Sust.

"She's the witch that's going to eat you when you're dead." Borin lifted his sword.

The youth said to him, "Tell the gods my name! My father—"

But the end of Borin's sword already had creased the front of the young man's throat so that he gagged, the blood came, and he was dead.

Dia-Sust now said to Oron, "You must do that to me, Nevgan."

"Do what?"

"I am nearly dead. I can no longer control my limbs. I am too weak."

"What must I do?" He looked down at her as the other three men approached behind him, concerned.

"Sever my head and leave the rest of me here. Wrap my head in this blanket. Cut off this dead man's arms. They will give me strength. I will grow new limbs."

Agol stepped up beside Oron and said to the witch, "I wouldn't risk it, woman."

"Old man, I know what I am about. This is how I will survive to kill Damu. Don't you think I've done this before?"

Oron took out his sword and stepped forward, kneeling to do it.

***

Late that afternoon, when they had nearly reached the top of the height their horses were climbing, the four took their rest again. The day's shadows were long, now, and the sun nearly gone, hidden as it was behind clouds and the tall trees. A drizzle had begun, and the air was damp.

"Tonight," Oron said. "I'll climb ahead to see where they are. Then we'll know."

"Wolf, I'll do it," Nadul said.

"Can we trust you?"

Nadul smiled. "I am more silent than air." He stood then and went off into the forest, and he was indeed so quiet that none of them heard him go.

The three sat quietly then and kept their eyes on the blanket in which Dia-Sust was wrapped. It had not moved in some time; Oron wondered if she had, in fact, died at last. Neither had they heard any sounds coming from her. He wondered what that meant, if perhaps she were indeed growing and changing like some bud before it blossoms, or the silent root as it grows under the earth.

The blanket quivered, and part of an arm dropped out, a clot of meat that had gone dry or been drained.

Following it came a glistening shoot, a fibril or white tendril, as young and clean as something in springtime. It retrieved the meat, curling around it, and pulled it back beneath the blanket.

Agol coughed, seeing this, then stood and went into the trees to empty himself.

When he came back, Nadul was with him. They sat on stones, and Nadul said, "Eighteen of them, as he said. At the bottom of the falls."

Oron grinned, stood, and walked to his horse to lead them the rest of the way.

5. The New Man

> The power which resides in
> him is new in nature, and
> none but he knows what
> that is which he can do. . . .
> Emerson

The moon had not yet risen, and the night around them was fully dark, when Oron ordered the men with him to dismount and go

102

up the steepness afoot. He did not wish to endanger their animals and, in any event, the three could proceed more quietly without them. They tethered the horses to some birch trees and continued on.

Oron carried Dia-Sust's head bundled in the blanket. He kept it by his side, tied to his leather belt, so that the thing bounced against his left thigh. And it was wet. Whatever sorcery Dia-Sust was concocting, it seeped through the cloth of the blanket and wet Oron's trousers. But the substance did not burn, and he heard little noise from the head. Only once did he ask the thing, whispering to it, "Are you alive?"

His answer was a shuddering of the bundle and a few syllables that might have been words, but that was all.

After a time, the men heard the sound of the waterfall to their left as moonlight broke through the tall foliage above them, and they heard other sounds, too, from the direction of the water. Someone or something moving.

Oron reached for the weapon at his side, but not quickly enough. A sharp point caught him along the left forearm, cutting him and warning him away from his sword hilt.

More spear points came toward the others with him, and Agol warned the two younger men, "Hold off! We know them!"

Six men of their former company came ahead, some of them with bandaged wounds, all holding Oron and his three at spear point and sword end. By the light of the moon, clean as it was and bright as it rested on sweating faces and tense, muscled arms, the six regarded Oron and the others as they might a wolf pack.

Oron lifted his head and said to the foremost of them, "Thon, where is Maton?"

"Close by, Nevgan. He suspected that you still lived." He called behind him, into the brush, "Damu! Here!"

The bundle at Oron's side quivered, and it seeped more liquid.

In a moment, the leaves behind the six parted and Damu, with two others, came through. "The Wolf," he said.

Oron told him, "I'm not surprised that you lived. Still having others fight your fights?"

"Insult me if you like, but I'm taking you to Maton."

"Good. I can kill him quick, then get some sleep."

Damu noticed the round, wet satchel hanging from Oron's belt. "What is that? You stole from the corpses on the field?"

"It's the head of an enemy."

"Is it?"

"I took it just tonight."

"Nevgans collect heads now, like other savages?"

"Only this one."

"Come." Damu stepped back and gestured for those with him to move Oron and the others forward. "And take their swords. Take their knives."

Oron and Agol, Nadul and Borin reluctantly unsheathed their steel and, grumbling, surrendered their weapons.

"Thon," Agol said to that one, "I saved your life only three moons ago."

"You did, old man. And I am grateful. Now give me your blades."

As they were pushed ahead, warned to move slowly and not attempt escape into the dark forest around them, Oron felt the trees on all sides move with more than the wind.

Did any of the others sense it?

Clearly not. Perhaps he was open to the sensation because Dia-Sust's head was bouncing against his thigh and she could share her thoughts with him by reason of that.

Perhaps he was indeed the only one of them who noticed branches and leaves twisting strongly, as though with intent, and not simply because they were touched by the night wind.

The witch had indeed created a powerful magic.

They came to something like a clearing, an area where the trees thinned and gave upon boulders contained by roots and other growth. The moon opened above them, startling in its brightness, and Oron and his three saw Maton sitting on a rock with what remained of his killers, no more than eight others, now, most of them bearing hurts from battle, some with bruised faces, others with arms or legs wrapped in clothes stripped from the recently dead. Beyond them was the river, not large, fed by the waterfall to the south.

Maton grunted as he stood and said to Oron, "I should have killed you outright. How did you survive? You escaped in the fog."

"I did."

"And what sorcery of yours was that?"

"Not my sorcery, but sorcery it was."

"Sent by Dasagak?"

"You should have asked *him*—before you ran away."

Maton looked at the three standing beside the Wolf. "I'm missing another of my men," he said. "Did you kill him, too?"

"We did," Oron told him. "My company and I."

"*Your* company?"

"Aye." Oron undid the satchel at his side and held it in his right hand.

"More sorcery?" Maton asked.

"It *is* sorcery," the Wolf told him. "That fog was sent by a witch with the powers of the earth in her. This is her magic." He held up the bag. "But not for you."

"Then who?"

Oron looked at Damu, who was only a short distance from his captain. "That one. Your guard dog."

Damu sneered.

"You killed a people southway of here."

"I killed many, Nevgan, in every direction under the sky."

"You awoke an angry spirit, Damu. This is for you."

"What is it?"

Oron cast the satchel onto the flat ground between himself and Damu. The wet blanket unrolled and from it, under the bright moonlight, came the head of Dia-Sust—yet now a head no longer. It was a green-brown knot with two yellow eyes, not human, and from it sprouted six, eight, ten branches, thin and wet, to push the knot of her head higher than a man's height.

Every one of the killers there lost his air, stopped breathing.

Damu fell back and reached for his sword.

But Dia-Sust, now a tall, spidery thing, reached for him with three of her branches. They had no hands on them, only points at the ends of them, and one of them took Damu high through the stomach, just below his breast bone, and lifted him from the ground.

"Witch!" Damu growled, as blood came from his mouth. He tried to hurt the sorceress with his sword, and he managed to graze one of the brown appendages near him, but then the end of that branch shot through his shoulder and, pushing hard, tore the arm from the body.

Maton, below, removed his sword, crouched, and yelled at Oron on the other side of the clearing, "*What sorcery is this, Nevgan?*"

Oron laughed out loud.

As Damu's arm fell to the ground, the thing shook him back and forth just above the heads of the men all around. His blood sprayed everywhere, and Maton's fighters held up their hands to avoid being blinded by the red drops.

Damu's bad left leg, the one nearly lost years earlier, came free, and its wooden crutch. He began to scream. Where did he find the strength? He was choking with blood, but still he screamed.

Two more arms, branches, pushed through his body, one at his neck, the other near his crotch, and shook his body so terribly that it was finally torn apart, the head dropping and rolling away, the torso itself pulled into halves with the organs of it spilling out, raising steam in the cold night air.

Still Damu screamed.

His organs and blood, his entrails on the wet ground, screamed, and his head. The entrails of him moved on their own as though they were fat, living worms, and in flexing and rolling on the grass and stones of the clearing, they issued wheezing sounds, perhaps echoes of Damu's howling spirit far below ground or in whatever hell awaits such men.

Now Dia-Sust, the thing, the spidery monster, used her ten branches to smash the pieces of Damu's body further, pushing his face apart to break the bones beneath, disarticulating his spine and his arms and legs, so that what remained was gore, merely meat and organs, with nothing left to show that these might once have been contained within someone alive.

The manner in which he had left Dia-Sust's southern village, burned to the ground, torn in every direction, with the pieces scattered, stones and lengths of wood, bundles of grass left to blow away in the wind, whatever remained—this was how she now left Damu, in pieces, with nothing left of him to show that he had ever been, with whatever remained left to sink into the earth or be carried away by dogs or be eaten by the worms and insects that live by such raw pieces.

"*Oron!*" Maton howled it, yanked his sword from its sheath, and moved toward the Wolf, taking care not to step in the blood and gore on the ground.

He had no wish to be contaminated by such sorcery.

Oron turned to Thon. "Give me my sword!"

"Give it to him!" Maton commanded.

Thon took it from a man near him and handed it to Oron.

Oron stepped ahead, moving into the center of the clearing, reckoning how best to meet Maton in his anger.

But Maton stopped several lengths away, moved his sword from his right hand to his left, and removed his barbed chain belt. He swung it around his head, with the heavy spiked ball on the end of it moving in a wheel.

Oron said to him, "You won't even meet me with your sword!"

Maton laughed and came ahead, prepared to tear the Wolf open.

But then he screamed in pain.

The ball was caught in the branch of a leaning tree.

Not Dia-Sust—

"The tree *moved!*" Thon yelled.

—but one of the tall birches nearby. It had reached with its branches, as though they were arms, and caught Maton's weapon as he whirled it, tearing it from his hand and sending a painful shock up his arm and shoulder.

Oron looked at Dia-Sust, the thing, the spider.

But she was already moving away.

Painful though his right arm was, Maton took his sword hilt in that hand and jumped toward Oron. "With my blade, then!" he said strongly.

Oron moved forward to meet him while the brilliant moon continued to brighten the clearing as though it were midday—and while the trees nearby, all around them, swayed, moved their branches and leaves, leaned in toward the fighting men—*observed.*

"You're full of surprises, Nevgan," Maton grunted.

Then he came in, swinging his long blade, forcing his way past Oron's guard and slicing the younger man along his right shoulder.

Oron cursed.

"More blood for your witch!" Maton spat.

But Oron circled to his left, held off several of Maton's strokes, then abruptly charged in, forcing the old dog back.

Agol, from where he stood, hooted out loud. "Do it, son!"

And kept at it. So that Maton, moving away, stepping backward as he searched for an opening, slipped on what remained of Damu, the gore on the stones, the wet blood.

He came down on his right side into the blood and the long stretch of entrails. Unable to use his sword, he tried to roll free and avoid Oron. But the Nevgan's steel caught Maton cleanly on the left collar bone, broke it, and sliced through his leather armor and his chest to come out low on the captain's right side.

Maton howled as what had been inside him squeezed out and was exposed in the moonlight to every man there.

He panted for a long time as he bled. The meat of him, where he had been opened, glistened and continued to push free of the wet leather of his harness. Maton moaned and moved his legs from one side to the other, back and forth, but at last he gave out.

Oron breathed deeply, pulling in the cold air with the smells of death in it, blood and the rawness of killing and cutting. He looked over toward Agol as the old veteran said to him, "Wolf."

Agol pointed toward where Dia-Sust had been.

She was gone now, or nearly so. She had been pulled into the trees nearby. The trees had reached for her and taken her into them, lifted her into their branches to hold her there, where she must die, although she had not been born as one of them.

Oron regarded the blood and gristle on his sword, walked in a small circle to get his air back, and surveyed what remained of two men on the stones and grass of the clearing.

The moon went behind clouds.

He looked at the trees that had taken the witch.

"We that are human cast many shadows. We are connected by shadows. Are our lives accidental, or is there a purpose to them?"

He regarded Maton's company and said coldly to those men, "I am Oron. I killed my own father, and I'll kill anyone else who deserves it. Do you understand?"

No one answered him until Thon came ahead, nodded, and

replied, "We understand, Wolf."

"I made a pact with that witch, and I'll do it with anyone or anything else that brings me what I want. I'll do it with you dogs if you still want what we started for. Or do I ride alone?"

One of them, not Thon but a man bigger than he and with scars to boast of, told Oron, "I am with you, Nevgan."

A second came forward then, and a third, and Thon also stepped forward.

"I'm with you, Wolf."

"And I."

"And I."

Oron lifted his right hand to them, a gesture of comradeship, despite the pain in his shoulder. He regarded Agol and the other two, Borin and Nadul. The two younger men ducked their heads and put their fists to their foreheads. We follow you.

Agol told the Wolf, "You've earned them, Captain."

"Aye," Oron said. "I have. Tomorrow, then," he promised his company, "I'll take you over those hills to women and plunder. This is our way, and anyone who joins us may have the same. Anyone against us takes what we give them!"

Loud hurrahs and shouts of agreement met his announcement.

"Now . . . let me sleep!"

Thon and Agol, Nadul and Borin slapped their chests as Oron went past them and found a place just inside the wood line to rest for the remainder of the night.

Agol and the two younger men settled themselves close by to guard the Wolf, keeping a watch for him through the night.

As he closed his eyes, Oron sensed movement in the trees above him.

He looked up.

Leaves and branches tossed gently in the night.

The wind moved them.

The wind—and something else.

The trees, too, would watch over him as he slept.

AMUOU'S BARGAIN

By Charles R. Saunders

The warrior trudged up a high flight of steps carved into the stone of a hillside. Vegetation shouldered the sides of the stairway, and the warrior frequently brushed aside fronds and branches as he ascended. The trees and vines cast shadows on the warrior. Searing heat from Jua the sun made little impression on him as he came closer to his destination — a notch between two hills that towered like sentinels above the others in the Nwanian range.

Tirelessly, the warrior's legs carried him up the steep stairway. He had travelled far to reach his destination. The Nwanian range was a land sought by few and shunned by most. Of those who sought it, few had ever been known to have returned.

At the top of the stairway, the notch loomed twice the height of the warrior, who was a large man. It was an upright rectangle of shadowy blackness that appeared to have been painted onto the rock rather than carved into it. Of what was on its other side, the notch revealed nothing other than the darkness of a night without moon or stars.

As he stood in front of the opening, the warrior saw that it was narrow ... his shoulders were too broad to fit through it. From the bottom of the stairway, the notch had appeared to be much wider.

To enter, the warrior would need to squeeze sideways into the opening. He did not know how deep the opening was, or how long it would take to reach the other side, which was obscured by the shadows ... or deliberately hidden.

The warrior did not hesitate. Turning to the side, he slid into the darkness. For a moment, a vague, filmy substance enveloped him, touching him lightly, like the wings of insects. Instinctively, the warrior closed his eyes as he sidled through the darkness. He reached out ... and touched nothing. But he did not turn and walk forward. He continued to slide sideways, eyes closed, until the touches ceased and he felt sunlight on his skin again.

When the warrior opened his eyes he blinked, bringing his keen vision into full focus. The notch was behind him ... but its orientation had changed. No longer was it set between two hills. Now, it was located at the bottom of an expanse of golden sandstone. Carvings covered every inch of the rock. Some were huge, some life-sized. Others were so small that the warrior could barely see them. The carvings depicted significant events in the Nyumbani continent ... the rise and fall of kingdoms, the comings and goings of gods and demons, the deeds of heroic and the misdeeds of the followers of evil ...

The warrior was not surprised to see his own image among the carvings. Nearly all the depictions of him were enormous. Sometimes, he loomed larger even than the gods.

Shaking his head in a combination of bemusement and annoyance, the warrior turned from the carvings. Ahead of him, he saw a broad, paved road. The road was flanked by walls that towered like the sides of cliffs.

Like the wall that held the notch, these were festooned with carvings, and also paintings. One side consisted of animals: nearly every creature known to exist in Nyumbani, along with others so rare that they were considered mythical. The images were so lifelike that the warrior thought he could see some of them breathing.

On the other side, images of people were carved and painted. Some were only faces; others, full bodies. The carvings showed individuals of every race, tribe and nationality in Nyumbani, each rendered in the artistic style of their homeland. The warrior had spent time in many parts of the continent, and he recognized most of the groups the images represented – including the people among whom he had experienced an unhappy childhood.

As he walked along the road, the warrior looked down and saw that he was stepping on designs carved into the paving stones. Some were geometric in form; others more abstract. Some were painted in bright colors; others were intricate patterns of lines scratched in stone.

Before long, the walls ended. Closer to the end, the decorations covered less space, until the surfaces became blank, as though they were awaiting the inscription of more images. The road, however, continued. Now it cut through a forest. The boles of most of the trees bore carvings of people, animals, spirits, deities, and amalgams of all three.

Interspersed among the trees were pillars of stone. Some were small, reaching only to the warrior's knees. Others were larger. The largest towered nearly as tall as the trees. Carvings covered nearly all the pillars.

Now, the warrior heard a tapping sound. The taps were arrhythmic: one, or two, or several at a time, interspersed with pauses of varying length. The warrior's strides became quicker, for the sounds signaled that he would soon reach the end of the long journey that had brought him to this place – a place that was sought by many, but found by only a few.

Before long, the pillars gave way to a clearing that was as circular as the fighting-pit of Mwenni, but many times larger. A wall of decorated stone surrounded the clearing. A waterfall descended one wall like a thread of silver, ending in a pool next to a cultivated field. Not far from the field was a typical West Coast dwelling: cube-shaped, but with embellishments a king would have envied.

Piles of masks, statues and drums littered the ground, along with pieces of stone and lengths of wood waiting to be transformed into exquisite shapes. The only objects not related to art were vases filled with water, and wooden plates that still bore scraps of food.

The source of the tapping was in the midst of the artifacts, any one of which would have fetched a fortune in the markets of the Sahanic cities, or even in those of fabled Cush. The warrior saw a small man, clad in the patterned *dansiki* and trousers that were common garb in the West Coast kingdoms. This man's garments were more colorful than most.

With his ebony skin and shaven pate, the man's age was indeterminate. Of all his attributes, the most striking was his hands, which were larger than would be expected for a man of his size. His fingers were long and delicate, yet they maintained a firm grip on the mallet and chisel he employed to coax a shape from the length of tree-trunk that lay in front of him.

Scattered wood chips surrounded the trunk, which was slowly becoming an image of a woman with elongated limbs. Only when the shadow of the warrior darkened the half-formed sculpture did the man look up.

He saw a huge, broad-shouldered man clad in the chain-link armor of a Sahanic soldier. But only a glance was necessary to discern that this warrior's homeland was not in that vast, semi-arid territory. His umber skin and broad features bespoke a different ancestry.

Beneath the brim of his helmet, the warrior's obsidian eyes glinted with an awareness that was almost feral in its intensity. But the disquiet in those eyes was all-too-human. The rest of his countenance was devoid of expression, save for a downward turn of his heavy-lipped mouth.

The carver's eyes strayed to the weapons the warrior carried. One of them was a Sahanian broadsword so huge that it could hardly be lifted, let alone wielded, by an ordinary man. The other was a short, hiltless blade of a design that bespoke a distant origin.

The warrior's hands did not stray toward either of his weapons. His eyes held those of the carver, whose mallet no longer tapped the chisel.

The carver was the first to speak.

"I know who you are," he said. "You are Imaro ... Death's Friend."

He spoke in Muluwa, the common trade tongue of the Sahan. The warrior responded in the same language.

"And I know who you are," Imaro said. "You are Amudu the Accursed."

The carver uttered a short, sharp burst of laughter.

"Do I look 'accursed' to you?" he asked.

Imaro did not reply. Amudu laid down his mallet and chisel, then rose to his feet in a fluid motion. Although the top of Amudu's head barely reached Imaro's shoulder, he showed no fear of the warrior.

"You did not come here to rob me, or kill me, or both," Amudu said. "If that were your purpose, the portal to this place would never have allowed you to reach me. So ... why did you come here?"

Suddenly, Imaro drew his broadsword, and then his *simi*, the short blade that was used by the Ilyassai, the fierce people among whom he was raised. Amudu's eyes widened in alarm, and he took a step backward. Then Imaro hurled both blades to the ground with so

113

much force that they bounded high in the air before lying discarded at his feet.

"I do not want to be Death's Friend anymore," Imaro said. "I want to learn to do what you do."

Amudu looked into the warrior's eyes and saw wells of pain and regret deeper than he would have thought possible. He knew of Imaro through tales of the warrior's deeds that were told throughout Nyumbani. Amudu had told those stories in carvings rather than words. To see Imaro in this place, speaking those words ... that was beyond Amudu's imagination.

"You are not the first to have come here with that desire," the carver said.

"Yes," Imaro said. "Some have come, and climbed the stair, and were afraid to enter the darkness. They returned and tried to drown their cowardice in palm-wine, which loosened their tongues to tell the tale. Others have sought you – and never returned."

He paused, awaiting a response from Amudu, whose expression remained noncommittal.

"It is said that most of those who never returned were killed by beasts or bandits," Imaro continued. "But a few are said to have entered the darkness, and found you, and remained with you, creating rather than destroying."

Imaro's eyes scanned the clearing.

"Yet I see no one here, other than yourself."

"The darkness took some of the seekers," said Amudu. "The ones who would do me harm are not caressed by feather-touches, as you were. The darkness seizes them ... and swallows them."

"And the ones who pass through, as I did ... what happens to them?" Imaro demanded. "Why do I not see them now?"

Amudu gave Imaro an appraising gaze before replying.

"That is a long tale to tell," he finally said. "But then, people like you and I have more time than most."

Imaro's eyes narrowed. This man had maintained his vigor far longer than most people. And the legend of Amudu spanned generations. Still, when the carver sat down, so did Imaro. As Amudu spoke, Imaro's discarded weapons lay between them like silent witnesses.

Amudu once lived in Yayuba, one of the many kingdoms that crowded the West Coast of Nyumbani. Of all the innumerable artists and carvers in those kingdoms, Amudu was considered the best, for he was an *isisiduya* – a master of all forms of visual art. His works enhanced the palaces of the region's kings and queens and were sold by merchants whose trade routes carried them to the Sahan and beyond.

Yet for all his accomplishments, Amudu was an unhappy man.

Of the three wives his fame and glory had attracted, none remained. All had departed, resentful of his lack of attention to them as he spent nearly all his waking hours in his workshop – and sometimes slept there as well.

Among them the three wives had produced only one child: a daughter named Emina. Unlike Amadu's wives, Emina did not desert him. Although she had neither the talent nor the interest to become an *isisiduya*, Emina found that she enjoyed the dealings of commerce. As his daughter's skill at bargaining grew, Amudu soon became wealthier than most of the people who eagerly sought his work.

Amudu knew that Emina would one day leave him as well, even though he had turned away every suitor who sought to wed her. Eventually, though, one would come who would not accept his refusal. When that one came, Emina would go with him, and Amudu would be alone.

Suitors were not the only ones who came to Amadu's compound. Many young painters and carvers sought him out in hope of learning the skills that had led to Amudu's renown. Amudu accepted a few of them as apprentices. None, however, lasted longer than a rain under his tutelage. For Amudu's standards were so high that no student could come close to meeting them.

Of all his difficulties, Amudu feared one the most: the inevitable encroachment of age. In time to come, his fingers would stiffen and his eyesight would become dim. No longer would he be able to produce the works that were the definition of his life, each one an extension of himself.

That time would come. It was unavoidable.

Or was it?

Amudu had often done work for the *nyim* – sorcerers. He never asked the purpose of the objects he crafted, for he had no desire to become embroiled in the machinations of the *nyim*. Now, the circumstances were different. This time, the sorcery of the *nyim* would benefit him alone. No one else – not even Emina – would know what he intended to do until it was done.

When he approached the *nyim*, and learned the price he would have to pay to stave off the advance of age, Amudu became so terrified that he shut his mind to the knowledge and begged the *nyim* never to speak to anyone else about their discussions with him.

As time passed, however, Amudu began to see deficiencies in his work. Only the best *isisiduya* could have detected the flaws. But Amudu knew that eventually everyone would be able to see that the quality of his work was declining. Ultimately he would be no better than the apprentices he turned away.

Amudu remembered then what the *nyim* had told him to do. And he decided to follow their impious counsel. He had no difficulty convincing himself that he had no alternative.

In Yayuba, the burial ground was also a forest, for a sacred tree was planted in the soil that covered each newly buried corpse. The Forest of the Dead stretched far across the land beyond the city. It remained unguarded, for who among the people of Yayuba would dare to desecrate the trees nurtured by their ancestors' decaying flesh and bone?

One would …

Late one night, Amudu entered the Forest of the Dead and made his way to the burial-trees of a clan that had long since died out. No one visited its trees anymore. From his garments Amudu pulled out an axe – a tool not usually associated with the work of an *isisiduya*. He selected a relatively slender tree that could have been the last one planted by the lost, nearly forgotten clan.

Then he began to chop. The crack of blade against wood echoed so loudly that Amudu was certain the sounds could be heard in the city. So did the crash that came when the tree fell. But no one arrived to challenge him. Only the other burial-trees bore witness to his act of desecration.

Cold perspiration slid down Amudu's skin as he cut a human-sized length from the fallen bole. Then he peeled off a piece of cloth he had draped over his garments, and used it to wrap both the axe and the length of wood. And he fled the Forest of the Dead as though all the vengeful spirits of Yayuba were pursuing him.

Returning to his home, Amudu went directly to his workshop. He took care not to disturb Emina's slumber as he shut his workshop's door. He set the wood from the burial-tree on a circular stone platform. Then, guided only by the wavering light of a torch, he began to carve the defiled wood into the shape the *nyim* had suggested.

When he was finished, Amudu could barely look at the shape he had created. Still, he knew it was the exact image the *nyim* had described: the image of an *omuludu*, a demon from the otherworld that neighbored the realms of the gods and the dead.

Amudu then chanted the words the *nyim* had whispered into his ear. With those words, and the sorcery imbued in the wood stolen from the burial-tree, and the power unleashed by the shape of the *omuludu* he had carved, Amudu now had a way to avoid the onslaught of age that must otherwise steal his skills.

When the final syllable of the chant was spoken, Amudu vanished. As did the effigy of the *omuludu*. As did Emina.

Once the Yayubans discovered that Amudu and his daughter had disappeared, rumors swarmed like gnats: Rival *isisiduyas* had abducted them. Assassins had slain them for a price. Demons had taken them to collect the price Amudu must have paid for his incomparable skills ...

Much later, someone discovered the desecrated burial-tree. No one connected that act with the disappearance of Amudu and his daughter. And the *nyim* said nothing of their earlier discussions with Amudu.

***

"The *omuludu* brought us to this place," Amudu said. "I have not aged since then, and I carved that image of the *omuludu* before your grandsire was born. Amudu the Immortal, they call me now. Or Amudu the Accursed. Sometimes, the *omuludu* sends dreams of this

117

place to *isisiduyas* from my homeland, and many other places. They come here, seeking to learn my secrets. They come ... and they learn nothing. But I learn much, for they tell me what has transpired on the other side of the portal. That is how I learned of you."

He paused and looked more closely at Imaro.

"Did you dream of this place, warrior?" he asked.

Imaro shook his head.

"I had no such dream," he said. "I asked where this place is, and I was told."

Amudu chuckled.

"Who would dare to deny anything to Death's Friend?" he mused.

"Where is your daughter?" Imaro demanded abruptly.

A sad expression fell like a curtain over Amudu's face. He pointed toward a faraway part of the rock walls that surrounded the clearing. An aperture similar to, but smaller than, the notch between the hills pocked the bottom of the wall.

"Why is she not with you?" Imaro asked.

"She serves the *omuludu*," Amudu replied in a flat tone.

Imaro's eyes narrowed in anger, and his hands reached toward the weapons he had flung to the ground. Amudu neither blinked nor moved.

"I thought you no longer wanted to be Death's Friend," the *isisiduya* said.

Imaro stayed his hands. But loathing continued to smolder in his eyes as he glared at Amudu.

"Your daughter 'serves' a demon so that you can spend eternity making things no one but you will see," the warrior said scornfully.

"You are judging me?" Amudu asked incredulously. "You, the greatest killer Nyumbani has ever known? You, the creator of an army of corpses?"

Imaro looked as though he longed to add another member to that army. But he made no move to carry out that desire. A long sigh escaped his lips as the flame in his eyes abated.

"I was created to kill," he said. "I was shaped for that purpose, just as you shape wood and stone. I was a living weapon, to be wielded against the Erriten and Mashataan. I served that purpose, at great cost. And when the Erriten and Mashataan were defeated, I was still a weapon ... and I needed other foes to fight.

"I have slain men, demons and beasts. I have joined wars, started wars and ended wars. The blood I have spilled would fill the Western Ocean. And now ... I want it to end."

Amudu gazed thoughtfully at Imaro. The warrior's face remained impassive, but his eyes revealed the anguish and conflict within him.

"And now, you want to become an *isisiduya*," he said. "Have you ever tried to make a work of art before?"

"I was once a blacksmith," Imaro said. "All I made was weapons. But if I spend the rest of my life trying to learn how to make things of beauty, the killing will stop."

Moments crawled ... then Amudu spoke.

"Emina did not come here of her own will," he said. "But that was not my doing. When the *omuludu* brought me here, its power was so great that it encompassed her as well. The *nyim* did not warn me of that. When we came here, the *omuludu* refused to return Emina to Yayuba. Her service to him would be the price for joining me in immortality."

"Service," Imaro said, contempt clear in his tone.

"It is not what you think!" Amudu said sharply. "The *omuludu* wants only her companionship."

Imaro waited for him to continue.

"My hands will make things for eternity, just as I wanted," Amudu said. "But my heart is forever filled with sorrow because Emina must dwell with a demon."

He gave Imaro a penetrating gaze.

"There is a way to end both Emina's service to the *omuludu*, and your service to the sword," he said.

"What way is that?" Imaro demanded.

"It requires a death," Amudu replied. "The death of the *omuludu*."

"Does the *omuludu*'s power not keep you and your daughter alive?" Imaro asked suspiciously.

"No. As long as she and I remain in this place, we will live, for time does not pass here as it does in the rest of Nyumbani."

Imaro's eyes narrowed.

119

"I am not the first to have heard this tale," he said.

"You are right," Amudu acknowledged. "I have told it to the seekers who passed through the portal to this place. I told them if they could slay the *omuludu* and free Emina, I would impart my skills, and one day their works would rival my own."

The *isisiduya* paused, gauging Imaro's reaction to his words. The warrior remained impassive.

"Some of them refused the offer," Amudu continued. "They tried to leave, but the portal took them. Others accepted, and they were defeated and devoured by the *omuludu*. I learned, eventually, that only a warrior or a sorcerer can overcome a demon like the *omuludu*. An *isisiduya* has no chance."

His gaze never left Imaro.

"Never did I imagine you would come here," Amudu said. "You are the greatest warrior of all – and there is sorcery in you as well, even though you are not a sorcerer, and you have warred against those who practice magical arts."

"Yes ... there is sorcery in me," Imaro admitted. "It made me what I am, and what I have always been – until now."

"But now you can be the one who frees Emina from the *omuludu*."

The warrior said nothing more.

"One more death, Imaro," the *isisiduya* said. "After the death of the *omuludu*, there will be no further need for you to be Death's Friend, with blood dripping endlessly from your blade."

Imaro eyed him speculatively.

"One more death," the warrior murmured.

Then a conflagration of anger kindled in Imaro's eyes. At the sight of it, Amudu wondered whose death Imaro contemplated ...

"If this thing involved only you, I would go back through the portal and take my chances with the *omuludu*'s sorcery," Imaro grated. "But your daughter is here through no fault of her own, other than having you as a father. One more death, then ... for her. And then I will leave this place."

"I thought you wanted to learn to create art," Amudu protested.

"I may learn someday," Imaro said. "But not from you."

The warrior then picked up the weapons he had thrown to the ground, and rose to his feet. With a final, scorn-laden glance at Amudu, Imaro turned and strode toward the dark opening in the decorated wall.

Amudu glanced at the incomplete carving of the woman. Then he turned his attention to the opening toward which Imaro walked. If the warrior's derisive words affected the *isisiduya*, his face didn't show it. Amudu's expression remained impassive as Imaro disappeared into the darkness of the aperture.

***

Weapons ready, Imaro stepped through the opening. His muscles tensed. He was poised to dodge any attack that might materialize from the darkness. None came. Even the spiderweb touches that marked his passage through the portal between the hills were absent.

The darkness lasted only a moment. Imaro blinked, then looked back toward the opaque opening. Then he turned and regarded the place of confinement the *omuludu* had prepared for Emina. And he saw Emina herself.

Her prison was a huge chamber carved with a high, curved ceiling. Light streamed through a hole cut at the center of the ceiling. Objects obviously created by her father filled much of the space. Like the walls outside, brightly painted images covered those of the chamber. Clearly, the *omuludu* permitted Amudu to enter and leave his daughter's ornate cell.

The reason Emina could not leave was plain to Imaro as he looked at her.

Emina appeared to be a woman of little more than twenty rains' passing. But her time in this place had lasted far longer than that. She was sitting on a stool that consisted of two U-shaped pieces of mahogany, with geometric shapes carved into the surface. A table, other stools and a low bed comprised the rest of the furnishings.

Like most women of the West Coast, Emina was short in stature, with a generously proportioned figure. Colorful, intricately patterned lengths of cloth swathed her body, leaving her arms and one shoulder bare. A head-wrap of similar material covered her hair.

Jewelry made from gold, silver and jade hung from her neck and circled her arms.

Her left wrist bore an object made from a different metal: steel. This bracelet was much thicker than the others. It was attached to a long, heavy chain that extended from Emina's wrist to a staple set in one of the decorations on the walls. The chain had enough length to allow her to go anywhere within the chamber – anywhere other than the black semicircle of its entrance.

Emina's skin was as dark as that of her father. As she gazed at Imaro, her eyes shone like pools of light in her broad-featured face. Those eyes expressed wonder … and hope.

"You are not like the others," she said in a soft tone that was barely above a whisper.

Imaro did not speak. His eyes rapidly scanned the chamber, searching for signs of the *omuludu*. He saw none. His *kufahuma*, the sense of danger he had honed many rains ago on the Tamburure plain, was silent. Yet the *omuludu* had to be present … somewhere.

"The demon is not here," Emina said, as though she were reading Imaro's thoughts. "Sometimes the *omuludu* is gone for long periods of time. But it always comes back … always."

Emina hung her head. Then she looked up again. This time panic fluttered in her eyes.

"The *omuludu* could return at any time," she said. "Break the chain, warrior! Break it, and free me!"

Without hesitation, Imaro swung the blade of his broadsword at the links that were closest to him. They shattered easily, as though they were made of copper rather than steel.

The section of the chain still tethered to Emina made a hissing sound against the floor as she approached Imaro. A radiant smile wreathed her features as she held out her arms to embrace him. The warrior's arms were at his sides, weapons dangling loosely from his fingers.

"Indeed, you are not like the others," she murmured as her arms encircled Imaro's neck and her body pressed close to his.

Then the flesh beneath Emina's garments began to writhe, and her arms tightened with surprising strength. Imaro's fists clenched around his weapons, and he shoved his arms forward in a violent motion. The woman fell away from him, chain clattering as she landed on the floor.

Imaro's sword and *simi* slashed downward. But the thing on the floor quickly scrambled backward, and the blades swished through empty air.

Even as the thing rose to its feet, all vestiges of Emina were disappearing. The clothing and jewelry melted into nothing; its body grew in stature; its face transformed from beautiful to hideous.

The being that now stood before Imaro bore the semblance of an emaciated ape, with sinewy arms and legs that were longer and straighter than those of a gorilla or chimpanzee. Its torso was thin but muscular, like the body of a snake. Hair the color of river-mud covered all of the creature's body except its face, which was only vaguely anthropoidal.

Instead of a nose and a mouth, a hooked beak like that of an eagle jutted from the middle of the creature's face. In place of hands and feet, its limbs ended in curving talons resembling those of a gigantic bird of prey. Unlike those of beast or bird, however, the being's slit-pupilled eyes blazed with malevolent intelligence.

And it spoke.

"How did you know?" the *omuludu* demanded in a voice that sounded like the rasp of steel against stone.

"I saw food and water outside this cavern," Imaro replied. "Yet in here, I saw no bowls, no gourds, no plates. Even immortals like Amudu need to eat and drink. Demons like you do not."

"Clever of you," the *omuludu* said.

"Where is the real Emina?" Imaro asked.

"Dead! Dead! Dead!" the *omuludu* cried. "Her father sacrificed her to win what I offered!"

"And the ones who came here to learn from him ... they, too, were sacrifices?" Imaro asked.

"Of course!" the *omuludu* said. "I take the ones who are worthless while they are still in the portal from outside. I allow the ones who interest me to try to rescue what they see as 'Emina.' How they scream and beg for mercy once I shed that guise."

The *omuludu* glared hungrily at Imaro.

"Never did I think you would pass through the portal," the

123

demon grated. "Imaro … Death's Friend … the scourge of your own kind, as well as mine. Without knowing it, Amudu has given me the greatest sacrifice of all!"

Suddenly, the length of chain attached to the *omuludu*'s wrist snapped twice. And Imaro's *simi* and broadsword were out of his hands. As the weapons clattered to the floor, the *omuludu* sprang forward, swinging the chain toward the warrior's head. But the links struck only air.

The *omuludu*'s revelation of what Amudu had done to Emina left Imaro with a deep loathing of both the demon and the *isisiduya*. Distracted by his disgust, the warrior's attention had wandered momentarily, giving the *omuludu* the opportunity to disarm him.

Even as the *omuludu*'s chain again snaked toward him, Imaro ducked under its sweep. Then he leaped forward and closed with his foe. As Imaro's body collided with the *omuludu*'s, the demon tottered off-balance, and the combatants crashed heavily to the floor.

Were he an ordinary man, Imaro's tactics would have earned him little more than a few additional moments of life. But Imaro had two fathers: a warrior of the Ngwika tribe, far to the south; and a Cloud Strider, one of the benevolent deities that stood against the Mashataan – the Demon Gods. It was the Cloud Strider's heritage that enabled Imaro to battle beings like the *omuludu* on equal terms.

Grappling fiercely, Imaro and the *omuludu* rolled across the floor. Furnishings broke to pieces as the two bodies crashed into them. Imaro wedged one of his arms under the *omuludu*'s beak to prevent its point from piercing his eyes. The demon's claws tore at Imaro's body. Were he not protected by his Sahanic mail, those talons would have opened his flesh to the bone. As it was, some links from the mail were torn away, leaving a trail of metal on the floor.

No longer did the *omuludu* taunt Imaro. Its eyes blazed hatred into those of the warrior, only to be met with enmity in equal measure. As it found its best efforts thwarted, the *omuludu* began to understand that the tales of Death's Friend whispered among demon-kind were true. And the demon began to realize that it should have slain Imaro while he was still in the portal, rather than allow him to enter this place.

Imaro knew the *omuludu*'s talons would eventually tear through his armor, and even he would not long survive the subsequent wounds. Even as he and his antagonist struggled on the floor, Imaro was steering their rolling bodies in a deliberate direction ... not toward his fallen weapons, but toward the remainder of the chain he had severed.

When they reached the chain, Imaro seized the *omuludu*'s beak in both hands and wrenched it sideways. Screeching in unaccustomed pain, the *omuludu* relaxed its grasp. That moment of respite was sufficient to allow Imaro to break free and seize a length of the chain.

Then a blow from the *omuludu*'s arm caught Imaro on the side of his head, denting his helmet and knocking him off his feet. Half-dazed, Imaro still managed to evade the *omuludu*'s charge. Momentum carried the *omuludu* past the warrior. With cat-like speed, Imaro wrapped the chain around the *omuludu*'s neck, then clamped his legs around the waist of the demon.

Imaro pulled the chain tighter, constricting the throat of the *omuludu*. Vainly, the demon flailed backward with its claws and its segment of the chain in an effort to dislodge its tormentor. Although the initial blows nearly knocked Imaro senseless, he continued to cling to the *omuludu*. And the pressure on the demon's throat became unbearable.

Gradually the *omuludu*'s wild struggles began to subside. But Imaro did not slacken his efforts, for he knew the *omuludu* could be feigning weakness while gathering its strength for a final assault. Only when the *omuludu*'s movements finally ceased, and its neck had been constricted to half its normal width, did Imaro relax his grip on the chain.

Muscles aching and blood dripping from the wounds his opponent had inflicted, Imaro slowly rose to his feet. He looked down at the inert form of his foe.

"Demons do not have to eat or drink," he said aloud. "But they do have to breathe."

His own breath coming in ragged gasps, Imaro bent and picked up his sword and *simi*. He did not sheathe the weapons. He looked toward the entrance to the cavern. The opaque darkness was gone; he could see the edge of the clearing on the other side of the aperture.

Weapons still in his hands, Imaro strode toward the opening. The time had come for a reckoning with Amudu.

***

When he emerged from the cavern, Imaro stood stock-still. The clearing had changed. Bright sunlight had given way to gloom, like that of a day during the wet season.

Looking behind him, Imaro saw that the colors of the paintings on the rock wall were duller, and the paint was flaking. As he stepped forward, he noticed that all the objects Amudu had carved were now broken, cracked or otherwise marred.

He did not see Amudu. Warily, he made his way toward the place where he had last seen the *isisiduya*. What he saw there caused him to shake his head and sheathe his weapons.

The statue Amudu had been fashioning lay in two jagged pieces. The clothing Amudu wore lay by the side of the broken statue, as did the *isisiduya*'s mallet and chisel. Gray dust, like ashes, spilled from the openings of the clothing. Vague outlines of head, hands and feet were still discernable.

Now Imaro understood the truth of the bargain Amudu had made with the *omuludu*. As long as the *omuludu* was supplied with the souls of those who yearned to be taught by Amudu, the *isisiduya* would live, with his talents and skills intact. But if the *omuludu* died, so would Amudu … and so would his works. So the old man had never intended Imaro to kill the demon, had not imagined a mortal capable of it. He had craftily sought only to feed the *omuludu* one more victim, a choice one.

Imaro's eyes swept the clearing. All the items Amudu had made were marred. Only the pieces of metal and lengths of wood Amudu had not yet begun to work remained intact.

Imaro remained in the clearing for a long time before he made his way to the portal, from which the darkness had departed.

***

A man stood at the top of the stair, and peered into the notch between the two tall hills. He was clad in the garments of the West

Coast. His clothing was tattered and dusty, and weariness showed on his face. So did determination.

His name was Kofi, and he had gained great renown as an *isisiduya*. Some said his skill was second only to that of the legendary Amudu. Kofi longed to learn the secrets that would make him Amudu's equal. Through tales and rumors, he learned where Amudu was said to have gone many rains in the past. And he heard that none of the seekers who stepped through the darkness of the notch had ever returned – or so those who did not dare to do so said.

Those words did not deter Kofi. He preferred to take his chances with the darkness rather than continue to be known only as the *isisiduya* who was second to Amudu.

As he looked into the notch, Kofi shook his head in bewilderment. The opening was shadowy ... but he saw nothing of the overwhelming darkness that that had robbed other seekers of their courage. He even detected a brightening that came from the other side of the portal.

Kofi stepped through the notch. As he walked cautiously toward the smudge of light, his footfalls echoed. No unseen tendrils touched him as he passed.

When he emerged, Kofi looked up at a gray sky, in which the sun was not visible. He saw the galleries of images that had been carved and painted on the stone walls. Of the carvings, only incomplete outlines remained. Faint flecks of color were the only traces left of the paintings.

A sense of foreboding gripped Kofi. Yet he did not believe he had anything to fear. He felt only sadness as he looked at the fragments that still bore unmistakable signs of Amudu's workmanship.

The sadness deepened as Kofi passed through the trees and stone pillars. The carvings on the tree-trunks were nearly overgrown with fungus, and the pillars were broken and crumbling. When he reached the clearing, Kofi shook his head at the sight of works he would have given anything to have created that were now shattered and decayed.

He hardly noticed the few scraps of cloth at his feet. He was certain, though, that Amudu had long since died, and had thus not been immortal despite story-tellers' tales.

Then he saw it ... a length of black wood that remained intact.

He picked it up and gave it intense scrutiny. He saw lines cut into the wood, but a moment passed before he recognized the markings as the outline of a face. Its eyes were little more than horizontal slits; the nose barely a suggestion. The mouth was the most prominent feature of the face: a jagged hole gouged deep into the wood. Anguish and anger screamed from that mouth ...

At first, Kofi could not credit such a crude item to Amudu. He thought it might have been made by a would-be apprentice. Then, with sudden insight, Kofi realized who the sculpture was meant to depict – Imaro, Death's Friend, whose legend continued to live long after the man was seen no more.

Kofi decided that this was, indeed, the work of Amudu ... perhaps his last. With simplicity rather than ostentation, Amudu had captured the conflicted essence of Imaro. Amudu had produced countless items of beauty, but never one of such understated power.

With no interest in further exploring the clearing, Kofi cradled the wooden sculpture as though it were made of gold. If he noticed a dark opening at the base of a far wall, he gave no sign. He turned and departed from the clearing, passed through the portal, and descended the steep stairway. And he carried the carving back to his West Coast home.

For the rest of his life, Kofi was known as the man who had found the last work of Amudu. He allowed other *isisiduyas* to see it but never permitted anyone else to touch it. It passed on to his family after his death, and for many rains thereafter it was an object of pride and renown.

Neither Kofi, nor anyone else, ever knew that it was not Amudu who had carved the face of Death's Friend into the dark wood. Imaro himself had done the carving, with his *simi*, before he departed from the clearing long ago.

THE SECRET OF NEPHREN-KA

By Robert M. Price

I. Return of the Past

One day, Simon of Gitta knew, there would come a mad prophet (or so many would deem him) who would carry a lit lantern in broad daylight, and would say many terrible things, including requiems for slain gods. He would say, "When you look into the Abyss, the Abyss looks back into you." And that is why Simon often resorted to the invocation to Morpheus so that he might sleep of a night. For often had he gazed into the Cosmic Pit of the Pain Lords, and communed with even worse Beings, and what he had seen was by no means easy to live with. Especially in the long night.

He found himself startled awake by an abrupt shock of plummeting temperature. He could imagine no natural explanation for the phenomenon, and so the discomfort that made him shudder was not of the flesh but of the spirit. Initially he thought it an invading nightmare. His brow knitted in apprehension above the broad planes of his prominent cheek bones. As if having waited for the Gittite to orientate himself, a blurred but rapidly crystallizing image appeared, and a hollow voice was coincident with it, without actually seeming to come from it.

"You know me, or do I underestimate you, O Simon Magus?"

The tall figure could now be seen to be draped in fabrics of sunset crimson. Barely discernible because of their hue against the darkness were a pair of tame panthers who licked the apparition's extended hands. His high forehead was surmounted by the double crown of Upper and Lower Egypt. His mien was haughty in implication, though his face remained in shadow.

As Simon sat up from his sleeping pallet, he replied, not with awe but with a guarded, implicitly defensive tone: "Thou art the Black Pharaoh, known to the few who remember as *Nephren-Ka.* Surely you are he?"

"I am. That, I am. In past ages I ruled forgotten Stygia, and before that, unknown Acheron. In every age my powers waned, atom by atom, until at last the priests of decadent Khem overthrew me."

"Are you his spirit, then? His ghost? Men say they slew you."

"As they do with many things, the priests lied in order to douse the fears of the common folk who must otherwise fear my return someday. Would that I might! But I did flee Egypt in those far-off days. I sent my faithful into exile in divers places, the acolytes of my servant Bubastis I sent to dreary Britain, the hierophants of Faceless Byagoona to Gaul, the minions of serpent-bearded Byatis to Greece. I myself accompanied my chief priests to a vast and unknown land across the seas. They kept my faith alive there with sacrifice and offering. Many belonging to one of the native tribes, awed by the miracles I performed among them by sorcerous means, rallied to me and called themselves Nephites after me. In turn, I protected them from their eternal foes, once come down from snowy Lomar, and called Lamanites.

"But not long ago, my vitality failed, and my life ebbed away. Now my people want for protection against the Lamanites, who, in my absence, have redoubled their persecutions. I have cheated death for so long, I never believed it would overtake me. That was foolish, I now understand. My spirit double can linger upon this plane for but a trifle longer. And before I go off to whatever awaits me, I must needs undertake to deliver my faithful from those who would destroy them. Thus I come to you this night. Only a man of your talents can be of help to me."

Simon, genuinely surprised, both at him who sought his aid and at the astounding journey the mission should entail, replied. "O Shade of Nephren-Ka! Forgive me if I speak my mind. Your worship is shunned and persecuted with good reason! I had thought it extinct and rejoiced at the thought! Black indeed are your rites, foul the deeds you have taught your disciples! Far be it from me to stain my soul by entering thy service!"

The revenant's enigmatic visage split with laughter.

"In truth, I suspected as much! But you have dealt with Dark Powers before. I know you have. But I am past nefarious designs. That is all behind me now. In my present infirmity I cannot so much as move a pebble with a finger, as you see. It is a good deed to which

I summon you, Simon of Gitta!"

An eyebrow arching in suspicious surprise, the sorcerer answered him, "What interest can you have in deeds of goodness, your Majesty?"

"You are correct, conjurer. Little good have I done in my many days. But some awful fate awaits me. The Hell of Endless Shrieking, perhaps. Or the Cavern of Ravenous Devourers. Mayhap the Black Dimension." Here the larger-than-life apparition's countenance flickered just a bit, as if momentarily daunted, pained by a conscience long since mummified. But he continued. "Perhaps if I can bequeath my followers a measure of safety as my last deed, through you, I may be able to mitigate my damnation by a farthing."

Simon barked a laugh of scorn.

"But the disciple is no better than his master! Why take the trouble on behalf of the devil's disciples? Best to let your ancient evil die!"

"They were no more than dupes! They served me out of fear! Left to themselves they would be harmless sheep. You must know that. It is always the way with helpless mortals. They feed off superstition and ignorance. But their present fears are quite real. In olden times, the Lamanites fought against the fierce Gnoph-kehs of the Commorian ice wastes. But in defeating them the Lamanites became like them. Furthermore, I have given them reason to take revenge on my flock, and their vengeance upon my Nephites must be terrible. But you can save them."

Simon was standing now, his eyes almost level with the glowing orbs in the otherwise-shadowed face.

"Save them? By myself? How?" He was beginning to reevaluate the situation and, with it, the strange appeal of the pleading ghost.

"Across the vast ocean that swells above the grave of Atlantis lies a land equally vast, verily a different world. There my followers await. Their deliverance lies with a potent talisman which men call the Golden Heart of Quetzalcoatl. It was long ago hidden away by the ancient Jaredites. They sold its power short, and their folly destroyed them."

"But suppose I am destroyed the same way? I know even less of the thing than *they* did!"

"The Jaredites were sages but not sorcerers. They left behind a wealth of bronze plates containing much of their science. But the Heart was a product of a science they knew nothing about. But you and I do. I could bring the amulet to life if I still occupied the body of flesh, but now? It is useless to me, for I myself am become useless. Of all the men of today, you, I judge, are the one best able to awaken and wield the power of the Heart. When you see it you will, I believe, know what to do. My servants will meet you and accompany you to the location of the amulet."

II. The Host of Ekron

Alone again, Simon returned to bed, needing sleep against what lay ahead. He had not asked his visitor how he might gain the far shores where adventure beckoned to him like a man waving from a beach. He already knew how he should accomplish that. Legend told that the ancestors of the Jaredites and, after them, of those now called Nephites had crossed the ocean in strange underwater ships. Simon had not the time for such a voyage if he were to rescue the persecuted Nephites. But there was another, quicker way. There was the Host of Ekron. These were the demon spirits commanded by the oracle of Baal-Zebub at Ekron, one of the pentad of ancient Philistine cities of which Simon's hometown Gath or Gitta was another. The demons ranged far and wide and could ferret out any and all secrets as they invisibly scanned the earth. These secrets they would vouchsafe to the Philistine soothsayers, who made their living passing on desired information to their clients who wanted to know where they had lost an expensive tool or if their daughters would ever get married.

Their whispering had the sound of the chittering of insects, hence the traditional costume of the Oracle: a man-sized effigy of a locust. Simon was no oracle-monger, but he knew how to call down the Host and to make them take him on their swarm cloud to whatever destination he desired, since all the byways of the world were known to them. This he knew from a scroll recording some of the secrets obtained from the demons by the Arab *kahins*, a text called *Kitab al Azif*, "the book of the buzzing." Many centuries hence, a descendant of the book would bring great troubles to mankind.

132

It was not long before Simon of Gitta stood, equipped with his pouch of magical chemicals and fetishes on one hip, and his gladius, retained from his days in the arena, on the other. He wore a bell-sleeved blouse under a tunic of rusty vermillion festooned with silver-embroidered zodiacal signs. He softly sang the chant that only the Host of Ekron could hear, wherever in the world they might be. By the time he had finished, a purplish mist was spinning around him. And he heard the cachinnation, which seemed a not unpleasant melody of its own. The familiar furnishings of his rented room swiftly faded until naught could be seen but the violet cyclone that bore him along at unimaginable yet unfelt speed. He felt as if dreaming, suspended timelessly until he felt solid ground beneath his feet and stumbled into the ready arms of a circle of robed men, their faces displaying a mixture of fear and awe. They led him, light-headed, to a wooden chair with only a thin cloth pad to provide any comfort.

Simon had reviewed a spell designed to make any foreign language intelligible but now found he did not need it. These people, the Nephites, welcoming him, were speaking a peculiar dialect of Hebrew heavily influenced by Demotic Egyptian. A hybrid tongue, it sounded like a kind of reformed Egyptian, no doubt introduced by the original priests of Nephren-Ka during the long years he had dominated the Nephites. Simon was fluent in both component languages and had little difficulty understanding his hosts.

His new acquaintances brought him more food than he could eat, and with it wine. They shared with Simon what they knew of the danger they faced and what they had guessed concerning the artifact from which their late god-king had promised deliverance should come. They showed him to a great and ornate bed, virtually a horizontal throne, which had belonged to Nephren-Ka. Simon had been largely passive in his magical transit, but somehow it had exacted the price of exhaustion, and he needed to refresh himself. At dawn the Nephites would lead him to the Jaredite ruins.

III. The Catacombs of Jared

The morning sky was intensely blue, the sun blazing. Simon thought himself inured to the hellish furnaces of the Negev and of the Nabatean desert, but this was new to him. He might have employed a meditation to lower his body temperature, but he preferred to endure the hardship and grow stronger for it. His companions, however, seemed little discomfited. Good for them. They had been born and raised in these scorching conditions.

Simon took advantage of the trek to sharpen his command of the Nephite language in conversation with the others. They were polite enough, even deferential, but none could conceal a pervasive unease. Of course, they had learned to keep alert for possible Lamanite harassment. No sooner had Simon asked one of the men about this than stones began to rain down on the party from a ridge above them. Some of the Nephites fled, desperate for shelter. Others raised crude metal shields, quickly pitted and dented by the larger of the pelting stones. The Gittite loosened the sword in his scabbard but quickly realized that none of the feathered and armored attackers were descending from their perch to engage in honest combat. So instead, the Magus extended his arms skyward and swiftly gesticulated, his hands weaving a complex pattern of silver-blue fire.

The hurled stones slacked in pace as the Lamanites found themselves distracted by Simon's fireworks. In another moment they dropped their projectiles and turned to flee. Seeing this, the Nephites started to emerge from their concealment behind some nearby boulders.

"O Magus! How did you dispatch them?"

Simon chuckled. "It was not me they feared, but rather the pack of winged and fanged hounds they imagined were springing for them. It is but a trick of the light, I confess, but the beasts they think they see will seem to pursue them for some time, wherever they go. We need not worry about them returning to trouble us further."

The surviving Nephite elders having given Simon thanks, nonetheless made a hasty departure, licking their wounds. Simon laughed at their timidity as he pursued his way. The directions he had received were simple enough; he would not have requested their escort and did not miss it now. But he found himself thinking, too, about his Lamanite ambushers. He might easily have destroyed them with his magic, like Elijah of old, but he had satisfied himself with simply scaring them off like panicky children.

Why had he shown clemency for these attackers? Perhaps he

had sensed something amiss. After all, the hostility of the sons of Lomar had been provoked by the atrocities commanded by Nephren-Ka. Perhaps they did not even realize the Black Pharaoh was dead! In any case, would they not share his own initial assumption that the devil's depravity lived on among his minions? And suppose they were right? Until he could sort this out, he was glad for now that he had not killed the Lamanites. There would always be another chance if necessary.

IV. The Golden Heart of Quetzalcoatl

Simon carefully treaded the labyrinth, having memorized the directions and aided by the eerie glow emitted by his blade, which had more uses than just to butcher men. But his way, he suddenly realized, was not clear before him. An advancing shadow alerted him before a giant of some seven feet lumbered forth from around a stony bend, its towering height all the more remarkable given that it possessed no head! As it lunged toward him, navigating, it must be, by means of some other sense than sight, the thing reached out to seize him and tear him apart like a chicken. Simon's observant eyes saw that each gnarled hand sported six fingers. At once he thought of his ancient countryman, his childhood hero, Goliath of Gath, one of the last of the fabled Nephilim whose number included Nimrod, Gilgamesh, and mighty Ishbibenob. Could this creature have been another? But who had ruined him, transformed him into this hulking juggernaut? Well, there was only one answer to that. It must have been the doing of the Black Pharaoh, posting him here to discourage any who coveted the amulet of power. Had his ghostly ally merely forgotten to call off this monstrous watchdog? Too late for that now!

Simon easily evaded the clumsy, club-like swinging of the massive limbs. He hopped from side to side, assessing the most opportune avenue of attack, quickly making his choice and stabbing at the heart. For a moment he feared his gladius lost, as it protruded harmlessly from the chest of the headless giant. Its animation did not, then, depend on the inner workings of mortal men's bodies, but on dark magic. Simon accused himself for a fool for not realizing that right off. But in a moment he found an opening to clasp the familiar hilt and yank the blade free. But of what use was it against this deadly marionette? He stepped away, sheathed the sword, and undid the draw string of his pouch.

There was no real opportunity to scrutinize the contents of his bag of tricks, so he just shook out all the powders in a random puff of mingled ingredients. What the effect might be, Simon did not know. Both he and the undead sentinel paused in their mutual struggle. In a few moments, his foe, though seemingly impervious to bodily pain, began to burst into flame over most of his huge form, flame shifting between blue and green, yellow to purple, and back again. Most of the rest of him suddenly stiffened into clear ice which shattered with every attempted movement. Inches of the dead flesh here and there began to sublimate directly into the air. As what was left of the thing collapsed with a blood-chilling sound, a kind of grinding groan rose from deep within its rotting torso. Simon gaped in delighted surprise and hoped he would be able to duplicate the recipe he had accidentally created.

The lingering stench was overpowering, abominable. Holding his breath, then his nose, he hastened on down the shaft, half-expecting another monster to bar his way. Accordingly, he was both surprised and not surprised to find himself circled by a veritable flock of feathered, flying serpents. Reflexively, he poised to defend himself, but none of the creatures swooped to the attack. And somehow he knew he must not strike with the sword. But why were they here? What was their purpose? It must be to protect the amulet, surely, a second line of defense in case the deadly Golem should fail. But then why did they not descend upon him? Unless perhaps they sensed danger arising from another quarter. What did they know?

The talisman was *here*. In a sudden, blinding flash of light it made its presence known. The winged serpents moved to circle it, but they made no move to prevent him as Simon extended his hand to grasp it, fearing the possible result. Would he be struck down for his sacrilegious effrontery, as the Jaredites were?

Now he held it in his sweating hand, its light illuminating his features from below, and waiting for the worst. And the worst arrived, though not from any direction he had imagined. Simon recognized a hollow voice and turned to face its possessor. As he now knew to expect, the luminous image of Nephren-Ka loomed above him in its clinging shroud of gloom. So it was, from the first, a trap.

"The goal, O Simon, was always to employ the peculiar power of the jewel, that of effecting soul-transference. My incorporeal shade will pass through it into the body of him who holds the Heart."

"Why me? Why go to such trouble? Surely any of your Nephite stooges would have sufficed, if all you need is a host body?"

"Ah, Simon of Gitta, how you underestimate your value! A soul of great power such as mine would overwhelm and destroy a human form unprepared, unfit to contain it. I required you not to find the amulet but to mediate its power. Your years of occult mastery, your conditioning by the forces of strange dimensions, have transfigured you. Of all men now living, you alone are an adequate vessel for me! And in your image the Black Pharaoh will once again walk the earth, blast it, and rule what remains. You are highly honored, my son!"

To his horror, Simon could feel the process beginning already as the fiend's words seemed to echo within his raven-haired head, as if originating there. The Black Pharaoh was beginning to supplant him. In the moments of shared consciousness, the Gittite suffered horrifying visions of the blasphemous deeds—and knowledge—of Nephren-Ka. Compared with this, a beckoning oblivion seemed a bright hope. It would not be so bad to let go...

But it was not to be. Suddenly pain overtook him as a *third* consciousness intruded. Simon knew, because the Entity knew, its identity. This was Holy Quetzalcoatl! He was a Light both glorious and terrible. Dreadful shrieks rang through Simon's skull (or through the catacomb of the doomed Jaredites, he knew not which) as the Golden Heart of Quetzalcoatl subsumed and devoured ancient Nephen-Ka.

This must be what had happened to the Jaredites so long ago. So Simon mused as in astonishment he beheld the Light of the Heart shrinking back into the gem, which had dulled but now regained its supernatural radiance. If the soul of Nephren-Ka was imprisoned there along with the ancient Jaredites, he would never be free again.

VI. The Vengeance of the Lamanites

Unstable from assaults both physical and magical, Simon finally retraced his path through the tunnel and into the merciless sunlight. The long shadows of the waiting Nephite elders folded as their owners bowed before him in groveling reverence. It was obvious they supposed the infernal scheme, to which they had been party, had gone according to plan. Their Master had returned! Or so they thought. They were in for a surprise. Weak as he was, Simon knew he could finish them all. He unlimbered his sword.

But the sound of a small, dislodged stone clattering down from the ridge above them caught Simon's attention, and he turned to see where it had come from. He could see the tops of many helmets. The Nephites' eyes widened in terror as Simon yelled up at their Lamanite enemies. "The Black Pharaoh is dead, never to return. But here you see," he said, with a gesture encompassing the frightened elders now rising to their feet, "the next best thing! Have at it, my friends!"

Not merely rocks but spears and feathered shafts fell like a destroying rain. It was over quickly, and Simon waited for the Lamanites to descend and surround him with raised weapons, hailing him for the deliverance he had won them.

THE DARK PHARAOH

Dark mage of ancient Stygia and Acheron,
   Thine awful thaumaturgies have for thee attained
Great powers, and for many ages thou hast reigned
   O'er empires fallen now into oblivion.

Thou didst invoke Nyarlat, that Mighty Messenger,
   Who set thee on Khem's throne in cruel and haughty pride
As Pharaoh Nephren-Ka, soon styled Death's Emperor!
   With his new Chosen One, Nyarlat is Satisfied.

Richard L. Tierney

THE TEMPLE OF LIGHT

A Changa Adventure
By Milton J. Davis

Market day in Mombasa brought the usual crowds to the city center, a discordant mix of buyers and sellers eager to fill their cupboards and coffers. It was also one of the few days that the various folks of the merchant city mixed without distinction, searching the various kiosks for life's essentials. Even among the variety of folk, one man stood out. He strode through the throng carrying two sacks of grain on his massive shoulders, a burden that would have bowed the average man. The brown leather vest he wore gripped his broad muscled torso; his cotton pants fit his legs like an extra layer of skin. He bore no sword or knife, but even one whose wits were sparse knew better that to approach him lightly. His presence spoke of a man capable of inflicting damage if need be.

Changa Diop reveled in the freedom of the market. He gazed upon the crowd with joy, ignoring the astonished stares as he made his way back to the dock. It was his third trip to the market that day and each excursion filled him with as much excitement as the first. He was free again, walking among folks without the burden of ownership weighing on his shoulders like the bags of grain he carried. There were still obligations, but they were decisions he made, not those made for him. The horror of the pit was behind him now, but danger still haunted him. Some things were persistent.

That thought alerted Changa that he was being watched. He kept his aloof expression as his eyes probed the swirling mob of the market. His eyes eventually found the source of his scrutiny, a tall woman who made no effort to hide her interest. Her head was immodestly bare, revealing her close cropped hair. She strode through the crowd covered in a black cloak that fell from her shoulders to her ankles. Her face reminded Changa of the Nuba, black smooth skin encompassing a beautiful yet stern face. Changa stared back and smiled; the woman's expression remained unchanged. She halted, watching him as he walked away, then melted into the crowd.

By the time Changa reached the docks the woman was but a pleasant memory. His new companions, Belay's *baharia,* waved to him as he approached the *dhows.* All were smiles except one small boy who stood with his fists planted on his sides, his eyebrows bunched and his small mouth set in a frown.

"Where have you been, Changa?" Tayari asked. Kasim, Belay's *nahoda,* had assigned his son the task of teaching Changa how to tie good knots. The boy took his job seriously and was not pleased that Changa didn't share his view.

"I had work to do," Changa answered. "You want to eat, don't you?"

Tayari continued to stare at Changa so intensely that Changa laughed. "Okay, *mwalimu.* I'll set these down and we can continue our lessons."

Changa spent the next hour with Tayari practicing the various knots required for the riggings and other items on the *dhow.* Some were simple and others complex, but Changa had no problem following the boy's swift hands. Afterwards he joined the crew with their various chores. He had yet to make any friends among them but at least they were friendlier than his former circumstances. For the first time in years he could fully extend his friendship to others. Unlike the pit, he didn't have to worry about facing any of these men later in a battle to the death.

The night eased across Mombasa, bringing a cool wind from beyond the horizon. Changa lay on the deck, gazing into the star-laden sky. He refused to sleep inside except when the rains forced him to. His life in the pit cells continued to influence him despite being so far away.

Sleep was laying its peaceful veil over his eyes when Tayari shook him back to consciousness.

"Changa, Bwana Belay wishes to see you right away," the boy informed him.

Changa dragged himself to a sitting position, then stood. "Lead the way," he grumbled.

Tayari led Changa to Belay's home in the center of town. The guard opened the gate to Belay's courtyard, eyeing both Tayari and Changa closely as they entered. Changa stopped suddenly as soon as he entered. Belay sat in his chair, a look of terror on his face. Before him stood the woman Changa saw in the market, the same scrutinizing look on her stern face. A third person stood with them, a man Changa did not recognize physically but whom he knew by heart. He stood a foot taller than Changa and seemed to weigh twice as much. His bulk was not that of a complacent merchant; hard muscles pushed against the cotton shirt and pants he wore. A black robe similar to the one the woman wore hung from his massive shoulders with a hood obscuring his head. The man's attention was focused on Belay.

"What is this?" Changa demanded.

"Silence, *mtwana*," the man rumbled. There was a tone in his voice that demanded obedience. Changa ignored him.

"What is going on, bwana?" Changa demanded. "Who are these people?"

The man looked up at Changa. His eyes burned with a malevolent light, hinting of something deeper than evil. Changa had seen such a look only once in his life from a man whose evil took the life of his father.

"Is this the one?" the man said.

The woman nodded. "He's the one."

Changa stepped towards them, and the woman came between them. Her hand disappeared into her cloak.

"Changa, stop!" Belay said. "You have no business with him, Dambudso."

"Quiet, merchantman," Dambudso said. "Shamsa said he's what I want. Her judgment is infallible."

"He is not my *mtwana*," Belay said. "He is a free man."

Dambudso looked Changa up and down. "He has the look of one. It doesn't matter. You owe me, merchant man. Our debt is erased if this man comes with me. If not, there is nothing you can give me that will erase it."

"What do you want of me?" Changa asked.

"Changa, no!" Belay yelled. "This has nothing to do with you."

"I'm a free man, bwana," Changa said. "This is not my business, but it's my decision."

Dambudso grinned, an expression that did nothing to make

him look more agreeable.

"What do you want?" Changa asked.

Dambudso approached Changa, then stood before him. "I'm taking a journey and I need special men to accompany me. Shamsa tells me you are a special man."

"Where are we going?" Changa asked.

Dambudso's grin became a smile. "A sacred place. There is something there I wish."

"How long will we be gone?"

"Long enough."

Changa looked at Belay. "Will Belay's debt be absolved when you get your something?"

Dambudso nodded. "Of course."

"I'll get my things," Changa said.

"You don't need anything," Dambudso said. "I'll supply you with everything you'll need for the journey."

The mysterious man took one last look at Belay. "Consider you debts paid...for now."

Dambudso strode for the door, Shamsa following. Changa followed them out of Belay's house and into the dark streets of Mombasa. He was taking a risk going with these two but he would not allow Belay to be in danger. The man had bought his freedom and saved his life; it was time for him to return the favor.

The mysterious duo walked through Mombasa's dark streets with no torch, but they moved as if the sun shone overhead. Changa stayed close to them; his eyesight wasn't nearly as keen in such darkness. They halted at the end of the road just before it entered the surrounding farmland. A wagon rested at the end of the road. Two oxen were hitched to it; an extremely tall man with facial scars sat behind the reins. Two saddled horses flanked the oxen. Men sat in the bed of the wagon, their faces hidden by hoods attached to cloaks similar to Dambudso's.

"Put this on and climb in back," Shamsa ordered. In her hand she held a black cloak.

Changa looked at the cloth skeptically. He was well aware of the ways of shamans and was not in the mood to be spellbound.

"You gave your word to Belay that you would do as I ask,"

Dambudso said. "Are you not a man of your word, Changa?"

Changa snatched the robe from Shamsa's hand and donned it. Immediately he felt refreshed. The inkling of hunger that teased him dissipated. His eyes fell on Shamsa and she smiled.

"It will nourish you during our journey. This way we won't have to waste time finding and eating food."

"I assume this task will require weapons?" Changa asked.

"You will get them when the time comes," Dambudso said. "Unlike you, some of your companions are not very trustworthy."

Changa climbed into the wagon, and his new cohorts reluctantly made room for him. They looked up at him, some nodding while others stared. One man finally spoke, uttering a name Changa recently relinquished.

"Mbogo" One of the mysterious men removed his hood and Changa grimaced.

"Katafwa," Changa replied. Both men locked stares, Changa frowning, Katafwa flashing a grim smile.

"I thought I killed you," Changa said.

"You almost did," Katafwa replied. "But no man can kill Death."

"Be quiet!" Dambudso ordered. "From now until we retrieve the Light from the Temple you belong to me. You will obey my every word."

"And if we don't?" Katafwa asked.

Dambudso appeared suddenly beside the wagon. His thick arm shot out like a serpent and his massive hand clutched Katafwa's throat before he lifted the man like a leaf.

"I cannot kill you because I need you," Dambudso hissed. "But there are things worse than your namesake, *mtwana*."

Dambudso dropped Katafwa into the wagon. The others laughed as Dambudso walked away and mounted his horse. Katafwa rubbed his neck. Changa said nothing, watching Katafwa with mild admiration.

"He's strong," Katafwa said. "Too strong to kill without weapons."

Changa didn't reply. He watched Dambudso and Shamsa mount their horses.

"Let's go, Luk," Dambudso said to the Dinka wagon driver. "We have a long journey ahead. I'm anxious to be done with this."

Changa expected a leisurely pace which would allow him to sleep. Instead the riders took off at full gallop. The Dinka did not follow. He sat still and began to sing a song, his voice low and insistent. The oxen crooned back, their bellows strong and agitated. And then they ran, darting off with a suddenness that caused everyone in the wagon to tumble into each other. Changa flung out his right hand and grasped the edge of the wagon. He pulled himself against it as the Dinka sang louder, his strange melodic voice rising over the rattling wagon. The jostling subsided, then ceased.

Changa peered over the side and his eyes widened in astonishment. The wagon drifted over the ground, the wheels perfectly still. He looked at the oxen; their legs moved as if they ran across flat ground, but their hooves touched nothing. Changa raised his eyes and looked farther ahead. Though Dambudso and Shamsa were dim shapes in the distance, he could tell their mounts travelled the same as the wagon.

"This is Dambudso's work," Katafwa said.

Changa looked to see the man sitting beside him still rubbing his neck. "We will not survive this task. They are speeding us to our death."

Changa didn't reply. He glared at Katafwa, remembering why he disliked the burly Nuba.

"I say we become friends if we want to survive this sentence," Katafwa continued.

His words forced a laugh from Changa's lips.

"Dambudso must have damaged your brain," he said.

"I'm not fond of the idea either, boy," Katafwa countered. "You almost killed me. But I know you better than that bundle over there. I trust your skills."

Changa glanced at the other men in the wagon. There were four of them, and they whispered among themselves. It was obvious they knew each other well. As much as he hated to admit it, Katafwa's words made sense.

"Who are they?" Changa asked.

Katafwa shrugged. "Who cares? They're *mtwana*, just like us."

"Like you," Changa corrected him.

Katafwa's eyebrows rose. "Maulani freed you?"

"No," Changa barked.

Katafwa nodded. "I didn't think so. You made too much money for him."

Changa didn't owe Katafwa an explanation but felt compelled to clarify his status.

"Belay bought me from Maulani and freed me soon afterwards," he explained. "He offered me employment as his bodyguard and I accepted."

"So why are you here? As a free man you have no obligation to him. Whatever business he has with that devil Dambudso is his own." Katafwa's eyebrows rose. "Are you his lover?"

Changa glared at Katafwa. "No."

The man shrugged. "Don't look at me like that. Many pious Swahili are only so among each other. Once in their stone houses a different master reigns."

"I owe him," Changa answered. "He freed me."

Katafwa laughed out loud, and the other men looked in their direction.

"Mbogo is a man with a conscience!" He leaned close to Changa, his hot breath annoying the Bakonga. "Take my advice and lose it as soon as you can. It will be the death of you."

"Seems it already is," Changa said.

The two reluctant cohorts remained silent the rest of the night, Changa wondering where their mysterious journey would end. The wagon's journey resembled that of a *dhow*, smooth yet undulating as if it rode gentle waves. Daybreak eventually emerged behind him; the sun's light creeping over the stunted treetops. Changa had journeyed a good distance from Mombasa a number of times, but never had he seen landscape like that which became clear in the growing sunlight. It was neither thick forest nor open savannah. It was barren like a desert, yet even the desert was not as sterile as the land stretching out before them. Signs of former life surrounded them; gray trees with empty branches resembling extended bones, bleached skeletons of creatures Changa knew well and others he didn't recognize at all. Whatever had reduced this land to waste was not natural. The wagon jolted, acquiring the normal cadence of a wagon connected to the ground. The Dinka ceased singing and his oxen responded with a short bellow. They halted, surrounded by the unnatural nothingness. Shamsa and her mount sauntered to the wagon, the woman's face still grim.

"We will rest here," she said. "The oxen need nourishment. Don't take off your robes until we reach the temple grounds."

"There is a temple in this waste?" Katafwa asked.

Changa didn't think Shamsa's expression could get grimmer, but it did.

"You talk too much," she spat. "Just do as I say."

Her piercing eyes fell on Changa. "You, come with me."

She reined her horse about and began to ride away. Changa hesitated, unsure of the woman's intentions. She stopped, then looked over her shoulder expectantly. Changa climbed from the wagon and followed.

"We go to retrieve an object very important to Dambudso," she said. "It is of extreme value to him."

"Dambudso appears as a man of great power," Changa said. "I'm puzzled that he would need our help...and yours."

Shamsa looked at him, and Changa thought he almost saw her smile.

"Under normal circumstances you would be right," she answered. "But everyone has a weakness. Dambudso needs you and the others to get near his prize. He needs me to retrieve it."

"And what is your debt to him?" Changa asked.

"I owe him no debt," she said. "I owe him a favor."

"Katafwa says we'll all die," Changa said. "Is that true?"

Shamsa sucked her teeth. "Katafwa talks too much. It was a mistake bringing him."

"You haven't answered my question," Changa reminded her.

"It's likely you will," she admitted. "But you have a chance to survive."

Changa's mood brightened. "How?"

"Stay close to me and do everything I say," she said. "Go back to your friends and say nothing of our conversation."

Changa nodded and returned to the wagon. The Dinka had

146

placed a blanket made of the same material as his robe over the oxen. He sat before them in his own robe that swirled with colors and symbols. He hummed as he stroked the beasts' muzzles, oblivious of the barren land around him. Changa climbed back into the wagon. No sooner had he sat than Katafwa scooted beside him.

"So what secrets did the stone princess share with you?" he asked eagerly. "And why did she share them with you?"

"She seems to think I can help her," Changa answered.

"With what?"

"I don't know."

"Keep your distance, Mbogo," Katafwa advised. "Trust no one."

"You seem to be full of wisdom," Changa replied, "yet you sit here just as vulnerable as I. Why are you here?"

Katafwa shrugged. "I am a *mtwana*. I had no choice."

"You don't seem like the kind of man who would agree easily to such a task."

"I was the best choice," Katafwa said. "My mistress's other *mtwanas* are domestic help. I am her only fighter."

"You're not much of one," Changa replied.

"With my hands, no," Katafwa admitted. "But give me a spear or a sword and the meaning of my name becomes very clear."

"So you are your mistress's shield," Changa commented.

A solemn look came over Katafwa's face. "I perform other duties as well."

It was Changa's turn to be surprised. "So you are her lover."

"You use that term loosely," Katafwa said with a bitter tone. "Apparently my mistress is one who craves the constant attention of men. When my master died she decided to request that attention from me. She is a lovely woman and I was happy to oblige. But like a fool I fell in love with her. I'm sure the feeling is not mutual, for if it was I wouldn't be here. I volunteered thinking she would say no."

"I have never been in love," Changa said.

"You're not missing a thing," Katafwa answered.

Movement on the horizon caught Changa's eye. The border between earth and sky faded into a roiling mass of sand.

"It looks like a sandstorm is coming," Katafwa commented.

"That is no storm," Dambudso said, his voice booming over them all. "It is an attack."

He dismounted and took a thick bundle from behind the saddle. Kneeling beside the wagon, he undid the leather straps holding the bundle tight then rolled it open, revealing eight swords. They were magnificent weapons, the curved blades shining in the dimming light, the pommels carved from perfect ivory and studded with jewels. Katafwa immediately jumped from the wagon and took up one of the blades. He caressed the weapon with his left hand, his eyes wide with wonder.

"Now this is a sword!" His smile was infectious despite the impending danger.

"The rest of you get down here and arm yourselves!" Dambudso barked. "I can kill most of them but not all of them. Hurry!"

Changa and the others climbed out the wagon and chose their swords. Changa was disappointed with the blade. Though pretty, it was lighter than he was used to.

"Don't be deceived," Katafwa said as if reading his mind. "These are Damascus swords. They can withstand the strongest blows yet cut like a razor." Katafwa grabbed the tip of his blade and bent it almost into a U shape.

Changa repeated the gesture. He still wasn't impressed.

Shamsa walked in their midst. "Close your cloaks and pull your hoods completely over your faces. If the sand touches your skin it will tear it away."

"We won't be able to see!" one of the other men argued.

"Do as I say if you want to live, fool!" Shamsa spat. "You will see enough."

Shamsa looked long at Changa before following her own advice. Changa pulled the hood over his face. His sight was obscured but not completely blocked. He stared at the advancing tempest and stiffened as the black mesh revealed the truth behind the storm. Shapes flowed within the sands, some human-like, some not, but all closing rapidly on them. Changa looked at his companions then to Dambudso and Shamsa, the only barrier between him and the coming menace. There was nowhere to run, not that he would. He hoped the sword he held in his hand was as mighty as Katafwa claimed. The

Dinka seemed oblivious. He covered his oxen with a black shroud, then lay against them, his singing constant and soothing.

Changa watched Dambudso push Shamsa behind him. The shaman stretched out his arms, his shoulders rising and falling in perfect rhythm. Tendrils extended from his fingers, thin wisps so frail it was hard for Changa to be sure they truly existed. They grew longer and wider, the air shimmering in their presence. They detached from his hands and expanded more, forming a translucent shell about them. The time could not have been better. The sandstorm and its creatures assaulted the barrier moments later. While the shield held back the swirling sands, it did not stop the beasts hidden within. Two serpent-like creatures leaped out of the sand at Dambudso, their maws wide. Shamsa stepped between the shaman and the beasts swinging her blade wide. Green fluid sprayed from them as their heads fell from their bodies and rolled by Shamsa's feet. Changa was so mesmerized by the sudden demise that he almost lost his own life. A bull-like creature smashed its head into Changa's ribs, knocking him into the air like a wind-blown leaf. He landed awkwardly but managed to roll to a kneeling position, his sword raised instinctively.

The bull creature was charging him again. Changa waited until it was almost upon him before rolling to his right as he slashed at the side of its thick neck. His blade bit into the strange flesh, and he was rewarded by the painful howl of his attacker. Green liquid sprayed into his face, never touching his skin but blinding him. Before he could wipe it away, something slammed into his back, knocking him forward into the sand. Small, sharp hands clawed at him, tearing at his shroud and trying to peel his fingers from the hilt of his sword. Changa let out a yell and pushed to his feet. He tore two of the monkey-like creatures from him, throwing them as far as he could, while cutting the others in two. More green ooze sprayed about him, turning into a clear thick liquid at it sank into the sand.

Sand stung his skin where his shroud had been torn. He took a quick look around and was dismayed. Dambudso still stood like a statue, arms outstretched. Shamsa danced about him, fighting off the various denizens emerging from the abrasive swirl. The other warriors struggled as he had, clawing the sand creatures from their bodies while swinging wildly with their swords. One man's shroud was ripped away and the sand swarmed him like locusts. His screams were drowned out, then ceased as his grit-eroded skeleton crumbled to the ground. Changa would not lose his shroud.

Another shout caught Changa's attention, although this was not a call of distress. Katafwa moved with a grace similar to Shamsa's, working his Damascus with a skill far beyond the ordinary. His flashing blade formed a shield around him more effective than Dambudso's tendrils, creatures piling at his feet in a morbid collection. With each kill Katafwa shouted, yelled or laughed. Katafwa hadn't lied to him earlier. He was a master with a sword. Creatures fell before him almost as fast as they fell to Shamsa's blade. It was why Changa stood unmolested; Katafwa's fury drew the attention of the other creatures. Changa took advantage, attacking them from behind. The other warriors offered Katafwa no such assistance. They huddled by the wagon, happy to be free of the onslaught. The creatures responded to Changa's attack and set upon him, but he was prepared. Together he and Katafwa battled the nefarious denizens until the attack trickled away, then ceased. Changa looked about; the sand storm had ceased and with it the attack. Dambudso slowly lowered his arms as Shamsa kept a focused vigil about him. As the sand cleared, Changa and the others were finally able to see the true threat to their lives. Hundreds of creatures lay dead beyond the barrier. He realized that without the shaman's mystical dome they would have been easily overwhelmed.

Dambudso scanned the area, then nodded his head. He looked at Shamsa.

"Gather their weapons," he said.

Shamsa immediately complied. She took the weapons from the tribesmen huddled near the wagon, disgust clear on her face. She approached Changa and Katafwa with an expression resembling a smile. Changa handed over his Damascus reluctantly. Katafwa did not.

"This is a fine blade," he said. "Too fine to give up so easily."

"Don't," Shamsa warned.

Katafwa's feet slid apart as he raised the sword. "You can have it if you..."

Katafwa disappeared, replaced by Dambudso's bulk. He held

the Damascus in his hand. Glaring at Changa, he absently gave the blade to Shamsa.

"See to your friend," he said. He pointed behind Changa.

Changa turned to see Katafwa sprawled in the sand face down. Changa trotted to the man and rolled him on his back. There was no obvious movement; he leaned closer and felt for his breath.

"He's alive," Changa shouted.

"Too bad," Dambudso commented. "I grow weary of him."

Shamsa folded her arms before her, clearly agitated by Dambudso's actions.

"We still need all of them. Besides, he's the best swordsman."

Dambudso shrugged. "His cloak will heal him eventually. Get them in the wagons. We must make up for lost time."

"Let us hurry," Shamsa said. "They are preparing for us."

Dambudso glared at her. "Don't state the obvious. Just make sure you are ready to perform your task. I will be very disappointed if you fail."

Changa felt the threat in Dambudso's words as he carried Katafwa to the wagon. As for Shamsa, she seemed unaffected.

"I will." She climbed on her steed. "As you said, we are wasting time."

Dambudso mounted his horse while the rest of the warriors climbed into the wagon. They looked at the bones of their comrade with sadness and fear, their hands tight on their weapons. Changa sat beside Katafwa, then placed his hand on the man's chest. He was breathing but barely. He did not question the healing abilities of the cloaks, but he was concerned lest the enchanted shroud not do its job before they reached their mysterious destination. He believed they would need the man's amazing skills.

The Nuba uncovered his bovine and climbed onto the wagon. He began singing the familiar song, and the wagon rose over the sand. Once again they were streaking across the land at an incredible speed, the sand blurring beneath them. The mountains in the distance were their obvious destination; what secret they held Changa would soon discover.

At least that was what he thought. Despite their speed, three days passed and they seemed no closer to their destination. The mountains slowly grew in stature until they could no longer see their snow-capped peaks. Changa was no stranger to mountains. His homeland was dotted with verdant peaks, but none was as massive as those looming before them.

"Damn it."

Changa looked down into Katafwa's disappointed eyes.

"Welcome back," he said.

Katafwa struggled to sit up. "It seems my plan failed."

"What plan?" Changa asked.

"I should be dead," Katafwa spat. "I was sure those sand things would kill me, but I guess I overestimated their ferocity."

"So you chose Dambudso."

Katafwa winced and touched his chest where the wizard slammed into him.

"Yes I did. I figured, since he almost killed me before, he would be happy to finish the job."

Changa smirked. "He almost did. You can thank your cloak that you sit among us."

Katafwa grimaced. "I'd rather sit among my ancestors."

Katafwa's eyes scanned the wagon. "We are missing one."

Changa controlled a shudder. "The sand consumed him. I saw it."

"Better you than me," Katafwa said. "Maybe we'll all be consumed by something before this is all over."

Changa refused to let Katafwa's morbid image enter his head. He looked ahead; the mountains now appeared as a massive stone wall before them. Details became clear: thick, wasted trees with canopies resembling mushroom caps towered over smaller, twisted brethren while the spaces between them were thick with shrubs. Changa thought he could make out some sort of a road through the dense foliage. He traced it up the mountain until his eyes rested on the entrance to a massive temple. The building was too large to have been built by men alone, he was sure. This was a structure assembled by the type of power Dambudso possessed.

The massive magic man suddenly reined his horse. Shamsa did the same. The Nuba's melodic coaxing ended with an abrupt command, and the oxen ceased their levitated run, drifting to the hard earth below with a grace belying their dense bulk. The wagon eased to the ground. Dambudso dismounted and marched to the wagon.

"Get out, all of you," he said, his eyes locked on Katafwa. Changa and the others clambered out to the wagon. Shamsa rode up to them and dismounted.

"You will follow Shamsa to the temple," Dambudso said, gesturing without looking. "You will obey her every command. If you return, you and your masters will be richly rewarded."

Katafwa folded his arms across his chest, then tilted his head to the side.

"And what will you do?" he asked.

Changa waited for Dambudso to strike, but he did not. Instead a frustrated look commanded his face.

"I will stay here," he said.

Katafwa's eyes widened and he grinned. "And why is that, great mage?"

Changa grabbed Katafwa's arm. "Be quiet!"

Dambudso grimaced before dropping his head. "Because I can go no further."

Shamsa strode to the both of them and shoved Katafwa.

"Be quiet, fool! You live on my grace only. Remove your cloaks and follow me."

For the first time since their journey began, one of the secretive warriors spoke.

"Why? Won't they protect us?"

Shamsa glared at him. "Not anymore."

The cohorts looked about fearfully. Katafwa was the first to follow. Changa followed, looking back at the others. The cohort finally fell in step.

Changa worked his way close to the warrior woman. "Why is it that Dambudso cannot come with us?"

Shamsa pointed at the temple. "That is the Temple of Light. Once it was the symbol of faith for all those who lived in its shadow. The priests of the Temple performed wonderful things and the lands prospered. But one of those priests was more talented than the others. He grew to high status, so much so that he began to think he was equal to his gods. The day came that he called the people to the temple steps and proclaimed himself a living god. He told the people they would worship and sacrifice to him from that day forth."

"Dambudso," Katafwa said.

"What happened?" Changa asked.

Shamsa's eyes narrowed. "He was punished."

They reached the base of the mountain. Changa could feel a change in the energy surrounding him. A sense of foreboding crept into his mind, a sensation that what they were doing was terribly wrong. He looked at the others; the cohorts shivered despite the humid heat. Only Shamsa and Katafwa seemed unaffected, Shamsa's face locked in her familiar frown and Katafwa smiling like a child. Shamsa stepped into the bush, following a narrow trail into the heights, Changa close behind her. The sensation grew the higher they climbed.

"No!" Changa turned to look behind him. The cohorts stood still, the four holding their weapons threateningly.

"We will not go any further!" Their spokesman was the tallest of the three, a man whose scarred face attested his long familiarity with conflict.

"We came to pay a debt for our masters," he complained. "We did not come to die!"

Shamsa pushed Changa aside, stomping down to confront the three.

"You mean nothing to your masters," she hissed. "That's why you are here. They don't care if you live or die, and neither do I. All that matters to them is that their debt is paid. All that matters to me is that you walk up this hill and do as you are told. Either you follow me up this hill or you die here. Your choice."

The man's fear faded from his eyes, replaced by fury. "I will not..."

Shamsa's arm flashed. The man's head jumped from his neck and disappeared into the close bush. His body stood before her for a moment, blood oozing from his neck, then collapsed at Shamsa's feet. She reached down with her left hand, lifting the man's body like a child's, then tossing it into the bush with his head.

"Either you follow me or you die here," she repeated.

The others glanced at the bush where their companion lay. They sheathed their weapons and lowered their heads in submission. Shamsa wiped her blade and strode back to the front.

"Katafwa, take position behind them. If they try to flee, kill them."

"Of course," Katafwa answered.

Shamsa continued up the trail, Changa following close.

"You have a problem with my actions, Changa?" she asked without turning to look at him.

"They will not fight for you," he answered, his foreboding replaced by anger.

"I don't need them to fight for me. I just need them to fight."

Shamsa stopped and raised her hand. They had reached the edge of the bush. Before them was an open area strewn with fallen timber and other debris. In the center of the ragged field stood the temple. The structure was more massive that it appeared from the distance, a granite monument draped with thick vines except at the towering entrance. A pulsing light shone from the aperture.

"What happened?" Changa whispered.

"Dambudso was not the only one punished for his arrogance. Those who chose to worship him were punished, too."

"They were killed?"

Shamsa looked at Changa with a mix of annoyance and worry. "Some of them."

Shamsa strode into the open. Changa and Katafwa followed immediately, but the rest hesitated. Their eyes darted back and forth, scanning the edge of the clearing. A quick backward glance by Shamsa ended their resistance; they crept into the clearing and made their way to the Temple.

Again size distorted distance. The trek to the Temple was much longer than Changa anticipated. The edifice grew higher and higher, finally reaching the height where looking at the top caused him to strain his neck. The staircase before them was as wide as a main avenue in Mombasa, fully capable of holding five ox carts side by side. They towered to a landing beyond their sight. Again Shamsa did not hesitate, attacking the stairs with impatience, her scowl deepening with each step. Changa and Katafwa followed. Changa ignored

155

the pain in his legs as he kept pace with Shamsa.

Close to the landing a strange sound reached their ears. Changa tried to recognize it, but nothing in his experience resembled it. Shamsa stopped, crouching low with her sword in guard position.

"Once we reach the landing, our task will begin. Fight with all you have and stay close to me. I will need you."

Shamsa sprang forward, leaping over the last five steps. Changa ran forward as fast as he could, but Katafwa sprinted by him. Changa caught the same crazed look that Katafwa held when he fought the sand demons. When Changa reached the landing Shamsa was charging across the stone floor. Warriors were converging on her, large, armored men bearing lances leveled at her. Changa reached at his side, then cursed; he had no throwing knives, for Dambudso had not thought to provide any. He soon saw that his intervention was not needed. Shamsa leaped high over the lances, then came down slashing. Blood spurted from the throats of the two even before her feet touched the stone. By the time the other warriors reached her, Changa and Katafwa were by her side.

Changa had no time to prepare himself. A guardian fell on him immediately, wielding his lance like a living extension of himself. Changa struggled to match his speed as the blade nicked his flesh with each thrust and slash. He ducked a swing at his neck, then kicked at the relentless man's leg. His foot met the shaft of the lance, but his sword found the man's torso, piercing his hardened leather armor. No sooner did he fall away than he was replaced by another warrior. Changa focused on the fight before him now. He moved with the speed and power of a leopard, dodging, parrying and cutting his way through the endless onslaught of armored foes. Occasionally a hearty laugh would rise over the din of ringing steel and grunts, letting Changa know that Katafwa was still alive. For a moment no one stood before him; he scanned the situation and was not encouraged. Shamsa was surrounded by warriors; Katafwa fought his way toward her, his face locked in a crazed grin. The cohorts were dead, their bodies strewn at the edge of the landing. Changa ran to one of them and pried a sword from the dead man's grip.

He fell into the rear of the horde converging on Shamsa, both swords flailing. Together he and Katafwa cut her free, although once with her they realized their help was not required. Temple guard swords had not held her at bay; only their numbers and mass had blocked her from her goal. With them slain, there was nothing standing between the three and the interior of the temple.

A blinding light pulsed at the end the column-bordered corridor, an illumination so bright Changa turned away, shielding his eyes. No sooner than he'd done so the light began to dim.

"No!" Shamsa shouted. She gripped Changa's shoulder, her nails digging into his shoulder and drawing blood.

"We must hurry!" She ran, Changa struggling to keep pace. He glanced backwards; Katafwa was not with them. He stood alone; legs braced far apart, swords in both hands. More warriors swarmed over the lip of the staircase, lances lowered and violent cries in their throats. Changa tried to break free from Shamsa's grip, but her fingers dug deeper.

"He will be fine on his own," she snarled. "I need you with me."

Changa glanced back. Katafwa ran at his attackers, his laughter mingling with their battle cries. He could look no more; he needed to keep pace with Shamsa.

When they entered the temple chamber the light had diminished to a glow. The chamber was vast, almost as wide as the clearing they traversed. The granite wall writhed with countless carvings, stark images of men, women and animals contorted in unnatural ways. Their footfalls echoed off the walls as they ran to the opposite side of the chamber. Their objective came into focus with each step. A cavernous hole punctured the granite, an opening filled with a massive carving. A feline head occupied the space, its mouth gaping open to reveal the light source. Paw-like hands lapped over the edge of the crypt, nails like swords extending from its fingers.

The eerie silence of the chamber was shattered by a deafening rumble. Shamsa stopped running. She turned to Changa, her brow furrowed in frustration.

"We are too late," she said. "But we still have a chance. Take this!"

Shamsa threw Changa her sword. He dropped one of his own, caught the hilt of her blade and immediately regretted it. The metal hilt burned the palm of his hand like fire.

"Don't let it go!" she yelled.

Changa grimaced as he fought to hold the blade. The heat subsided to pulsing warmth. He looked at Shamsa puzzled.

She smiled. "It will not fail you now."

The chamber rumbled again and the floor trembled. Changa's eyes went to the feline face. The light was almost gone, but that was not what caught his notice. The paws that had first rested on the edge of the cavern now touched the ground. The stone feline had moved.

Shamsa sprinted out of his vision. Changa back-pedaled, his blades wavering in his tense hands. A constant rumble vibrated the chamber, the carved images in the wall animated by the disturbance. A mighty grating sound accompanied the rumble as the great cat emerged from its narrow chamber, blinking its gray eyes. The light disappeared as the being closed its maw, then stood. It was enormous, a wide living being of stone standing the height of twenty men. Changa did the only thing he could do. He ran.

The cat-thing released a deafening roar. Its footfalls boomed like a drum as it pursued Changa, stone shattering underfoot with each step. The floor quaked beneath the warrior's sandaled feet. At once the shaking stopped, but Changa did not look back; he continued to run for the chamber entrance. Suddenly darkness descended before him. The ground pitched and he flew off his feet, then landed on his face. He scrambled back to his feet and stiffened. The stone cat crouched before him, a deep snarl escaping its clenched fangs.

A paw flashed at him, and Changa instinctively raised Shamsa's sword. He expected the blade to fly from his hands, but instead it cut into the stone as easily as flesh. The stone cat howled and jerked the paw away. A bolt of confidence shot though Changa; he was not so defenseless after all. Still, he knew he was no match for the massive stone beast. He had to get out of the chamber.

The cat stalked toward him, its eyes focused. Changa circled, trying to work his way toward the opening while keeping an eye on the massive predator. He thought he glimpsed movement just beyond his sight; then focused without taking his eyes off the cat. It was Shamsa. She crawled along the figurines in the wall, stealthy working her way over to the cat beast. Changa waved his sword, partly to keep the beast's attention and partly to let Shamsa know he saw her. She responded by increasing her pace.

The cat suddenly rose onto its hind legs and howled. It dropped with both paws together, hurtling down at Changa. He waited, then rolled away. The paws slammed into the floor, punching a hole where Changa had stood. He was about to regain his footing when a paw slapped him. He slid across the floor before slamming into the opposite wall. Dazed and wounded, he scrambled to get back on his feet as the cat ran across floor toward him. Changa leaned on the wall, fighting to remain conscious. The cat jumped, paws outstretched and mouth wide. Shamsa leaped onto its head, and Changa felt a surge of hope. That hope was dashed as he saw her jump from the feline's head and into its mouth. He had resigned himself to death when Shamsa reappeared. She tumbled from the cat's maw, her body strangely illuminated. She landed under the cat, then rolled away. The cat became rigid in mid-jump. Its eyes lost the glow of life, its limbs stiffened. It crashed onto the floor sending a shower of dust and stone upon Changa. He fell to the floor and into a ball as flying stone slammed the wall above, around, and on him. Changa clenched his teeth, absorbing the battering until it ceased. He lay buried, barely holding on to consciousness. The burden atop him slowly diminished until he felt a warm hand on his back, tugging at his shirt.

"Get up," Shamsa said. "We are not done."

Changa stood, dust and stone falling away from his frame. Shamsa was walking away, her path lit by the glow she had absorbed from the fragmented stone idol. Changa stepped from the rubble and limped after her. He followed her out of the Temple to the stairs. There he found Katafwa. He lay dead among a pile of temple guardians, swords still clenched in his hands. He'd finally received his wish. He was among the ancestors.

Changa slowly gained on Shamsa as they crossed the temple field. By the time they reached Dambudso, Changa stood beside her.

Dambudso's wide eyes were illuminated by the glowing object in Shamsa's hand.

"At last!" he shouted. "The gods now know I cannot be denied! They will taste my vengeance!"

He extended his hands. "Give it to me."

Shamsa nodded, and then plunged her sword into Dambudso's chest. Dambudso's shocked expression faded as life drained from his body. Shamsa extracted her blade as he fell to the ground.

She turned to Changa. Changa stepped away, preparing for her attack. Instead she dropped her sword and began to disrobe.

"At last," she whispered.

Shamsa stood nude before Changa. She gave him a sly smile then slowly pressed the luminous object against her breasts. The temple light disappeared into her chest, then slowly spread throughout her body. The features of her face melted away; soon all that remained of the stern woman was her female outline. Her blue form metamorphosed into a red-orange light that emitted heat like a roaring flame. Changa covered his face and staggered away.

"Go home, Changa," she said, her voice ringing inside his head. "Your work is done. Belay's debt is paid."

"What are you?" he asked.

"Dambudso called me down from the World of Light and seduced me with the pleasures of this flesh. But then it became a prison. I have sought a way home for a long time," she answered. "One day he spoke of a temple that contained the light of heaven. I persuaded him to seek it, to renew his bid for godhood."

Her light grew more intense, and Changa shielded his eyes.

"I care little for the beings on this plane, but even I could see that Dambudso was not one to support. But he served his purpose. I have the light that is my birthright; my reward to you was to rid you of such a vile man."

Changa was cowering now, the light and the heat becoming unbearable.

"You have the strength of the spirits inside you, Changa. Use it well. I will be watching you."

The being Changa knew as Shamsa slowly rose into the sky. By the time she reached the treetops she was formless light, illuminating the land like a small sun. She lingered for a moment, then streaked away into the heavens.

Changa watched her disappear into the wide sky. He stood stunned, attempting to comprehend what had just occurred, then stopped. He was injured but he was alive. He looked about him to get his bearings. The Nuba and his oxen rested patiently, the animals chewing on the grass, the Nuba singing softly as always. Changa limped to the wagon and looked inside. The cloaks were still there; he took one out and donned it. The healing sensation rushed through him, Dambudso's magic lingering after his death. Changa took another robe from the wagon.

"Do not leave," he said to the Nuba. The man looked at him and nodded. Changa made his way back to the temple. The silence was unnerving; he expected to be attacked at any moment, but that was not the case. He climbed the temple steps then found Katafwa's body. Wrapping it in a cloak, he lifted him onto his shoulders and descended the steps. He half hoped the cloak would revive his newfound friend, but it was not to be. When he reached the wagon Katafwa was still dead. If no one else would mourn him and give him the proper burial, Changa would.

He laid him gently into the wagon. Changa climbed in the back.

"Take us home," he said.

The Nuba answered by singing loudly. The oxen broke their feast and walked, the wagon rocked gently from side to side as it slowly disappeared into the surrounding forest.

kiss of the succubus

By Charles R. Rutledge

At the heart of all beauty lies something inhuman."
— Albert Camus

Mortlake, England 1570

The young man hadn't come for learning. This much Doctor John Dee determined simply from looking at him. His hair was wild and disarrayed from the wind and rain, but it was his eyes that gave Dee some idea of the young man's state of distress. If ever a pair of eyes could be said to be haunted, it was those belonging to Dee's visitor.

"You are Doctor Dee?" The man said. "Please tell me that you are he, for no one else on God's Earth can help me."

Dee said, "I am Dee. Come in, young sir, out of the rain."

With the approach of night and of a heavy storm, all of the patrons of Dee's externa bibliotheca, the open reading room Dee had added to his residence and private library, had sought their homes. Dee himself had been about to head for the warmth of the house he shared with his wife and his mother, but something in the young man's face had kept Dee from refusing him entry.

"Please forgive me for coming here this late, Doctor Dee, but I am desperate."

Dee led the man to a table near the reading room's small fireplace. "Sit here, lad. Tell me what has distressed you so."

The young man sat down with a great sigh. He stared across the table at Dee and said, "I am haunted by a demon. A fiend from hell."

Dee said, "That is indeed a serious matter."

"You believe me then? You don't think me mad?"

"I know that such things occur. As to your madness, that has yet to be determined. Tell me your story, beginning with your name."

162

"Of course. Forgive me. My name is Henry Fletcher. I live in the city. My family is known there."

Dee nodded. He wasn't familiar with the Fletchers but he didn't wish to interrupt Henry and thus slow his tale.

"I will tell you, Doctor," Henry said, "That I am not proud of the way I have lived my life. My father has always been perhaps too generous with his money and I have squandered no small portion of it in the pursuit of the pleasures the world can offer."

"I take it that one of these pleasures is the cause of your current distress."

"Indeed, sir. Oh that I had never looked upon her face."

A woman? This was the demon that Henry had spoken of? Dee could feel his interest waning. All young men who have been treated badly in love think that they are the victims of some great calamity.

"No sir," Henry said. "I can tell that you think me some lovestruck buffoon, betrayed and deserted by his lady love. If only that were true. If only she would desert me and leave me alone. I wasn't speaking poetically, Doctor Dee. This woman is truly a demon. A succubus, sent to destroy men and consign their souls to her master in hell."

"Calm yourself, Henry," Dee said. "You are right to chide me for leaping to conclusions. Tell me more of this woman."

Outside the rain had begun to fall in earnest and Dee could hear it rattling on the roof. The wind howled around the eaves as if seeking a way inside, and the fire guttered and danced, casting flickering shadows on the book-lined walls.

"She calls herself Lady Frances Hardwick," Henry said, "And she owns a great manor house North of Mortlake."

It seemed to Dee that he had heard the name before, but he couldn't recall where.

"That house," Henry went on, "Oh God, that house. The things I saw there." He paused for a moment, collecting himself. "I met Lady Frances at a party thrown by a mutual friend. I was taken with her immediately, as was every other man in the room. She is a beauty, Doctor, with hair black as raven's wings and eyes that seem violet in the firelight.

163

"It seemed that she preferred my company to that of the other men there and soon we were walking in the garden under the moon. She spoke to me of her home and said that I should come there very soon, and a few days later, I did."

"She made no secret of what she wanted with me. I had never seen a woman of high breeding act in such a wanton way. I was besotted with her, and I took her to bed, or rather she took me. It seemed that our love play lasted for hours in her great bed. She inflamed my passion as no woman ever had. It was as if she were devouring me, Doctor, and I suppose she was. And when we were done...oh God..."

Dee waited, sensing that he should allow the youth to find his tongue in his own time.

"When we had exhausted our passion, or mine at least, she rose from the bed and left the chamber. After a little time had passed I felt the chamber grow cold and I sat up to see if the fire needed tending. The door leading to the hallway was open and it seemed to me that a gray mist was rolling in through the door. I got out of the bed and pulled on some of my clothes.

"I began to hear strange sounds coming from beyond the door and I stepped out into the hall." Henry had lifted a linen cloth from the table and he was twisting it in his hands. "In the hallway I beheld an army of phantoms drifting along the halls and down the stairs. They weren't the shades of men, but of some horrible creatures, all wailing and moaning and staring at me with eyes that glowed like a will o' the wisp.

"I staggered, leaning my back against the stone wall for support. As I watched, lady Frances came dancing down the hall, leaping and cavorting through the hideous creatures, her eyes as wild as theirs and her red lips pulled back in a terrible grin to reveal teeth like those of some ravening beast."

Watching Henry's face, Dee had no doubt that the young man was telling the truth. He had never doubted the existence of demons.

"And then Lady Frances looked deep into my eyes and she raised her lips to mine for a kiss. I screamed and ran down the stairs. I could hear her wild laughter ringing behind me. I ran out the door and sought my horse, but the poor beast had bolted, doubtless sensing the terrible things going on around it. I ran through the woods and fields, and behind me I heard the demons of hell in pursuit.

"Somehow I made it to an inn and I sat in the common room until dawn before making my way back home."

Dee said, "You were fortunate indeed to escape with your life."

"I was, but that wasn't the end of it. When I got home I tried to convince myself that it had been all some mad dream and I drank until I fell into a restless sleep. She came to me in my dreams, Doctor, she and all the loathsome things I had seen in her home. And she told me that I was hers and that if I didn't return to her house I would never know a moment's rest.

"And now, whenever I close my eyes and try to sleep, she and her demons come to me. I have had no rest for days."

Dee said, "That is the way of the succubus, Henry. Once they choose their prey they do not relent."

"But there must be some way to make her release me from her power. Surely you know of some spell or incantation that will save my soul."

Dee said, "I will not tell you that such a thing can easily be accomplished. The desires of demons are not easily thwarted. I must think upon this. You may stay here tonight and together we shall seek an answer."

Any reply that Henry would have made was cut off by a loud hammering upon the outer door of the reading room. Henry's frame went rigid at the sound, but Dee said, "Easy, lad. I do not think that demons would bother knocking."

Dee rose from the table and made his way to the door. It seemed that this was his night for visitors. Of course it might merely be one of the servants, sent by his wife to inquire about his absence from the evening meal.

Dee opened the door and a gigantic figure filled the doorway. The largest man Dee had ever seen pushed his way into the room. Dee said, "One moment, sir. By what right do you barge into my chambers?"

"You're John Dee," the man said. A statement and not a question.

"That is my name, sir, though what concern that is of yours

I..."

"You have grimoires. I need to see them."

The man was well over six feet tall, with a broad chest and massive shoulders. His hair was long and tied back with a cord and his face was scarred and weather beaten. He wore a cloak of oiled leather to keep off the rain.

"You will have to come back tomorrow," Dee said, refusing to be cowed by the man's size. "The reading room is closed for the night."

The big man said, "I've no interest in the books you allow scholars to look through and copy. I know that you have a private collection of spell books and it is those I wish to see."

Henry, who had sat at the table watching the exchange, stood up. He was armed with a smallsword, the weapon carried by most gentlemen, and he drew this now and advanced upon the giant.

"You would do well to heed Doctor Dee and return upon the morrow, sir," Henry said.

Almost too quickly for the eye to follow, the big man swept one arm from under his cloak. Something silver gleamed in the firelight and Henry's sword went flying away, its blade shattered. The man's other hand struck Henry a backhanded blow, sending the youth sprawling.

The giant turned back to Dee and now Dee could see that the man carried a huge axe of an ancient design. It had two blades like the weapons carried by the fabled Varangian Guard of Byzantium.

"The grimoires," the man said. "Now."

"Come this way," Dee said, casting a sidelong glance at Henry, who lay senseless on the floor. Better to give this brute what he wanted and get him out of the building than to risk being severed in twain by the great axe.

Dee led the intruder down a hallway to a locked door. He said, "Please do not break down this door sir. I assure you I have a key."

To Dee's surprise the man grunted a short laugh. He said, "You've got some backbone, old man."

"I do," said Dee, "And I would prefer that you not separate it from my body."

The large man hung the axe back on the belt from which he

had taken it. "I've no interest in harming you or anyone else. I'd not have drawn steel on the boy had he not drawn first. But I must see your books. It's a matter of grave importance."

Dee turned the lock on what was the most private room in this part of his library complex. Beyond lay his *interna bibliotheca*, the room that held his most rare and valuable, and yes, dangerous books. He hoped that this man wasn't here to steal them for some jealous rival magician.

"Here," Dee said. "This is what you seek."

Dee lit several candles to illuminate the room. The big man stepped in and examined the shelves. He lifted out one weighty tome and looked at it. Dee doubted that the brute could even read.

Dee said, "Please be careful with that. It is quite valuable."

"Yes, it's a fine copy of Agrippa's *Occulta Philosophia*," said the man. "Not what I'm looking for, but interesting."

"Er... yes," said Dee.

"Burgo's *Treatise on Magic*," the man mused. "Haven't seen one of those in a while. Ramon Lull. Norton. Ptolemy's *Tetrabiblious*. Impressive."

The man turned from the shelf and his eyes fell on Dee's desk. He made a sound of disgust and crossed to the desk. He spent a moment looking at the ancient manuscript and the stack of new papers, which Dee had been working on earlier in the day.

The man said, "You're translating Alhazred's *Necronomicon* into English."

Dee could contain his curiosity no longer. He said, "Who are you, sir? You can obviously read several languages and your knowledge of the occult seems formidable, and yet..."

The big man grinned. "And yet I look like some godless savage, eh? Make no mistake, Doctor Dee, that's what I am. My name is Kharrn and yes I know of your blasphemous books, but I don't trade in magic. You're most unwise to translate this book, so that others can learn its secrets."

"Is it the *Necronomicon* you seek then?"

Kharrn shook his head. "No, though I urge you to destroy it. The book I'm looking for is called the *Silent History*."

Dee's eyes went wide. "Why, you had only to ask and I would

have told you that even I don't possess that dark volume."

"I find it better to look first and ask later, lest the one I'm questioning seek to conceal what I'm looking for."

Kharrn's head snapped around toward the door as a shriek of utter terror rose through the house. Kharrn said, "The boy!" Then he lunged back through the door with Dee close behind.

When they reached Henry he was writhing on the floor and screaming. His eyes were wide open and he was staring into the darkest corner of the reading room. For a moment Dee thought that he saw two points of light in the darkness, but they vanished before he could be sure of his eyes. He crouched beside the young man and grasped him by the shoulders.

"Henry! Be calm, lad. You're safe now."

Kharrn said, "What's wrong with him?"

"He is beset by demons. They come when he tries to rest."

"I thought I saw something right when we entered this room. A shadow in the corner with burning eyes."

Dee said, "Then you saw it, too. The succubus was here, in this room."

"She was here," Henry said. "I felt her sharp teeth at my throat. Oh I am accursed."

Dee said, "I can stop her from returning, I think. At least to this room." He turned to Kharrn. "If you've satisfied your curiosity, then please be on your way. I have much to do."

Kharrn said, "Go and make your preparations. I'll stay here with the boy. No demon will enter the room while I'm here."

"Oh?" said Dee. "Have you some charm to stop them?"

Kharrn slid his cloak back and placed his hand on his axe. "This is my charm. It will kill a demon as readily as a man."

Dee said, "Wait here, Henry. I'll be back soon."

Henry cast a fearful glance at Kharrn. "With him?"

"I'll not harm you, lad," Kharrn said.

Dee went to the room where he kept some of his equipment. He chose several items, then returned to Henry and Kharrn. Without speaking to either, he went first to the door. Here he made several marks on the floor with a stick of chalk, then placed one of the candles in the center of the markings and lit it. He did the same on the sill of the room's only window.

"Warding the portals," Kharrn said. "That should do it. At least for now."

Again Dee wondered at his visitor. The man looked as if he would be more at home drinking and carousing in the taverns of London, and yet he knew exactly what Dee was doing.

"Tell me about this demon," Kharrn said. "Perhaps I can help."

Henry said, "Dr. Dee doesn't need your help and neither do I."

Dee said, "Tell him your tale, lad. I begin to think there's more to our visitor than is readily apparent."

Henry's expression was petulant, but he told Kharrn the same story he had told to Dee. When he was done, Kharrn turned to Dee and said, "What will you do?"

"I shall go to the home of Lady Frances Hardwick and insist that she release the boy from her power."

"And you think she'll do it, just like that?"

"I am not without powers of my own, sir."

"If she's truly a succubus, your knowledge of sorcery may not be enough," said Kharrn.

Dee said, "What would you suggest, then?"

Kharrn shrugged his massive shoulders. "I can think of no other plan. So I shall go with you."

"You do not fear demons?"

"Any man with half a brain fears demons. But I've killed them before."

"What about me?" Henry said.

"I think it best if you remain here," said Dee. "Nothing can get to you in this room, and I'll have my wife send one of the servants to sit with you. Now give me the address of this lady."

The rain was still falling when John Dee and Kharrn stepped out into the night, though it had lost much of its intensity. Dee could make out the rough lines of Mortlake Church looming against the dark clouds.

"My horse is tethered across the lane," Kharrn said, "He can carry the both of us since it is no great distance to the house."

"You are very familiar with Mortlake for a stranger, sir," Dee said.

"Only from necessity," said Kharrn.

"Indeed? You have never told me why you seek the *Silent History.*"

"Perhaps I will if we live through the night."

Kharrn's horse turned out to be a great black stallion. Dee thought that it watched him with a thought to bite if given a chance. Kharrn swung into the saddle and, when Dee had some difficulty climbing up behind him, the big man simply caught Dee's arm and lifted him up. Dee noted that the strength in that momentary grasp was amazing.

The pair rode slowly over the rain slicked cobbles, and soon the horse was trudging along a muddy road beyond Mortlake proper. Dee could see the occasional dull gleam of light from a farm house or cottage, but aside from that all was darkness.

Not so, the manor house of Lady Frances Hardwick when it came into sight. It seemed as if every window were ablaze with light, as if the lady knew they were coming and was offering them a welcome. But what sort of welcome would they receive?

Kharrn reined in his mount near a stand of trees across the road from the house. He said, "No point in dooming this poor beast if you and I meet our deaths at the hands of this demon. I'll leave the horse here."

"I am taken aback by your sentimentality," said Dee.

"I like horses," said Kharrn. "Better than I like most people. And keep a civil tongue, magician, if you would keep it in your mouth."

An acid reply stuck in Dee's throat as he looked at the big man's cold blue eyes. He said, "Let us be about this grim business."

The two men crossed the road and started across the broad lawn in front of the manor house. Dee noted that the house was almost as impressive as the nearby Barn Elms, home of the Walsinghams. He thought it strange that he had never visited there or really even noticed the place.

Kharrn made no attempt at stealth, but instead marched up to the front door and hammered on it with one huge fist. The door was opened by a footman, a lean, gaunt faced man in dark livery.

Dee decided he had best take charge of things before Kharrn cleaved the servant shoulder to waist. He said, "I am Doctor John Dee, and I wish to speak with the mistress of the house."

The man said nothing, but stepped back and gestured for Dee and Kharrn to enter. Still without speaking, the man left them in the front hallway and disappeared through a doorway to one side. Dee glanced about him at the expensive decorations and furnishings. A fine house indeed.

"So you are the famous Doctor Dee."

Kharrn spun as a voice spoke from behind them, his hand darting to the axe on his belt. Dee turned more slowly, though he was as surprised as his companion by the sound.

Henry Fletcher's description had not done justice to the Lady Frances Hardwick. Dee had never seen a more beautiful woman. She stood there, her ripely curved form sheathed in a filmy gown of some white sheer stuff, her lustrous hair rolling in ebony waves around her oval face. Large dark eyes. A wide scarlet mouth. She was the very substance of desire.

Dee shook his head, as if trying to dispel the languor of sleep. Glancing at Kharrn, he saw that the big man seemed just as besotted. He said, "Yes, I am John Dee, madame. I have come to speak with you about Henry Fletcher. You must release him from whatever spell you have cast over him."

"Why of course, my dear doctor," Lady Frances said. She moved closer to Dee and placed one slim-fingered hand on his chest. "Why would I bother with a boy when such a man is before me?"

This close the woman's scent was intoxicating. Dee tried to concentrate, but all he could see were the woman's hypnotic eyes and soft, full, lips. The entrance hall receded and Kharrn no longer existed. Dee was alone in a misty realm with this vision of beauty. His hands slid to her trim waist. He leaned down toward her upturned face, toward the moist and parted lips.

Dee was snapped out of his erotic stupor by a loud bellowing. The entrance hall snapped back into existence and he saw Kharrn slapping the Lady Frances, sending her backpedaling away. For a moment Dee was seized with fury that the giant would dare treat his beloved so, but then he saw that Lady Frances had regained her balance, landing catlike in a crouch near the foot of a long staircase.

The red lips pulled back, revealing sharp teeth and as Dee stared in horror Lady Frances began to change. Her arms and legs elongated. A pair of ribbed, bat-like wings sprouted on her back and spread behind her. Her fingers became claws and her eyes took on a yellow cast. She opened her mouth and howled in fury.

Dee staggered back, his heart pounding in his chest. All his life he had believed in demons and night creatures, but the sight of one, the actual proof of their existence, threatened to send his very reason to the edges of madness. He had indeed been mad to think that he could challenge such a thing armed only with his knowledge of magic.

"You," the thing that had been Lady Frances said, pointing one long clawed finger at Kharrn. "You are not of this world. What are you?"

Kharrn said, "You are wrong, demon. I am of this world, but not of this time."

"No matter," the demon said. "You are mortal and can die in any time."

She raised her hands and a roiling mist formed all around her. Dee could hear weird tittering and gibbering echo through the hall. As he watched, vague shapes began to appear in the mist, and then a host of horrors spewed forth from around the succubus. It was as if she had opened a doorway into the pits of hell and allowed the denizens to escape. Creatures large and small scrambled and slithered toward Dee and Kharrn. Dee's overtaxed mind couldn't take it all in as the sea of limbs and tentacles and claws and teeth rolled toward him. He heard himself screaming as he stumbled backwards.

Then he heard Kharrn bellow out another battle cry. The big man threw off his cloak and snatched the great axe from his belt. Taking the weapon in both hands, Kharrn leaped into the onrushing tide of monsters. There was no finesse in his technique. No feints, blocks or parries. He simply swung the axe, yelling and cursing as he went. Severed limbs and foul, brackish blood filled the air. Something that looked like a giant lizard with a man's face lost its head, and a crablike monstrosity's shell was split. Dee saw claws rake the giant man and slithering limbs seek to grasp him, but the relentless axe whirred and the creatures gave way. It was then that Dee realized that there was a purpose to Kharrn's seemingly berserk attacks. He was cutting his way toward the demoness.

The succubus had seen Kharrn's purpose as well, and she began backing up the stairs, all the while exhorting her horde of vile minions to finish her enemy. As Kharrn broke through the mass of creatures, the succubus spread her wings and lunged from the stairs. One clawed hand swept out, catching the big man across the face and drawing blood. Beating her wings like some crazed harpy, the succubus bowled Kharrn over, sending him tumbling down the stairs. His axe clattered away and, with a shriek of triumph, the demoness leaped atop the prone man and latched onto Kharrn's throat with both hands.

Dee, still almost mad with terror, managed to stumble forward. He knew that once the succubus had finished Kharrn he would be next. He reached the axe, and though he could barely lift the weapon, he half dragged, half carried the axe toward the struggling pair.

The succubus strained, trying to crush the big man's throat. Kharrn gripped her forearms with all the strength in his massive arms. The corded muscles bulged with the effort as he tried to break the creature's grip. Kharrn pushed the succubus back far enough that he was able to bring one foot up and wedge it against the demon's chest. With a grunt of effort he kicked, managing to break her grip and send her staggering back.

"Kharrn!" Dee said, holding up the axe.

With amazing speed for one so large, Kharrn rolled to his feet and snatched the axe from Dee's hands. He grinned a wolfish grin and advanced on the succubus, who crouched against a wall.

"Stop!" The succubus said. "If you kill me the boy dies as well."

"You're lying," said Kharrn.

The demoness smiled with her sharp teeth. "Am I? I have taken part of his soul, you savage. If you strike me down then he shall wither and die like a fruit cut from a vine."

"Dee?" Kharrn said.

"I don't know. It's possible she speaks the truth."

Kharrn stood rigid for a moment and it seemed to Dee that the big man was weighing the importance of one young man's life against the existence of the demon. Finally Kharrn rose from his crouch and lowered the axe.

"You've won for now," Kharrn said. "But this isn't over."

The succubus smiled. "Oh I know, my fine savage. Leave my house. But I will find you some dark evening." She turned and grinned at Dee. "And you, dear Doctor."

Kharrn turned and stalked away, and Dee, not wishing to be alone for a moment with the demoness, hurried after him.

The two men rode in silence through the rain, but Dee's mind was racing. So many things he had only suspected had been made clear for him. The world was a much larger place than even he had imagined. There were dangerous things out there in the dark.

When they reached Dee's home he said, "Come inside, Kharrn. We may not be defeated just yet."

"You have an idea?"

"The beginnings of one. But I need to make use of some of those books you covet."

Dee led the way into the house and they found a servant sitting with Henry Fletcher. Dee told the servant that he could go and then asked Henry if he was all right.

"I am well, Doctor Dee," Henry said. "Did you see her?"

Dee said, "We did, and she was all that you described."

"And can you help me, then?"

"It will be difficult but I believe so. First I must consult some of my texts. You may sleep on that couch. The wards I placed on this room are still intact and Kharrn and I will be only a few doors away."

As they left the room, Kharrn said, "You suddenly seem very resolute, Dee."

"The succubus threatened me and mine. I cannot allow that threat to hang over my family. I believe I can find a way to protect the boy and then we may proceed with destroying that creature."

"If we can find her again," said Kharrn.

"What do you mean?"

"She is powerful and not a fool. She will know we are seeking a way to thwart her and she won't stay here and wait for us to find it.

We will not find her at that house again."

Dee said, "I may have a way that we can locate her, but first I have many preparations to make."

Venice Italy.
Two Months Later.

She no longer called herself Lady Frances Hardwick. Now she was the Lady Jelena Moneta, and when Dee caught a glimpse of her across a crowded ballroom, he noted that her features and skin tone had changed subtlety so that she now appeared to be an Italian beauty.

Dee made certain to stay far away from her as he crossed to the opposite side of the room. Once there he stepped out onto a balcony and waved toward a gondola which floated in the shadows of one of the city's multitude of canals. The gondolier used his pole to push the gondola closer to the balcony and then leaped up to grasp the edge of the balustrade. Seconds later, Kharrn pulled himself up and over, onto the balcony.

It had taken time to find her and Dee had hoped to confront the succubus someplace less public, but she had set herself up with a country villa guarded by a small army of paid bodyguards. Catching her in public was the only choice he and Kharrn had. A ball arranged by the young nobles of the Compagnia della Calza had given them the opportunity they had needed.

"You've seen her?" Kharrn said.

"Yes, she's inside. So are several of her bodyguards."

"I'll deal with them. You just do what you came to do. Now I'll draw the attention of her retainers."

Music swelled and people hurried to find dance partners as Kharrn stalked into the ballroom. Kharrn made a straight line for Jelena, shouldering his way through the crowded room. He produced his axe from under his cloak. The demoness's eyes went wide as she spotted the big man.

"Assassin!" the succubus cried. "He's come to kill me!"

Half a dozen men came from various parts of the room, drawing swords as they hurried to interpose themselves between their mistress and Kharrn. Dee moved along the side of the room, keeping his head low, hoping to reach Jelena before she noticed him.

The first man to reach Kharrn had both his sword and the bones in his arm shattered. The second and third fared worse, being caught in the back swing of the huge axe. One lost a hand and the other was almost decapitated, his head left barely attached by a thin strip of flesh and muscle. Blood sprayed as both men fell.

The other three bodyguards stopped their forward rush and tried to circle the giant man. Their strategy looked to be to try and use their long swords to stab at Kharrn from beyond the range of the axe.

Kharrn didn't wait to be circled. A battle axe isn't a defensive weapon. He lunged forward, splitting one of the men from neck to waist. One of the other men managed to leap in and stab Kharrn in the side, but the giant man ignored the pain and twisted away. Even as the sword point was pulled from his ribs, Kharrn struck out with the axe and crushed his attacker's skull. The last of the bodyguards, seeing what had become of his comrades, dropped his weapon and fled. Kharrn wheeled toward the succubus, who had backed into a corner.

"Will no one save me from this madman?" Jelena cried.

Those of the crowd who could flee had done so. The rest had pushed up against the walls to get as far from Kharrn as possible.

Jelena glared at Kharrn and said, "Nothing has changed, savage. Kill me and the boy still dies."

Dee, who had managed to slip up on Jelena's right side while she had been watching Kharrn, said, "No he won't."

Jelena's head snapped toward Dee just in time to receive a face full of powdered silver. The succubus snarled and spat, and her illusion of beauty fell away. People all around gasped as Jelena's great, ribbed wings appeared.

"What have you done?" Jelena screeched.

"Severed the connection between you and Henry Fletcher. And shown these fine citizens your true nature." His studies had revealed that silver, crushed into powder and combined with other ingredients, could temporarily rob a succubus of most of her sorcery.

"You will die for this, John Dee," the succubus said. She

176

leaped forward, wings beating.

Kharrn struck the wing closest to him, tearing the veined webbing between the ribs. Dark blood flowed and the demoness cried out. She whirled toward Kharrn with fangs bared and talons spread. Her lower jaw distended, revealing far too many teeth. Her yellow eyes blazed with hatred. There was little even remotely human left of her.

Another man might have flinched away from the very sight of the creature's fury, but Kharrn leaped inside the reach of those long arms and swung the axe at the succubus's unprotected neck. Her head was still screeching as it bounced upon the floor.

"That's it, then," Kharrn said. "The bitch is dead."

"And we should go," said Dee. "I do not wish to explain this to the local authorities. Criminals here are often executed without trial and left in the streets as a warning."

Kharrn nodded and started toward the balcony. Dee followed. The two men clambered into the gondola and Kharrn began to pole the vessel away. No one tried to follow. They left the gondola at an old dock where they had hidden their horses.

As they mounted, Dee said, "Will you return with me to England to see that young Henry is well?"

"You don't need me for that, Dee." Kharrn said. "There's a war brewing here with the Turks. I think I'll stay awhile."

"What about your search for the *Silent History*?"

"It goes on. But a man has to live, and being a mercenary is a way to make gold."

"There are other ways," Dee said.

"Not for me. Farewell, Doctor. Get rid of Alhazred's book like I told you."

Dee nodded but he made no promise. He watched as Kharrn rode away. Then he sighed and turned his mount toward home.

I rejoice whenever I find a story that is Lovecraftian in essence and conception but which steers clear of the usual parade of names, titles, locations, etc. Naturally I love the ones that don't avoid these things, too, but it is mighty nice to enjoy the freshness and variety! Ken Asamatsu, one of the top tier of horror writers in Japan today, has supplied stories of both kinds. The present tale is of the first type, while his wonderful novel The Queen of K'n-yan is more traditionally Lovecraftian, and both are top-notch! This one embodies fascinating Japanese Buddhist lore and makes me wish Lovecraft had set a few fictions in the same land.

Ken served as editor of the four volume set, "Lairs of Hidden Gods," to which I wrote all the volume and story introductions. I hope we will be reading much more in English by him, thanks to translator Ed Lipsett.

THE LIVING WIND

By Ken Asamatsu
Traanslated by Edward Lipsett

– 1 –

The sunset clouds floating in the May sky suddenly flowed off southward, as if chased, and suddenly the bowl of the heavens was cloudless. The sun had dipped below the distant hills, coloring the air in pale lilac.

A strong wind swept down from the mountains to the north, as if waiting for the instant. It was cold enough to sting, freezing Ikkyu's hand on his staff, so cold that he dropped the staff in shock at the frigid impact. As he bent to retrieve it, he saw a white woman's arm lying on the dark blue of the road, its long fingers hooking an invitation.

"What in the...?"

He frowned at the unexpected sight, staring, and saw that it was not a woman's arm after all. It was a *shimenawa*, a sacred rope from a local shine used to repel evil spirits, still decorated with the little twisted paper *shide* that summoned the gods. The twists of paper were merely fluttering in the wind.

"Heh... I guess I must be hungrier than I thought if I mistake a *shimenawa* for a woman's arm," he chuckled to himself, and pulled out the box lunch he had purchased back in Tsuyama. It was pounded *mochi* rice, and still fresh enough to be soft. He pulled off a piece, and as he popped it into his mouth the keening of the north wind came again.

"This wind is freezing! People warned me about cold wind around here, but they said it didn't gust until September or October!"

Swallowing the rice, he looked upwind... toward the dark mass that was Mt. Nagisan, said to be the place where the gods who created Japan first descended to the earth.

"I guess I had better stop wandering around where the wind blows me. Or run into something even worse..." he said with a wry grin, stuffing the rest of the rice into his mouth.

It was true, though. Ikkyu really had no reason to be out here. He was supposed to be on his way back to Jozuian, the temple where his master Sodon Kaso awaited. Kaso had ordered him to deliver a picture scroll of the three Buddhas who guard past, present and future to the Rinzai shrine in Suo-no-kuni, Tokuyama, which he had done.

On the journey home, though, he had suddenly recalled that the Emperor Godaigo, one of his ancestors of over a century ago, had visited Tsuyama. And once he remembered the story, he couldn't put it out of his mind, and his path veered until he finally arrived. Here.

It was the strange wanderlust that had always affected him, his special sickness. If the rest of the world chose the right-hand road, Ikkyu would surely choose the left. Even when he knew he'd regret it, looked upon as a fool by even children and village idiots, he couldn't help but risk his life, at times, upon these whims. His fellow monks all knew by now that his bizarre sickness—or was it possession, of a sort?—caused him to do unusual and unexpected things.

Still wandering, with no destination in mind, Ikkyu left Tsuyama on the road to the east.

The road had taken him to Shinsho, then Katsuyama, Ochiai, and finally to Tsuyama, but he heard that it originated at Izumo Shrine where the gods of Japan assembled. Travelers who continued on to the east from Tsuyama would eventually reach the distant capital of Kyoto. For a monk like Ikkyu, Izumo was a place of power and awe, and now he found himself walking on the road from Izumo.

As the road left Tsuyama, farmhouses grew sparser, and the ruddy, iron-rich hills became hidden behind rising undergrowth, or more distant bamboo forests. He saw a small settlement far off to his left, but nothing else.

Ikkyu picked up the fallen *shimenawa*, for no particular reason, balled it up and tucked it away in his robe.

I thought I would be sleeping under the stars tonight, only the full moon and my own voice for company, but not in this freezing blast! If it gets too bad I can always burn the shimenawa. *It's fat enough and long enough to keep me warm for a long time.*

He began to look about for a place to camp for the night.

The underbrush should keep the north wind off. And without the wind, it's easy enough to make camp here, he thought, and turned toward the edge of the road.

Suddenly the wind hammered past with a human shriek, then closing to encircle him in the warmth of summer. The unseasonable wind toyed with his uncut locks, and Ikkyu wondered if the wind was blowing from a different direction... yes, from the west. But even as his body felt the warmth of that wind, he felt something icy slither down his spine, like an icicle pressed against his back, a *frisson* strong enough to make him want to hug himself and shrink, trembling. The wind shrieked again, shaking the tree branches and underbrush, howling and sobbing like dozens of women in anguish. And as he heard it, Ikkyu saw a cloud of silvery lights to his left in sort of a wine-glass shape, up high, illuminating him.

The thin, freezing-cold fingers of the wind slipped into his chest, digging into his very heart.

"A demon!" he cried, reflexively raising his staff and concentrating his *ki*. With surer eyes now, he saw the scintillating lights that looked like tiny bolts of lightning, or minute silvery arrows in flight.

That I should be entrapped in such a vision! I need more training, he thought to himself, and began chanting a sutra deep in his heart. The icy fingers snapped back, out of his heart, taking with them the quivering horror his body had felt. Instant quiet.

"...it must be this strange, warm wind," he muttered, looking upwind toward the low hill the sun had so recently slipped behind.

"Huh...! I thought that hill was much farther away," he said, looking more closely to discover a huge boulder on top of it. It was a deep red, no doubt with the iron ore so common in these parts, red enough to be plainly visible even from here.

Suddenly, as if summoned by the warm wind that had so recently died out, a bluish-white light flashed on that darkening hilltop.

"Lightning!"

He checked the sky quickly, but there was still not a cloud in sight. Maybe just the lightning, with no storm? It flashed again, this time accompanied by a thunderous crash from the west. A huge tree to the side of the road to his left shattered, split in two, and as Ikkyu turned to watch, he saw beyond it a young girl racing toward him through the underbrush. As if fleeing for her life, she was running with all her strength, glancing back over her shoulder as at a wolf at her heels... but there was no wolf, no wild dog, no pursuing villain. And still she fled toward him!

Still searching for the cause, he felt the warm west wind falter, and again the frigid north wind battered him. His eyes teared up with the cold, and the stars in the dark skies above wavered. White lightning crashed into the earth, driving her towards him with bolt after bolt striking at her heels like arrows from a master of the bow. One strike shattered a giant boll just in front of here, knocking her off her feet. Galvanized, Ikkyu leaped into action, racing to her side.

"Are you all right?" he cried, slipping an arm under her shoulders and raising her body slightly. Her eyes regained their focus and looked into his. She must be only fifteen or sixteen at the most, he thought, then struggled to maintain his balance as she pressed both hands against him, trying to escape.

"Forgive me... Forgive me! Please, let me go! Let me go home!" she entreated him.

"It's all right, you're safe now. I am a monk. Nobody will hurt you now."

"But they are chasing me! The people of Kazaishi, the people of the windstone!"

Terrified, her eyes searched behind him for her pursuers.

"It's all right. No matter who may come, I will protect you now," he soothed, and looked at her features more closely. Her face was finely sculpted, with delicate nose, large eyes, and lips as cute as a gentian bud. The robe she wore was far from luxurious, but it was of a good, sturdy fabric. Probably the new wife—or perhaps the daughter—of a wealthy merchant, he guessed.

"What is your name?" he queried gently.

"Chisato. My father runs the Kuraya oil shop in Tsuyama."

"Chisato, I am Sojun Ikkyu. I'm a Zen monk in training. There is no need to be afraid any more. Tell me, what happened?"

"I don't know what's happening! I was just walking along the Izumo Road toward Tsuyama and all of a sudden a bunch of strange men surrounded me, saying I was the eighty-eighth vessel, and now the *kantsuma* would open. They dragged me to a little village to the west."

"...A vessel? *Kantsuma*?" he wondered, thinking aloud. They must be talking about a vessel for possession of some sort, he figured, suggesting that a god or demon would use this girl's body. The Japanese *kami* used sacred mirrors, swords or statues in shrines as vessels of power, and the Japanese people worshipped these objects as a result. When people were the vessels, it was usually girls no more than about seven years old, or at any rate young and beautiful.

The priests of Kazaishi must have kidnapped this poor girl to be the mortal vessel for their god... I've heard that there are old villages out in the country that still carry on these ancient rites, but that a village so close to the Izumo Road should be one!!

He frowned.

But what in the world is kantsuma? And how does it "open?"

Suddenly, Chisato opened her eyes wide, still safe in his arms. He saw the silhouette of a man with a tall, Heian-style hat reflected in them. Someone behind him...

Still crouched holding the girl, Ikkyu swung around, whipping his long staff against the ankles of the other man. He yelped and toppled, dropping his dagger, as Ikkyu stood, still holding the girl. He leapt into the underbrush on the other side of the road, and ran for a short distance to a secluded spot before he set her down

"Hide!" he whispered, and pulled her down next to himself, looking through the branches to see a number of figures moving on the road. He saw the man with the hat that he had hit, and a man with what looked like a bamboo spear. The man with the hat bent over to pick up his knife... he must be a ruffian, Ikkyu guessed, judging from the way an old sword scar on his cheek shone in the full moon.

They must be the men from Kazaishi, the ones Chisato ran away from. But using a girl as a vessel is a religious rite! They sure don't look like any priests I've ever seen. They act more like they're hunting down escaped prisoners, or putting down a peasant rebellion.

Chisato reached out a hand to him, grasping his black robe in her cold, sweaty palm. She gripped hard enough almost to pull it off his shoulder.

"It's all right, Chisato. Don't be afraid. I'll protect you," he whispered again, and saw her pale face jerk up and down in understanding. She must have realized that he could be trusted, in spite of his ratty appearance. She scrunched deeper into the bushes, and together they watched their pursuers.

A smaller shadow ran toward the group from the West, joining them in their search for the girl.

"You're late, hierophant!" snarled the man with the spear.

"Sorry, sorry... The one who owns this body is, as usual, fighting me," said the newcomer. Standing only four feet tall or so, with a high voice and small frame, he looked like a child. He was speaking to the other man more like an equal, though, and an adult at that.

"...So? Where's the vessel?" the slight youth asked of the others.

"She got away with some wandering monk. We're looking for her now," snapped the man with the tall hat, furiously waving his knife.

The hierophant sniffed insultingly in response.

"You are always so weak and pitiful!" he sneered. "I'll take care of it."

The youth brought his palms together in front of his chest, focusing his *ki*. An eerier voice began to issue from deep in his throat: the susurration of a snake, the croaking of a toad, and yet the whisper of a wind slipping between withered branches. Whatever it was, it certainly wasn't any sutra or prayer. It was closer to a snore, or just noise! It repeated again and again, and gradually a warm wind arose from the west with the sound of many sobbing women, carrying with it the reek of something raw and bloody. The stench reminded him of rotting fish guts at a wharf. His stomach began to roil and he covered his noise and mouth with his hand, motioning Chisato to do the same.

The stench is getting stronger, he thought, and suddenly he saw silver sparkles flashing in the air. They were little glints of light, almost like human eyes, exactly as he had seen before when that warm wind blew, flashing like tiny bolts of lightning, on and off again. The stench grew overpowering and the lights blindingly bright as the wind from the west blew as warm as summer.

Goose bumps rose all over this body.

He looked at Chisato, clutching him. *I'm trained, and even I'm about at my limit! It must be incredible fear and torture for this poor girl!* And even as the thought occurred to him, her hand fell away from her face, and she began to groan. The west wind intensified, countless tiny flashes of silver dancing in the air. She looked away, her body arching like a bow in agony, hand falling from Ikkyu's robe.

An eerie voice began to issue from her throat, like a cat in heat, a raven, or a beast growling in threat... it was not human. Ikkyu hurriedly covered her mouth with his hand.

"Chisato! What is it?"

Writhing, bent, she did not answer, merely continuing to growl.

"She's possessed!"

He struck her in the solar plexus with his staff, trying to knock her out, but she suddenly grasped his staff and tore it out of his grip with incredible strength.

Then she turned and shouted toward the pursuers, "Here! Brothers of the Wind! The vessel and the monk are here!"

It wasn't Chisato. It was the same manner of speech as the young hierophant, standing with palms pressed together in the road!

Before he had time to register what was happening, somebody rapped him over the head with a club, knocking him forward. He was pummeled by clubs, kicked and trampled, but before he lost consciousness he heard someone speak.

"Idiots! He is the blood sacrifice we need to open the *kantsuma*!"

It was the hierophant, and Chisato, speaking in two voices fused into one, with the susurration of a snake.

That hissing... that's their laughter, he thought as he slipped away, and once again felt the warm wind blow. Then the club knocked him into blackness.

– 2 –

Ikkyu awoke, the air smelling of dust and bone-dry straw. His eyelids were so swollen they felt heavy, but he finally managed to get them open properly to semi-darkness. There were countless tiny lights flickering, but they were not shaped like the human eyes that had come with the warm west wind.

Fireflies? …or maybe starlight?

He reached out to see, but gasped at the sudden agony in his elbow and shoulder, noticing for the first time that he was bound with a rough rope. His eyes had grown accustomed to the dimness, and he could see he was in a tiny hut, its sunken dirt floor full of straw. The roof seemed to be made of reeds, and he could see the stars through the huge hole in it.

He suddenly recalled Chisato, and as his mind cleared he wondered where she was. *And why did she suddenly call out to the men from Kazaishi, when she was trying to escape from them? Who were the "Brothers of the Wind?" The Kazaishi villagers? And why in the world did she suddenly use the voice and manner of speech as the young hierophant?*

He shook his head to stop the questions he couldn't answer.

I can't sit here thinking… I have to make sure Chisato's all right!

And as he thought that to himself, he heard a quiet voice: "So, the monk is finally back with us again."

It was not a man's voice. *Chisato?*

It was too high to be Chisato's voice, though. It was a woman, no, a *girl*, he realized.

"At last!" said the other, and a girl dropped down from above into the straw. She was only about four feet tall, with spindly arms and legs and long hair uncut and untended hanging down. She looked to be about ten.

"Who are you?" he asked.

The girl smiled broadly, like an adult.

"I'm Tsubaki. You're pretty cool, monk, worrying about others. I think you should be worrying a bit more about yourself, don't you?"

"Yes, no doubt," replied Ikkyu, smiling sourly. He wiped the smile off his face, though, and countered bluntly, "But even when tied up like this, we monks still worry about others."

Tsubaki was unimpressed.

"Hmph. I'd say you were just asking for trouble, myself," she sniffed, strolling around behind him. He felt a dainty hand checking that the knot on his heavy rope was still tight.

"Good... that won't come off easily," she muttered.

"You sound like you might be from the capital?"

"That's right, from Kyoto. Very good, monk!"

"People from the capital tend to talk to everyone in that pushy manner... but why is a Kyoto girl here? What happened to your parents?"

She merely sniffed again, not deigning to reply.

"Are you a villager, too? Is that why you came to check my bindings? Why does a Kawaishi girl speak with a Kyoto accent?"

"You're pretty noisy for a monk," she snarled. "Too noisy!"

She suddenly kicked him in the back a few times, but she was only a girl, after all. It didn't hurt at all, and in fact he thought she probably hadn't intended to hurt him in the first place.

"Where is Chisato? Did you beat her up and kick her, too?"

"Worried about the girl, are you?" teased Tsubaki, mouth twisted in a malicious grin.

"Yes. Surely you didn't let the men have their way with her! Or kick and beat her like you did me!"

Her grin vanished, and she suddenly grew still, looking down. She was silent for a moment, then admitted, "She's fine. Nobody did anything to her."

She shook her head slowly, then suddenly snapped out of it and sat down next to Ikkyu.

"She's the eighty-eighth vessel, after all. Nobody will even lay a finger on a blood sacrifice until the *kantsuma* opens. But that doesn't apply to you, monk: you're not one of the eighty-eight. You're gonna be drained dry, and that's all."

As she spoke, it finally dawned on Ikkyu... the way she said "vessel" and "blood sacrifice" and "*kantsuma*'" were not at all girlish. They were identical to the way the hierophant had said them!

Not one to dance around, Ikkyu said straight out, "You're the hierophant."

"No, not now," she answered, sounded a bit bewildered. "I'm just me; Tsubaki, from Mt. Funaoka in Kyoto."

"What do you mean, 'now?' So you were the hierophant a minute ago?"

"Sometimes he just barges into me, takes me over. I'm pretty tough, though, and he usually can't get in that easily!"

"I don't quite follow,..." he said, brow furrowed.

"You will, all too soon. The eighty-eighth vessel has come, and tonight's the night the *kantsuma* opens. It's waited for tens of thousands of years. Tonight will be special!"

She laughed out loud. Suddenly the shy girl was gone, and the icy, superior smile was back.

"Tens of...? What has waited for tens of thousands of years?"

She stood, cutting him off.

"You are one noisy monk!" she sneered. She walked about behind and began kicking him again, but it still didn't hurt. She began to pant, perhaps from exhaustion. But suddenly the warm wind came blowing in through hut's half-collapsed wall.

"Stop it! Stop it! Stop!" she screamed, covering her ears and turning her face to the sky. It was clear she wasn't shouting at him. She was screaming at the warm wind blowing, the countless silver lights that looked like eyes in the darkness, the shudders of terror that ran down his spine and the long, icy tentacles he felt probing his innermost heart. The warm west wind grew stronger, and the hut began to rock with its force. It felt like an earthquake! Dust clouds rose from the heaped straw, and the hoes and rakes along the wall toppled.

"Stop! Go away!" she screamed, flailing her tiny hands, and he heard a low rumble.

Earthquake? No, he realized, *not an earthquake... but the earth is groaning in pain.* He bent to place his ear against the earthen floor and heard the ground rumbling far, far below. It shook as if in answer to the west wind shaking the hut.

What's happening? And what in the merciful Buddha's name is this village? He listened to the rumbling uneasily.

He suddenly heard a deep sigh, and looked at the girl.

The straw was whipping up into a vortex, but only around her. The countless glints of silver, like eyes, surrounded Tsubaki as she tried to protect her face with her hands, sparkling as they raced around her. Her uncut hair whirled up straight, and her thin arms jerked again and again. Suddenly she collapsed in agony to the straw-strewn floor, clutching her throat, eyes wide open. Unable to breathe, she spun like a wheel on her back.

"Epilepsy," breathed Ikkyu... *if only my hands were free I could hold her until the attack passes, and protect her from this bizarre wind and those lights*, he thought, unable to do more than watch helplessly. He wriggled his wrists again, straining to get free of the ropes.

Sensing someone watching, he turned his head toward the door and saw he had visitors: the man with the spear, the man who had carried Tsubaki, and the man he had knocked over, with the high court-style hat and the knife. And there was a woman, too.

"What are you gawking at!" he shouted, "Help Tsubaki!"

They said nothing, and stood, immobile, watching her writhe in pain.

"Help her, please!" he entreated again, and the man with the hat and the scar on his cheek listlessly shook his head.

"She's becoming the hierophant. Nothing we can do."

The woman standing next to him, fortyish and holding a staff, explained, "Her heart and body are so very strong. No doubt that's why the hierophant chose her, but it is difficult for even him to enter."

"Possession...?" he murmured in astonishment. As if answering him, the warm west wind began to blow again. He felt goose bumps rise, and felt the ground roar again.

"It is done. The true lord of this land is pressing us to hurry," said Tsubaki.

No, not Tsubaki. It was the heirophant's voice.

They dragged him out of the hut.

— 3 —

A bonfire stood in the middle of the village, and as he approached he heard someone say "The blood sacrifice!"

The orange flames pierced the darkness, reflecting off Ikkyu's eyes, and as they adapted to the night he finally saw what kind of hut he'd been in. It was uninhabitable, with the thatched roof barely standing for all the holes in it, and the entire structure leaning, supported only by the twisted corner pillars. It looked ready to collapse at any time.

He looked around.

All the other houses here were in the same shape. The thatch hadn't been changed in years, walls showed gaping holes and leaning precariously, and the buildings still standing were lopsided and shaky.

This is Kazaishi Village?! It's not a village, it's a ruin! Nobody's lived here for decades! A sudden thought occurred to him: *Are the villagers the spirits haunting this place?*

He'd seen things that strange, and worse, in the thirty years he had been afflicted with his wanderlust.

He shook his head. *No, these are not spirits. Tsubaki actually kicked me, and the others beat me. They physically carried me to that hut.*

He looked around the village again, and noticed a larger hut built of rough-hewn logs, standing outside the village proper on the road sloping up onto the hill. All the other buildings looked as if they'd been abandoned for years, but that hut looked fresh.

Kazaishi Village isn't just mysterious, he thought. *It's downright unnatural!*

He began hunting for Chisato, to see if she was all right, as he lay where he had been dropped and using only his eyes. People were gathering around the bonfire, but the faces revealed by the dancing flames did not seem to be all from this village. The man with the tall hat was a ruffian from Kyoto, no doubt, but there was a middle-aged woman who looked to be a merchant's wife, and the man with the spear looked more like an elderly trader. That man over there had the build and muscles to be a freight hauler, whether on horse or by cart. But Tsubaki was the only child present.

A village with no children? And without anyone dressed like a peasant?

As he continued to search for answers, Tsubaki appeared, a group of people trailing. Ikkyu lifted his head to see what was happening.

"The blood sacrifice! Put the vessel with him!" said Tsubaki in that strange voice, and somebody pushed Chisato down in front of Ikkyu. She was wearing the white robes and scarlet *hakama* skirt of a shrine maiden. He wondered at her clothing, but this was not the time to seek an answer.

"Chisato!" He called to the girl lying on the ground. "Are you unharmed?"

She raised her face. It was pale with fear, but she didn't seem to be injured that he could see.

"Yes," she answered in a small voice. Her eyes were free of possession.

He relaxed, relieved that she had regained her own mind.

"Stand them up!" ordered Tsubaki. The man in the tall hat roughly pulled him to his feet, while the middle-aged woman grabbed Chisato's shoulder and made her stand.

"Walk! To the *kantsuma*!" ordered the man from behind him and to his right, pushing.

"Wait," interrupted Ikkyu, and turned to the hierophant dressed as a shrine maiden.

"You are the hierophant now?"

"Yes," she replied, with the gravity of an old priest performing a sacred rite.

"Do you still remember what you thought and did when you were Tsubaki?" asked Ikkyu.

"Thou art a fool!" sneered the hierophant. Her expression was the scornful look of an aged man.

"Why should the hierophant for yon sacred rite remember the thoughts of a mere womanchild?"

His language grew increasingly formal and archaic.

His speech, and his very thoughts, are becoming ancient as this ancient, mystic rite approaches. Or perhaps it is deliberate, to prepare himself for the rite?

Ikkyu tried again: "So you remember nothing of Tsubaki?"

"Nought," agreed the other, then turned to the waiting throng and shouted. "Go!"

They proceeded along the path sloping out of Kazaishi, from the log hut up to the top of the hill. The torches they held illuminated the narrow path on both sides, revealing that the slopes had no fields, no orchards planted... it was a barren wilderness, with only stones scattered in the darkness.

I've never heard of a village with no fields or orchards surrounding it, he thought, straining to see more clearly. It was hard to be sure in the flickering torchlight, but judging from what he could see peeping out though the weeds, this had once been a soybean field. And it was clear that it hadn't been tended for decades.

No harvest from this *field! And with no harvest, they won't be able to render up their yearly tithe. Usually when that happens the lord of the region comes to check, to see if there's been an uprising or the peasants have fled or died. No sign of lord or tax collectors here, though...*

Ikkyu thought for a moment.

That must be what happened. Kazaishi has been abandoned for decades. These people don't live here at all!

As they continued up the hill be tried moving his wrists; the rope was quite a bit looser now. Tsubaki had helped by kicking the knots before the hierophant had possessed her. He realized now that she had checked on the tightness of the knot, and kicked him in the wrists, merely to help loosen them.

But why would Tsubaki do such a thing? he wondered. She had seemed nothing more than a mere child then, but unless she had some deeper plan in mind she surely wouldn't have just decided to try to loosen his bonds. Suddenly the knot slipped open.

Ikkyu quickly slipped the ends of the rope into his obi, as unobtrusively as possible. His black-dyed obi was old and frayed, and it was unlikely anyone would notice the rope... and in any case the pitch-black darkness of the hill made it impossible for anyone to see anything below his shoulders. Even so, just to be on the safe side, he turned to the scar-faced man behind him to the right.

"By the way, what happened to my staff?"

"You're gonna be dead pretty quick, monk. I wouldn't waste your breath worrying," the other replied, surly.

"I've travelled with that staff for almost twenty years now; it's a close friend. It certainly has a spirit, perhaps even a soul. If I die separated from it, I'm quite sure it will transform into some monster."

"Turn into a monster?" repeated the man, obviously unhappy at the prospect. There was still a deeply rooted folk belief that inanimate objects had spirits of their own, and could come to life. It was hard for this man to deny the possibility when a monk told him so.

"That'd be bad..." he muttered to himself. "Your staff is in the log hut. You go right ahead and tell it that it ain't getting out even if you are sacrificed and it does turn into some monster."

"I see," said Ikkyu. The log hut had been the only newly built structure in the whole village.

"No talking!" snapped the hierophant, suddenly turning back at their voices. They both fell silent, continuing to trudge up the hill.

A few minutes later they finally reached the summit. The hierophant walked over to Chisato, then turned to point ahead: "Look! The *Kantsuma*!"

Ikkyu and Chisato both looked. At the very apex of the hill was a huge boulder, as large as a Noh theater stage, lying there like some giant's forgotten toy. It shone red in the torchlight, and Ikkyu thought it must be rich in iron as well. It was more than just red, though... the surface seemed wet, shining in the light, as if the entire boulder were drenched in blood.

Maybe spring water bubbled up through a split in the rock and has wet it? But what is that incredible stench? It smells like rotten meat... and it certainly didn't come from any spring water! They must have slaughtered a lot of animals near here.

He looked around, peering into the darkness. The torchbearers were all clustered around the scarred man, making that area bright and gradually bringing the giant boulder ahead into view—along with its surroundings.

"By the merciful Kannon!" he gasped. He couldn't help himself when he saw what lay strewn around the boulder that was the *kantsuma*. At the same time Chisato also saw what lay there, and recognized the source of that terrible smell. A small squeal of terror and disgust slipped from her mouth, and she tried to wriggle free from the woman who gripped her shoulder.

The ground was littered with dozens of corpses. Most of them were rotting, torn open by wild dogs and crows, arms and legs lying scattered separate from torsos, and many even lacked their heads. From the scraps of red and yellow robes left on the pitiful remains, the black-dyed scarves nuns used, or the wide belts and cords used by the samurai families, it was obvious most of them had been women. And from the ripped flesh left hanging from the scattered arms and legs, and the breasts still visible on hollow ribcages here and there, it was obvious most of them had been young.

Ikkyu and Chisato hurriedly looked away... but not because of the scattered cadavers. The heads left by the wolves and wild dogs lay in disarray, long hair streaming over the earth, and their white teeth shone in every case, lips torn off of each face. In the flickering torchlight they seemed to grin in death.

"Grinning skulls... But why dishonor the dead so?" wondered Ikkyu almost silently as he tried to stop from retching.

Chisato could no longer speak at all, merely trembling in terror, on the verge of flight. The villagers held her tight, grasping not only her shoulder and arms but even wrapping their hands around her waist to hold her still. They dragged her in front of the *kantsuma*, forcing her down to kneel. The rest crowded in close around them, clubs and bamboo spears ready to stop them from fleeing.

Chisato dredged up her last fragments of courage, sobbing out "Please! Help me! Ask my father in Tsuyama! He'll pay ransom! Please, don't kill me!"

Her voice rose higher and higher, turning into a shriek of terror no longer distinguishable as speech. And, as if summoned, that warm wind began to blow in response.

The wind was shrieking.

Not the rush of moving air, but the wails of terror and anguish of dozens of women.

With it came the foul stench of fish offal. The wind was not blowing from the west, but from the huge boulder they called the *kantsuma*. The shrieks of the women, the stench of offal and the warm wind all emitted from the giant rock, glinting red and wet in the torchlight.

The hierophant turned toward the *kantsuma*, illuminated by torchbearers standing on both sides. Ikkyu could clearly see the surface of the boulder now, and was able to see it *change* suddenly... and hideously!

There were small lumps of flesh scattered across the boulder, a richer hue than the reddish rock. They covered its surface in pairs, opening and closing in unison... and he realized with a start what they were.

As if spitting poison, he gasped: "Lips!"

The *kantsuma* was covered with the blood-red lips, dozens and dozens of them, of young women!

The youthful face of the hierophant broke into a smile, then an evil laugh.

"Aeons ago there was a war between the gods of Taka-Amahara, the high heavens, and the gods of Akitsushima, the gods of the Land of Yamato. It was in this spot, the same sacred spot where these islands were created, where Sabae Nasuashiki Futsunushi, the God of the Wind known as Hfutzn'sie in the ancient tongue, was imprisoned.

"The *kantsuma* is the seal, what was once known as the *kami tsumari*, the place when the *kami* is held. And the land here is possessed by His power!

"The people of ancient Akitsushima have visited this sacred site for thousands of years, working to free Hfutzn'sie from His imprisonment in the bowels of the earth! *We* have come here over the centuries, but the Imperial court in Kyoto still worships the gods of Tama-Amahara, killing us, trying to destroy our rites and our tomes, to extinguish us from the face of the earth! They have called us monsters and demons!"

"You are their ghosts?"

The hierophant giggled.

"And you have possessed the people of Kazaishi, kidnapping women on the Izumo Road, and sacrificing them to your Hfutzn'sie?"

Ikkyu finally understood it all.

"Close, monk, but not in the cup," said the hierophant, sneering at his guesses. "Our rites are very different from the rites performed by your Emperor as head of the land, and from the esoteric rites of

Buddhism. You are right that we have kidnapped eighty-eight virgins, but *we* will not be the ones to break open this *kantsuma*. Those eighty-eight virgins are not sacrifices!"

Ikkyu waited, silent.

The hierophant sneered yet again, and laughed aloud in his childish voice.

"Foolish Buddhist monk! You cannot guess what we do! I wish I could show your foolish face to Prince Umayado, who first brought Buddhism to these shores centuries ago!

The man in the tall hat carried a pottery jar over to the hierophant, who was still giggling. The lip of the jar was sharp, as acute as the tip of a spear... and while pottery would shatter if hit, it could cut sharper and deeper than steel if fashioned right.

He showed it to the hierophant, who pointed at Ikkyu with his chin and ordered "Show it to the monk."

The razor lip of the jar was shoved up under his nose. He turned his face away at the smell of blood welling up from its depths.

"This is for the blood of those other than the sacred vessel. Those women who were not virgins filled this with their heart blood, washing the sacred *kantsuma*."

"What foul magic keeps these women's lips alive on this rock?"

"Ah, how delightful!" laughed the hierophant. "Thank you, monk. We've kidnapped any number of nuns, but every one was merely a whore in a nun's robe. They were all fools unable to read a sutra, and merely washed the *kantsuma* with their heart blood. But you, monk... You can read the sutra! You know how to talk to the dead, and are under the protection of the Buddha...."

Ikkyu cut him off. "Tell me! What magic is in those lips!"

The hierophant smiled, and leaned to whisper into Ikkyu's ear.

"The Great Sabae Nasuashiki Futsunushi is not so weak a god as to be freed by the puny rites of humanity! Hfutzn'sie will use the body of the virgin vessel, kneeling at the sacred *kantsuma*, to Himself sing the chant needed to break the seal and free Himself!"

"This Hfutzn'sie, imprisoned in the depths of the earth, will possess Chisato and free himself!?"

"I suppose that's how you would look at it, ignorant as you are."

"But why these lips, so many lips, wailing on the face of this boulder?"

"Living proof that Hfutzn'sie reveals Himself here to sing the chant! After these virgins sang the chant, their lips flew to the *kantsuma*, becoming a part of it to sing His praise in the tongue of the gods. You foolish humans only perceive the sound of the wind and a fetid odor!"

"...that wind from the boulder, and the stench, and the wailing of the women... that is the language of the gods!"

"Hfutzn'sie has changed the *kantsuma*—a sacred object here in Taka-Amahar—to an object to praise Himself with the lips of virgins." The hierophant pointed to Chisato, continuing, "*She* is the eighty-eighth vessel, the final vessel to free Hfutzn'sie from His prison! We cannot wait to see how she will shatter the *kantsuma!*"

The grip on Ikkyu's shoulders suddenly grew painfully tight, and the man in the tall hat brought the pointed tip of the jar toward his breast.

Smiling in anticipation, the hierophant spoke almost to himself. "She will be His bride!"

Chisato was still kneeling, palms together and head down, in front of the *kantsuma*. The ground began to quiver and he heard—or felt—a roar from the deep.

All eighty-seven pairs of lips on that crimson rock opened at once. The sight of all those meaty flowers bursting into bloom at once was beautiful, and hideous!

The warm wind blew that stench toward him, and he heard the wailing of the women. Behind the boulder a greyish mist began to form, mist streaming from those eighty-seven pairs of lips to congeal and spread in the darkness of the night.

It was like dropping lead-colored liquid into a dark blue pool... a gray vortex swirling in the darkness, surrounded by the night. Tendrils extended from the edges of the vortex like living things, approaching Chisato's face.

The sharp lip of the jar approached Ikkyu's breast, and the hierophant giggled as the ground rumbled even louder. The eighty-eight pairs of lips wailed out their anguish in a paean to Hfutzn'sie, and the stench intensified as the chant progressed, with the smells of those scattered corpses helping to "purify" the area for the rite.

"A rite of the evil gods..."muttered Ikkyu to himself, clenching his teeth together.

Something peeked out of his torn black robe... the rope?

No, it was the sacred *shimenawa* he had picked up on the Izumo Road. The white paper *shide* wrapped around it fluttered palely in the darkness.

If Hfutzn'sie was imprisoned by the gods of Taka-Amahara, then he must be weak against their powers! Realized Ikkyu suddenly. He didn't know if it was true or not, but he had nothing to lose by trying!

And I am a descendent of the Emperor Gokomatsu, the lineage that still practices the sacred rites of Taka-Amahara!

He snapped his right shoulder down, pulling free of the hands that had held him tight until then. They were taken completely by surprise, as he hadn't resisted them at all until then.

With his right hand free, he punched the wrist of the man holding his other shoulder, and jumped up, kicking the jar out of the hands of the man with the tall hat. Before the other had time to do more than begin to look surprised, Ikkyu smashed his fist into the other man's face. In years past he had fought barehanded against brigands and deserters to protect starving peasants. He had been training at Saigonji Temple in Kyoto then, training under the monk Ken'o, but he was still more than capable of ramming his rock-hard fist precisely into the spot between the other's nose and lips.

Before he could check to see if the other was down for the count, the middle-aged merchant's wife came thrusting at his back with the bamboo spear. He twisted to avoid it, letting it pass under his armpit as he grasped it and ripped it out of her hands.

He quickly wound the *shimanawa* around the spear and thrust, shouting "Demon worshippers, bound to a god the world has damned! Come on! Come on and die!"

Half of it was bluff, but he was serious, too. He would save the lives of Chisato, the unwilling vessel of an ancient god, and of Tsubaki, also possessed by the spirit of the long-dead hierophant, or die trying.

The wailing from the *kantsuma* grew more intense, more frantic, and the offal wind blew into his face.

It would be so much easier if I had my old staff...

The thought flashed across his mind suddenly, perhaps caused by the foul magic of the *kantsuma*, because suddenly Tsubaki was thrusting at him with her knife, with bamboo spears coming hard behind. He parried furiously with his own spear, smashing the butt into throat or solar plexus to knock them out when he could.

They fell back momentarily, and he raced to Chisato's side. She still knelt, immobile, waiting to be taken by Hfutzn'sie. He yanked her to her feet by her clothing, and with a hurried "Forgive me," slapped her hard across the face.

The *smack* exploded through the night, and the tendrils of mist stretching toward her from above pulled back sharply, seemingly afraid of the sound.

"The forces of evil are ever afraid of sharp noises," his mother had taught him years ago when they visited the Imperial court. *"That's why we clap our hands when we visit the shrine."* The daughter of Munefusa of Kazanin Shrine, she had been a noble well versed in the rites and rituals.

He looked into the swirling mist... no time to be reminiscing about how useful Court knowledge had turned out to be!

Chisato's expression was back.

"Can you stand?" he cried.

She nodded.

"And run?"

"Yes," she answered, voice stronger.

"Good! Then run, girl, run from here as fast as you can!"

Without waiting, he thrust the *shimenawa*-wrapped spear in his hand into the darkness below the gray vortex, and began chanting a Shinto prayer at the top of his lungs.

He called on the gods of Taka-Amahara to help him, crying out that the *kantsuma* would be breached. He cried to the eight million gods of Japan for aid.

And as he chanted, the vibrations of his voice and body shook the *shimenawa* and the white *shide* hanging from it. The vortex alternately expanded and shrank, as if in agony.

Ikkyu waved the spear toward the vortex, the *shimenawa* and its *shide* fluttering white against the dark blue sky. Unlike the refined waves and gestures of the shrines of the Kyoto court, these were

Ikkyu's own raw motions, more primitive and more powerful.

Pulsating in response, the vortex suddenly shot up high into the night sky. The onlooking crowd shouted in response, incredulous to see their god attempting to flee from this scruffy monk.

Watching them out of the corner of his eye, Ikkyu called to Chisato: "To me! We have to save Tsubaki!"

With her behind him, he turned to face the hierophant.

He was standing, blankly staring at the vortex high above him. He had been the one to bring Hfutzn'sie back into this world, and now he had seen his god flee from Ikkyu, even if temporarily. He was shattered.

"Tsubaki!"

Ikkyu called to the girl, and the hierophant suddenly turned to face him. The other was terrified, unable to believe that the quiet monk had beaten him.

"What god possesses you?" whispered the hierophant, but Ikkyu did not answer.

"Forgive me," he said instead, and lightly chopped the young girl on the back of the neck. She collapsed without even a whimper into his arms.

"Take care of her," he ordered Tsubaki. "I've got to take care of that god, or demon, or whatever it is."

He turned back to the *kantsuma*.

If my quick prayers had that much effect, a full sutra should work even better... after all, it was Buddhism that destroyed the believers of that foul god the first time!

He began to chant the Prajna sutra, that the Rinzai sect said would cleanse all sins, looking upward as his did. The lead-colored vortex was still spinning, painfully. Thin tendrils stretched out from the periphery, almost as if beckoning.

In response, one person after another craned to face the sky, looking up into the grayish mist. Their eyes were already dead, the clouded eyeballs of a dead fish.

Ikkyu gripped the spear, arm back to throw it into the vortex, still chanting. The *shimenawa* and its *shide* shook in the stench.

He felt a voice rumble within his mind: *You may not! I forbid you!*

Ikkyu aimed carefully, knowing he would have only one chance.

And just as he leaped forward, arm swinging to throw the spear, something silvery-white cut across his field of vision.

He froze, gripping the spear tightly, and reflexively turned toward the light. They looked like eyes, shining silver in the darkness, but they flew like arrows toward the center of the vortex, driving deep into it and gradually, ever so gradually, making it brighter. One by one they flew home, and were absorbed.

The same eyes I saw before!

He suddenly noticed a hissing noise, like a jet of air, and turned to see that the tiny lights and the noise were both coming from the same place: the villagers. Mouths gaping wide, eyes fixed on the vortex, pinpoints of light shot forth from their throats. Behind them, the men and women collapsed, eyes turned up white.

The ghosts of those worshippers from centuries ago!

Hfutzn'sie was eating the spirits of his own people to survive!

Ikkyu exploded with rage, focusing his anger and prayers on the spear... it was no longer a mere shaft of bamboo, but a sacred object imbued with all the power of the gods of Taka-Amahara and Buddha. Ikkyu *knew* it to be true.

The vortex was growing steadily larger, absorbing countless silvery glints from the people below, and the tendrils continued to wave, to beckon the souls of the worshippers.

"Die, demon!" Ikkyu screamed, throwing the spear with all his power.

At the same time the spear left his hand, a shortsword came flying out of the darkness, knocking it off course to fall onto the path.

The man with the Heian-style hat strode into the light, sneering at Ikkyu. The scar on his cheek shone whitely in the light from the torches guttering on the ground as he leaped toward the shortsword.

Reading his move, Ikkyu leaped to the spear, while overhead the vortex slid gradually to spin directly above the *kantsuma*, stronger than ever.

Still half sprawled on the ground, the other man swung his sword up, but Ikkyu had already recovered his spear. He dodged the blow, driving the butt of the spear into the other's stomach. He wanted to knock him out of the fight, not kill him.

Unfortunately, his target had other plans. He twisted to avoid the spear, thrusting again and again from below. Ikkyu dodged using his advantage of height to move closer for a better shot.

The vortex began to drop down, silently, onto the *kantsuma,* greeting by countless lips open wide in greeting. Or were they screaming in ecstasy?

Shrieks pierced the night, and the odor of fish entrails grew over-powering. A warm wind blew, and the ground shook at its touch, the giant boulder beginning to spin like a top.

Hfutzn'sie was coming.

Finally, Ikkyu was in the right position, and punched the butt of the spear home into the other's solar plexus. His enemy collapsed, half-grunting and half-moaning, unable to breath. He grasped his throat, sword and Ikkyu forgotten, rolling over to try to catch his breath facedown.

Ikkyu turned back to the vortex, advising the fallen man in passing "Be at peace. You'll be fine in a little while."

Chisato started hunching toward him, the weight of Tsubaki on her back.

"Thank goodness you're all right!" she gasped, and when Ikkyu turned to look at her his eyes widened.

"Hurry! Run! *Run!*"

Unable to hear what he was shouting, Chisato halted, unsure of herself, and Tsubaki began to whisper from her back.

"You had better do as the monk says. The *kantsuma* is opening; Hfutzn'sie is come!"

Chisato looked toward the *kantsuma.* Something red was spin-ning there, illuminated by the countless silvery-white lights. The whole boulder looked like a chunk of raw meat, spinning like a cy-clone. The shrieks of eighty-seven women echoed in the stench... the top of the hill was becoming something out of a different world.

The *kantsuma,* still spinning wildly, lifted off the ground, and light streamed forth from the gap under it, a *slimy,* greenish light. It was as rotten as the smell of fish offal in the air, suppurating and foul.

He could make out something in the greenish light. It was well-muscled wrist, with a shackle on it. The band around that arm was not steel-gray, though, but the color of dead fishbelly.

But by the Buddha! It was enormous! Each of those fingers was thicker and longer than a log! Compared to the huge palm, even the gigantic boulder of the *kantsuma* looked small!

Even the kantsuma *would be nothing but a teacup to that hand! He would reach the clouds!*

Chisato was frozen like a frog transfixed in the snake's gaze, unable to resist or flee that terror. She could only wait to die.

"You stupid girl! Don't just stand there! Come here! Get off the crest!" he bellowed, but her feet didn't stir.

Tsubaki suddenly gave a grunt and slid off her back, apparently recovered from the shock of having that ghost sucked out of her by the vortex.

Recovering with the speed that only the young can achieve, she took Chisato's hand, and pulled her toward Ikkyu.

"Come on!" she cried, but Chizato was petrified with terror, overpowered by the sight of Hfutzn'sie being reborn from the depths of the earth. "It'll eat you!"

Ikkyu checked the *shimenawa* to make sure it was still tight on the spear, then tied the end of the spear to his wrist using the rope from his robe.

He knew he was no hero, fit to battle a god... only an insect, fighting this ancient evil with a bamboo spear.

He breathed in deep, calming himself, then turned to face Mt. Nagisan, where the gods who created Japan had first descended.

"I am Sojun Ikkyu, of the Rinzai Daitokuji Temple! I come to cleanse this earth of Sabae Nasuashiki Futsunushi, the God of the Wind known as Hfutzn'sie in the ancient tongue! I call upon the gods of Nagisan, Izanagi, all the gods of Nippon! *And I call upon the Buddha, upon Kannon, upon our founder Eisai to aid me!*"

And he threw the spear with all his might into the spinning *kantsuma*. It flew, a shaft of light through the darkness, like a bolt of lightning from his hand straight toward that giant hand.

The wind whipped him off his feet, pulling him through the air to the *kantsuma*, hanging onto the end of the rope with both hands. He leapt with it, leveraging the rope to land atop the boulder amid the greenish light, the wailing of the eighty-seven virgins and the unbearable stench.

He felt nothing for the lips under his feet. They had once been women, but now they were merely objects of evil, talismans to bring Hfutzn'sie back to our world.

Standing on the bloody rock, he called yet again to the gods of light.

"Evil is but an illusion born of the loss of purity, and if we but remain pure all evil can be dispelled by the sacred radiance we all hold within! Help me, O gods and Buddha, to save the earth from this abomination!"

And he plunged the spear with all of his force into the body of the *kantsuma*. A blast of wind rushed over the hilltop, frigid and clean air from Mr. Nagisan, announcing the descent of Izanagi and Izanami, the creators of Nippon.

Hanging on for his life, Ikkyu smiled.

He knew.

Izanagi and Izanami had created this land, these islands of Nippon, and they would protect it from being fouled by the stench of Hfutzn'sie's offal. But more than that, by praying for their assistance *and in the same breath asking for help from Buddha,* he had made them furious, he was sure. They wouldn't take kindly to a prayer that included Buddha, who wasn't native to Japan at all!

A brilliant light shone in the north, golden radiance bright enough to wash away the sickly green, and with it came the clean fragrance of living things, cleansing the air of the stench of rotten fish. The shrieks fell quiet, and the boulder stopped spinning, throwing Ikkyu off to the ground as it dropped back to lie snug on the hilltop.

There was no sign of that giant, shackled hand.

He picked himself up, and ran over to the girls, laughing aloud.

Joining in the laughter without understanding why, Tsubaki asked "Why the laughter, monk?"

"I've angered my fellows, my superiors, the monks of famous temples and shrines throughout Japan, and even the lords who rule this land, but I've never angered the gods before! And now they've pushed him back deep into his prison again. And I've survived to tell the tale!"

As he laughed once again, the reddish light of dawn broke over the distant mountains. The sky was a deep blue without a cloud in sight.

They slept until noon, exhausted, until hunger woke them. They wandered down the path to the log hut in search of something to eat, and pulled open the door.

It was packed full of staffs, baggage, scarves, clothing and all sorts of things that men and women might carry or wear when travelling.

"There never were any villagers here, just travellers ensnared by the ghosts of the worshippers," said Ikkyu almost to himself.

Tsubaki looked down.

"And it is all my fault."

Ikkyu asked her what she meant, but she didn't answer.

The three of them walked back to Tsuyama, and when Chisato was returned to the safety of her family Ikkyu and Tsubaki were repaid with three days and nights of feasting, and a large pouch of gold.

Ikkyu tucked the gold into the sleeve of his robe, and together with Tsubaki set forth east along the Izumi Road.

Walking, he asked, "So what did you mean when you said those travellers had been possessed because of you?"

She told him that the *shimenawa* had been torn off the boulder and discarded by the man with the tall hat. He was a slaver from Yamaguchi who had bought her from her parents, and had been leading her off to a life in the pleasure quarters in Yamaguchi.

He had led her off the road and into the underbrush, suddenly attacking her. They fought, and as she resisted him, the *shimenawa* had been broken. A flash of eerie light came from the boulder, and they were possessed.

Possessed, the man in the hat had torn the rest of the *shimenawa* off, throwing it to the ground. The winds must have carried it back to the road, where Ikkyu found it.

"Slavers never touch their own wares," mused Ikkyu. "For him to touch you, a mere girl... he must have been touched by Hfutzn'sie already! That evil waited hundreds, nay, thousands of years for that chance!"

When they reached Kyoto, they first went to meet Tsubaki's parents. He handed them the gold he had received from the Chisato's father, and forced them to promise never to try to sell a daughter again.

"I'll be back every so often to see Tsubaki, and I'll be asking my friends in the court here in Kyoto to let me know how she is. I'm sure she'll have no worries, though. Any more."

* * * * *

Upon his return to Jozuian, he told his master Sodon Kaso all that had happened.

When the tale was done, his master frowned, silver eyebrows drawing tight. He sighed, deep in thought. The story of Hfutzn'sie deeply interested him, it seemed.

"I fear I must have offended the Buddha and Eisai, too, though," added Ikkyu, chuckling.

"No, I think they would have approved. After all, you did save the possessed."

"Yes, but I was unable to help those poor travellers."

His master looked him in the eye.

"I'm not talking about anything so trifling as the girls!"

"What...?"

"With that spear you cleaned the land of Kazaishi Village itself of the evil."

"The land was possessed?"

"Evil does not possess only people, but the earth as well. You destroyed that evil using your spear as your prayer beads, and the force of Izanagi instead of your mastery of Rinzai's *mu*, nothingness. Whether Buddha or god, saving the people demands using the tools at hand. That is the very core of Zen!"

As he left the temple, Ikkyu grinned at the thought of the people believing in heaven and hell, and stuck his tongue out like a roguish boy, whistling through the gate.

The Last Temple of Balsoth

by Cliff Biggers

Illuminated by the dancing flames of two iron sconces, the young woman seemed resigned to her fate. Her head slumped forward slightly, framed by the thick dark hair that fell forward to shadow her flawless face and cascade below her shoulders, contrasting with the creamy whiteness of the fine silken dress that struggled to cover her breasts, clung to her narrow waist, and followed the roundness of her hips before flowing in folds to her ankles. Her placid expression betrayed not the slightest bit of fear--or any other emotion, for that matter. Less evident was the fact that it was the crushing grip of the two altar guards on either side of her that kept her upright, still, and steady. Left alone, she would fall to the floor, largely due to the soporific effects of the contents of a goblet that the priest's guards had forced her to drink less than an hour earlier. The brew's effect would last for several hours... which was longer than the woman herself could be expected to endure what was planned for her.

After a moment, an elder priest approached the altar in a solemn, obviously rehearsed processional, marching in time to a resonant and dirgelike drumbeat. He walked slowly; it was unclear whether his slow, hesitating stride was an element of the ritual or a result of age. The priest stopped in front of the young woman, gazing intently at her. Had the light been better, one might have seen a hint of desire in his eyes; no matter a man's age, some urges never fully subside.

The processional drums halted. The altar guards stood mute, maintaining their firm grasp of the woman's arms, their faces obscured by their hooded ceremonial cloaks. The priest reached behind the altar and withdrew, in a melodramatical guesture, a double-edged athame. He held it flat in his hands, extending it in offering while loudly calling out a ritual recitation in a tongue so ancient that no man alive fully knew its meaning.

At last, the recitation came to an end. The priest nodded

twice, and the altar guards recognized the cue. One of them held the woman's right hand in his own right hand, drawing it forward while gripping her elbow in his left hand. He drew her arm over the altar, positioning her wrist over a gaping orifice in the weathered stone surface. Shallow grooves ran from the hole to the outer edges of the stone in a sunburst pattern; they appeared to be decorative, but in reality served to channel blood offerings into the central hole, a sort of stone drain that directed the blood into the altar's lower chambers—chambers that none but the high priest himself was allowed to enter.

The priest extended both of his hands, the athame resting across them. He waited for a moment, then looked at the second guard. The irritated expression on the priest's face was easy to see, even in the dim light. He tipped his head slightly towards the athame once, then twice; the guard standing on the woman's left hesitated for a moment, then extended his left hand in response to the priest's hint, grasping the athame by its ornately embossed handle. The priest recited another incomprehensible line as the guard stood there, blade at ready. The priest stared at the guard, then thrust his chin down slightly towards the woman's extended wrist, his expression of irritation giving way to more obvious anger at this failure to follow in the ritual.

The guard seemed to recognize the cue: he lifted the athame and positioned it over the woman's wrist with a dramatic flourish. He placed his right hand over his left as if steadying it, while the other guard bent the woman's hand down and back, extending the right to make tendons and veins more evident. The knife-wielding guard adjusted his stance slightly, moving the knife in a feint as if lining up the ritual cut.

Suddenly his right hand shot forward, grasping the other guard's right hand at his wrist. The guard scarcely had time to flash a quizzical look in the knife-wielder's direction before the blade thrust forward, down, and back. Blood pumped into the air and spattered onto the stone--but it was the guard's blood, not the woman's that ran into the stone channels and trickled down the ancient drain.

The guard released his grip on the woman's arm; she dropped to her knees as he struggled to grasp his own wrist in a futile effort to stanch the rapid flow of blood. It might not have been futile, of course, had the knife-wielder not thrust again, driving the blade firmly across the guard's left wrist. The guard looked at him in shock and confusion; the knife-wielder looked him in the eye, then grinned.

"Balsoth will feast tonight... but not on her blood." With that, he grabbed the guard by the back of the neck and slammed him forward onto the altar, thrusting the blade through the guard's exposed neck until the metal rasped on the stone beneath. Groan gave way to gurgle as blood flowed freely across the thirsty stones.

"What... what have you done?!" The priest was too startled to retreat and too ineffectual to do anything else.

The remaining guard pushed his cloak back to reveal a broad, grinning face, framed by unkempt dark hair that hung almost to his shoulders. His broad nose had been reshaped by countless fights over the years, the indentation of the scar across his left brow discernible thanks to the angle of the flickering torch light. "You wanted a blood sacrifice to Balsoth? I gave you a blood sacrifice to Balsoth-- same as I've done in every damnable temple between Norheim and here."

"You fool! Balsoth demands the blood of a virgin! Your actions are futile!"

"Tell that to this fellow--" he nodded in the direction of the dead guard. "He might have some thoughts on the futility of my actions... if he could have any thoughts at all."

The priest trembled slightly as he lifted his hands, fingers bent and spread apart in the first phase of an unholy spell. The dark-haired man let the girl sink to the floor, propelling himself over the stone altar to grasp the priest's bony fingers in his sinewy hands. The sharp report of breaking bones resonated through the temple, punctuated by the priest's high-pitched wordless scream.

"No magic, old man! No tricks! Balsoth is going to feast tonight--first on the guard, then on you." He grabbed the priest by his ritual robes, lifting him off the ground and dashing him onto the stone altar.

"Why are you doing this?" asked the priest, his voice querulous from the pain. "Why do you attack the High Temple of Balsoth? Do you know what happens to those who cross the gods?"

"Balsoth is no god, old man--he's a devil. Only a devil would demand the lives of young women season after season. I was willing

208

to look the other way for too long... then your priests brought their temple to my homeland. I returned from battle to discover that my only sister had been taken as an offering to your god. I determined then and there to make the priests pay... and Balsoth as well.

"I signed on as a temple guard--that's where I got the uniform. I slaughtered that priest the same way he slaughtered my sister. Then I went down to the temple's holy room beneath the altar. I saw the temple bloodstone, old man--I saw it soaking up the blood that flowed onto it. I know about your bloodstones--unholy eggs for the devils that you worship. So I took a war-hammer to that stone and shattered it into pieces, then torched the temple. Since then, I've done the same thing over and over again. And every time I do, the remaining devils that you worship get a little weaker. Now there's only one left.... and it should be an easy kill."

"You fool," the priest spat. "Those were temple outposts. This is the holy temple itself. They spread the worship of Balsoth--we are the home of the god himself!"

"Then it will be a fine day to kill a god... and his priest." As he spoke, he thrust the athame into the priest's chest, twisting it firmly as it pierced the withered heart. The old man's eyes widened, and blood poured from his mouth, running into the altar channels and disappearing down the opening still red with the guard's blood.

On the other side of the altar, the intended sacrifice began to stir, moaning softly. The man dropped his cloak and cowl, revealing both a sword and a short-handled axe that had been pushed back and out of sight in the voluminous folds of the cloak. He repositioned and tightened them around his waist so that the weapons hung in easy reach on either hip. He then bent down and placed his fingers on the woman's ear lobe, pinching with his rough-hewn, dirty thumbnail. The woman jerked upright and howled in protest.

"Good--you're awake. I didn't expect you to sleep for too long, since I poured half the liquid down the side of your face rather than in your mouth."

Her momentary confusion gave way to dawning fragments of memory. Her eyes widened to take in the vision of the temple and the guard who loomed over her--one of the same guards who had drugged her to bring her here. She reached up with her right hand and raked her nails across his cheek. He jerked his head back as he grabbed her slender hand in his crushing grip.

"Stop! I'm not here to hurt you. They had other plans--" he gestured towards the two bodies on the altar-- "but I put a stop to them. Now I'm going to take you out of here."

"Who are you? Why?--"

"My name is Gondar. That's all you need to know about me for now, other than the fact that I mean you no harm. Who are you?"

"Ysidra... my name is Ysidra."

"Well, Ysidra, I need to get you out of here--I have a temple to destroy, and that will be easier if you're not in the way."

"How did I get here? What happened?"

"That was my doing. You were the first attractive woman I saw when the priest called for a sacrifice, so I lied and said you were a virgin and--"

The resounding slap echoed through the stone temple. Gondar put his hand to his face, grinning.

"You nearly had me killed, and now you insult my purity?"

"You weren't going to die--I was one of the guards, remember? I needed someone like you, large enough that one guard would have trouble handling her..."

She swung at Gondar's face a second time, but his large hand enveloped hers before the blow landed. "Ahh ahh ahh--the clawing was understandable, and I gave you the first hit, but that's it."

"Why do you keep saying such horrible things about me?"

Gondar laughed. "Horrible? There's nothing horrible about a big woman like you--tall, strong, sturdy, and rounded in the right places. What I meant, though, was that I didn't want some weak wisp of a girl that a lone guard could whisk up and haul to the temple." Gondar rubbed his face a second time, sure that it must be red where her hand struck. "And I can see that I made the right choice."

The woman was about to reply when she became aware of the corpses on the altar. She pulled away from Gondar and the altar. "They're dead... you killed them!"

"It was them or you, woman. The priest intended to sacrifice you, and the guard was here to make it happen. You should be thanking me."

"You stupid oaf--you're the reason I'm here to begin with, remember?"

Gondar smiled again. "We can do this all day, but it's best that you get out of here. Stone may not burn, but all of these draperies and furnishings should be easy to torch, and..."

Ysidra's eyes widened in horror. Gondar thought for a moment that his words had frightened her, but he saw that her gaze was not directed at him but beyond him. He turned just in time to see a groping tentacle-like appendage rising up through the stone drain of the altar, reaching in his direction. This was a sight he had never beheld at the other temples; perhaps there was something to the priest's claim that this was the home of Balsoth himself. With one arm, he swept Ysidra out of the way while his other hand grasped at the short-handled axe now hanging by his side.

Even as he lifted the axe, he could see the change in the form and structure of the limb before him. In less than a second, what was gelatinous became rigid--it almost seemed to Gondar as if it had become bony or tusk-like. Its motion became purposeful as it first pointed, then lunged in his direction. He dodged the main thrust, suffering only a shallow incision across his bicep. As he pulled back, he struck with the axe but lacked sufficient leverage to deliver a killing blow. Instead, his axe glanced off the stone-like surface, doing little damage.

The appendage swayed, snakelike, pulling back and then drifting from side to side. It was searching for him--or was it searching for his motion? Testing his theory, Gondar moved his arm, which was below the table's edge and thus invisible to the creature before him. He grasped the ankle of the dead priest and began to pull. The dead weight of the corpse shifted; the body slid to the floor in a heap. Sensing the motion, the appendage struck again. Seeing his opportunity, Gondar slashed with the axe--not at the bony end of the appendage, but at the soft, bloated, slimy flesh of the lower end of the extremity, where it rose above the stone hole in the altar. The limb offered little resistance; it fell to the floor in a spray of translucent crimson fluid, spasming and writhing. Gondar hacked at it a second time, and a third, cutting deep into the soft tissue until there was no motion.

Gondar wiped the ichor from his face with the back of his muscular forearm as he turned to address Ysidra. "A moment later and it would be *me* lying there and not this hellspawn. If you had-n't..."

His ceased in mid-sentence. Ysidra, still wide-eyed, lay on the ground before him--but her eyes saw nothing, and her terrified ex-pression would never change. Just below the collarbone was a jagged gash. The blow that he had dodged had found another target--the young woman whose shocked gaze had first alerted Gondar to the abominable threat behind him.

Gondar knelt and brushed her face with the back of his hand. Then, with gentle touch uncharacteristic for such a mighty warrior, he closed her eyes.

After muttering a childhood blessing that he only vaguely re-membered, Gondar walked to the temple's back wall and tugged at the tapestries. As each panel fell, he piled it on the altar. With a little lamp oil, the fabrics would suffice as kindling. But he wasn't just pre-paring to torch the temple; he was also searching for something.

Behind the fifth tapestry panel, he found it. To the unin-formed, it would have appeared to be nothing more than a mis-matched stone. But early on in his quest to destroy the temples of Balsoth, a guard eager to live had told Gondar of the secret stone. The secret and the guard had died within moments of one another.

Gondar pressed. The stone gave. He put both arms into it, muscles bulging. As he did so, a passageway to the stone's left re-vealed itself. Gondar holstered his axe in the metal loop that hung from his belt. Unsheathing his sword, he stepped into the shadowed passage.

The stone steps descended in a spiral towards the temple's inner chamber. The priests referred to it as a sanctorum, but Gondar scoffed at that: there was nothing sacred about this place. As he made his way down the steps, he could hear a noise from below--a wet burbling sound unlike any he had heard in the other temples.

By the time he reached the last step, the noise became loud-er, sharper--a moist, fleshy sound that raised the hairs on his neck. He stepped into the chamber, and in the wavering light of the oil lamps, he saw the thing responsible.

The amorphous mass reminded him of the countless jellyfish that he had seen during his years aboard ships. This creature was a translucent red in color, however, with the richest ruby hues radiating from the amputated limb whose extension now lay on the floor of the temple. But it was already healing, re-forming itself--and it was just one of many tentacles that branched from the swollen, gelatinous body. At the very center of the mass was a dark spot---the bloodstone from which this creature had arisen, no doubt. Now Gondar realized that the bloodstone wasn't an egg at all--instead it was an unholy *seed*, watered with the blood of the sacrificial victims.

He stepped towards the mass, which seemed to sense his presence. A tentacle whipped in his direction--but rather than striking at him, it stopped in front of him. The shape changed, becoming bulbous, then elongated, reminiscent of the body of a snake that had consumed a large rodent. Gondar stood at ready, sword prepared to strike, as he watched the tentacle undulate, swell, and reshape itself.

Within a matter of moments, the end of the tentacle began to engorge, taking on the shape of an embryonic figure. The shape continued to coalesce, with rudimentary arms emerging from either side and a misshapen head at the end of the appendage. Those arms, while roughly human in shape, moved with a fluidity that betrayed the absence of a bony skeleton beneath the flesh. But even that was changing as the transformation continued; beneath the translucence of the tentacle Gondar could see a jagged opacity as a stony skeleton crystallized. But it was the form of the body, not the skeletal growth within, that disturbed him in its familiarity: it was taking the shape of Ysidra, whose body lay lifeless on the floor above.

For a moment, the transformation had mesmerized Gondar. Now it repulsed him. He turned his and witnessed similar transformations taking place at the end of other tentacles, each in varying degrees of readiness. One he could recognize as the dead priest, another as the guard. Beyond that a form was just emerging--the largest of the homunculi that the creature was manipulating like demonic puppets. Gondar rarely looked into a mirror, but he had seen his own reflection recently enough to recognize the distorted shape of his own body.

With a roar of rage, he rushed forward, slashing at the almost-complete shape of Ysidra. His blow would have been enough to cut through a normal human being--but the stony skeleton forming inside these creatures was stronger than bone. Gondar hesitated, then remembered the strategy that had proven so effective in the temple above. Rather than slashing at the form, he directed his sword at the amorphous tentacle that manipulated the unholy effigy. As he struck, the corrupted form of Ysidra opened its mouth as if to scream--but lacking lungs, it unleashed its torment and anger in silence. Then the disconnected limb fell to the ground, and its motions quickly ceased.

Next fell the form of the priest, then the guard. It had not been his intention to attack them first; he had hoped to amputate the appendage that mimicked him in form, since it was more massive than the others--and he knew that could not be a good thing. But the creature seemed to know his plans, and it had moved the other figures like pawns on a chessboard. Gondar was able to deal with them, but each passing second allowed his own repugnant double to gain strength and solidity.

He rushed forward, sweeping his sword in a downward arc intended to strike at the soft flesh of the lower half of the appendage. His replica parried--not with a sword, but with its right arm. The sword slashed through the outer flesh, but its swinging motion halted abruptly when it struck the stony skeleton beneath. The fleshy thing looked at Gondar intently and grinned--just as Gondar himself had grinned with battle lust so many times before.

Gondar slashed a second time; again, the creature parried with its arm. A third strike, a third parry--but this time Gondar could see that the hand was beginning to reshape into the same sort of rigid spike that the creature had used to kill Ysidra. He realized that he had only moments before the transformation was complete.

He thought for a second, then swung his sword again--a bold, powerful overhead swing that came down directly onto the skull of his unholy double. Had his opponent been human, the blow would have been sufficient to cleave him to collarbone. As it was, Gondar managed to drive the blade into the stony skull... where it remained.

The devil jerked its misshapen head backwards, ripping the sword from Gondar's grasp, then swung its head forward again, using the hilt of the sword as a cudgel to knock Gondar to the ground. The duplicate grinned again, sword jutting from its skull, as it lifted the spike to thrust it through the body of the warrior before him.

But the duplicate had failed to account for Gondar's axe, which the warrior had removed from its holster. Now he could see the soft tissue of the lower appendage in front of him, unguarded. He looked up to see his duplicate pulling its arm back for a deathblow; sensing that this was his last chance, Gondar swung with animal rage. The axe met no resistance as it sliced through the soft flesh, and his doppelganger fell to the ground.

Balsoth continued to move its few remaining tentacles ineffectually, its vitality sapped by the many wounds Gondar had inflicted. Gondar placed his boot on the face of his duplicate, then ripped the sword from the bony skull. He worked swiftly and effectively, wielding the sword like a warrior and the axe like an executioner. Balsoth's fetid ichor soaked Gondar, but it meant nothing to him. He had been covered in the blood of his enemies before; gods willing, he would be so covered many more times before it was *his* blood that flowed over his body.

The unstable flesh lost its reddish color, turning gray and gelatinous. In the center of the mass, Gondar could see a small, stony core. The shrunken mass of the bloodstone, no doubt, largely depleted by Balsoth's assaults. He had destroyed the other bloodstones; this was the last. Once it was shattered and the temple was destroyed, the horror of Balsoth would be done.

Gondar holstered his axe, slashed with his sword, then thrust his hand into Balsoth's remains. A moist, sucking sound resonated in the stone chamber as he felt around in the slowly seething mass; then he withdrew, an object in his hand.

But what he held no longer resembled the dull, asymmetrical rocks he had shattered at the other temples. Instead, this was a single fist-sized gem, deep red in color, crystalline and multifaceted. For a brief moment, Gondar considered hammering the stone into a thousand shards. Then he realized that a blood ruby could purchase a great deal of wine, a good horse, new armor, a sumptuous feast, and the attention of several lovely women... And eventually, a libation in honor of a dead woman named Ysidra.

LONO AND THE PIT OF PUNHAKI

by Paul R. McNamee

The yearly tribute festival spread from the coastal village onto the beach. Children splashed in the waves, adults sang and plucked musical instruments or beat on drums. Outrigger canoes arrived to cheers and greetings. Tributes were unloaded, placed at the base of the wooden throne which had been moved to the shore for the event. The king nodded in pleasure at each tribute received.

Lono, chief of the Maoli, found Makani seated on a long bench, cracking crabs and flirting with the women placing flowers around his neck.

"Why don't they roast the boar on the first day instead of the last?" the ka-man asked. The women departed, giggling and gossiping as they went. Undoubtedly, they had been asking Makani for magic in love and fortune.

"Who could prove their worth if the boar had already been hunted before the festival?" Lono asked as he sat beside his friend. "Would you leave all the glory to the Aurwa? There is an abundance of food."

"Fish and crabs," Makani scowled at the purple-gray goo on his fingertips. "And root-mash. I need something substantial to fill my belly."

Makani was stout but not rotund. A broad muscular chest and large arms framed his small paunch. His dark hair was cropped short over eyes gray as flint. His face was round with hard lines of cheekbones and a prominent chin with a sight cleft.

As the day wore on, the people glanced nervously at their king. He drummed impatient fingers on the arm of his throne. A summons went through the crowd and the sub-chiefs assembled in front of King Kapua, Chief of chiefs.

216

Kapua turned a baleful eye upon Lono. Lono folded his arms across his chiseled chest and met the king's gaze with equal fortitude. The king was large, taller than Lono and wider than Makani. Some of the king's girth was fat but underneath were strong muscles.

Lono was muscular, tall and lean. His curly brown hair just reached the nape of his neck. A scar on his left cheek was the only blemish on his handsome, square-jawed face.

After a moment, the glaring contest ended. Kapua leaned back into his throne and the wood protested.

"The Kanaka are your people, Lono," Kapua said. "Why are they not here?"

"They are their own people now," Lono replied. "I do not answer for them. I am not their keeper."

Seven years earlier, a combination of volcanic eruption and strong magic had created a new island. The Kanaka had split from the Maoli and had settled there.

Two years later, Kapua, a chief of the Aurwa, had consolidated the islands under his one rule. He was a formidable warrior. His ascension to kingship had not softened his combat prowess.

Kapua feigned disinterest in Lono's flippancy. His stubby fingers traced the contours of the grotesque face carved in the heel of his leaf-shaped, hardwood patu war-paddle.

"You, Lono, chief of the Maoli, are a subject of this kingdom," Kapua said. "Is this so?"

"It is."

"As a loyal subject, I task you. Find out why the Kanaka and their chief, Matiu, are not here to pay their tribute."

Lono nodded in begrudging obedience.

Satisfied, the king shifted his bulk on the royal seat, trying to get comfortable. The seat had been made for smaller men but ceremony and tradition were important.

"I will not be slighted in this way." Kapua shook his head, his thick black hair waving with the motion. "Matiu must return with you and with his tribute before the end of the festival."

A half of one day had already passed. It would take two-thirds of a day to reach Kanaka - if the sea cooperated. They wouldn't have much time. Five days would mark the great feast and the end of the festival.

"Go!" Kapua ordered. "If Matiu will not return with you, be sure to return with his tribute."

"What if Matiu will not pay the tribute?" Lono asked.

"Then I will be most displeased," the king answered with menace in his voice.

***

Four of his Maoli warriors and Makani joined Lono on the voyage. The winds were not fair, the plated leaf sail caught no breeze. They rowed hard in the dark, using the stars for navigation.

"I could almost taste that boar," Makani muttered ruefully. His muscles rippled as he paddled his oar in the swelling water. "King or not - who is Kapua to order us to run errands?"

"He favored the Kanaka." Lono said. The civil discord between the Maoli and Kanaka had aligned many non-combatant chiefs into voicing support for one side or the other. "Apparently he favored them enough for them to believe they have impunity now."

Makani grunted. "To save face, he puts the burden on us to prove he did not back an ungrateful ally."

Lono nodded. Kapua's command had another potential purpose. Lono was favored among the sub-chiefs. Lono had no desire to be king over all the tribes but Kapua did not think the same way as Lono. The king might assume Lono thought as Kapua would think. If Lono failed to return with the Kanaka tribute, what form would the jealous king's displeasure take?

Their outrigger canoe approached the island of Kanaka just after dawn. The waves washed gently onshore and the timid sea breeze listlessly stirred palm leaves on the edge of the forest. No other movement caught Lono's eye. No people were at the shore. No birds flew in the sky. The stillness sent gooseflesh crawling over Lono's body.

Makani grunted, mumbled something quietly under his breath. Lono saw the unease in the faces of the other warriors, too. They didn't need a ka-man's talents to tell them something bode ill on the island.

After beaching their canoe, the six men marched along the strand, spears at the ready. They fanned out to cover ground between the lapping waves and the edge of the forest. At the first creek, they found a trail into the thick rainforest.

The trail led to a ruined village, not far inland. A faint scent of stale smoke still wafted among the blackened husks of burned dwellings. When they found the heaped pile of human bones, they knew the conflagration had been no accident.

"What happened here?" asked Ano. He was tall and lanky but his muscles and posture were as firm as his heftier companions.

Makani knelt, pulled a bone from the pile. A few skulls rolled down and settled at the bottom.

"Leg bone." Makani examined the knobbed end of a femur. "Gnawed and cracked for marrow."

"Ghouls," said Kamea. He was an older warrior, gray-haired and covered in more tattoos than any of the others. His voice strangled to a whisper. "Spirits of the hungry and damned."

"Or man-eaters." Lono was in a grim mood. He flashed a toothy smile, anyway.

"Man-eaters. No ghouls here," Makani said. He nonchalantly tossed the bone at Kamea's feet.

"What do we do now?" Holokai asked. He was a portly one, the same size as Makani.

"I don't think we're going to find Kapua's tribute here," Lono tapped his toe against the heap of bones.

"Unless you want to pick apart this pile."

***

Deeper in the interior of the island, a second village had not been put to the torch but it was deserted. Damaged dwellings still stood. Bloodstains and discarded weapons indicated a recent struggle.

Nohea looked to the sky. "It grows dark. We should return to our canoe. Get back to Kapua. Let him send a proper war party."

"Do you want to be the one to show Kapua your empty hands?" Lono asked. "He might cut them off."

"We cannot bring back a tribute we don't have," Ano argued.

"I agree with Lono," Makani said. "We must bring back some-thing - information, at least. If we return with nothing, Kapua will brand us cowards - say we ran off like frightened game.".

"We sleep here," Lono said.

"In the open," Holokai added. "I don't want to be ambushed in a hut."

It was good advice, and Lono did not argue it.

***

Lono woke. Makani had been shaking his shoulders. The ka-man clamped a hand over Lono's mouth.

"Sleep when you're dead, eh? Wake the others. Men are com-ing."

Lono rubbed his eyes, nudged the nearest slumberer. Dawn twilight steeped their surroundings. Clouds would keep the sun sleeping late into the morning.

"I don't hear anything." Lono sniffed at the light breeze. "I smell nothing."

"There!" Kamea hissed in a strangled whisper and pointed to-ward the edge of the forest. Furtive shadows moved among the trees.

Lono gave a silent order with his hand. The other men spread through the village, hiding behind dwellings and tree trunks.

Men of reddish skin, faces streaked with ochre paint stripes, emerged from the trees and moved into the village. They clutched clubs inlaid with jagged black fragments of rock. Three were swinging slings, waiting for something to move.

Ano struck first. He had maneuvered between the forest's edge and the back walls of the dwellings. He flanked the slingers and charged. His spear found purchase in the belly of one. He crossed the space to the next man, pummeled the slinger with bare fists.

The third warrior lobbed his stone before Ano reached him. The main body of warriors clustered in groups of twos and threes and attacked the Maoli.

Lono turned his lean body, avoided a swinging club and closed the gap with his opponent. His patu caught the man under the ster-

220

num. The man dropped his club, bent over clutching his chest. The patu swung again and crushed the man's temple.

Two more warriors stood in Lono's path. One grinned a mouthful of teeth filed to points.

A large club swung at Lono's head. He barely deflected the blow with his patu. The other opponent's club jabbed. Lono felt the air punched out of his belly, felt the sharp cut of the obsidian nuggets. He withstood the blow and did not double over. Enraged and breathless, he fought in mad desperation. He dropped his patu, clutched at the neck of the one man, and spun the man's body around to serve as a shield. The other attacker tried to step around. Lono tripped the man he was holding, let go of his throat and sent the two men bowling to the ground.

They scrambled but Lono was faster. A few hard punches disabled them long enough for Lono to snatch up his patu and finish them.

Lono wheezed in air, forcing his lungs to breathe despite the blow to his stomach. He had a moment to survey the rest of the fight.

Kamea was down, two men over him, their clubs rising and descending. The blows crushed the old warrior's tattooed body.

Nohea, the youngest of Lono's party, fared better. Three red bodies lay at his feet. He let out a war cry as another duo rushed him. A club swing nicked the top of his left shoulder. His shark-toothed knife slashed across the club wielder's throat in a spray of ragged crimson. Another red warrior raised his club and Nohea grabbed his arm. His opponent clutched Nohea's wrist to prevent the knife from striking. Grappling, the two fighters fell to the ground. Nohea's wrist slipped free and he sliced his knife through the man-eater's groin. The red warrior shuddered and died.

Holokai and Makani surrounded the largest of the warriors. He kept them at bay with deft club work; swinging, thrusting, turning. The two men couldn't flank him. The two warriors who had killed Kamea ran to assist their comrade.

Lono killed one man with a patu strike to the base of the neck. Holokai wielded his shark-toothed dagger, gutting the second man.

Weaponless, Ano leapt, his spindly limbs tackling the last man

-eater. He brought the large man down, straddled his body and punched hard at his head. After a time, the man was still. Ano leapt to his feet, swept up a spear. The enemy warrior rose to his knees.

Ano drew back his arms to plunge a spear into the man's guts. The warrior waited, chin held high and proud.

"No, wait!" Lono took the spear and stabbed a long, deep gash in the man's calf. The man collapsed clutching his ruined leg. "I want him alive, for now. I have questions."

***

Their prisoner had a reddish skin tone, unlike their own swarthy appearance. The bright feathers of the man's bracelets and anklets were from birds unknown to the Maoli. His teeth were filed to points like the other man-eaters. His wide smile was unnerving.

Lono had made a mistake in his desire to question a prisoner. They did not understand his language. After a few frustrating attempts, they learned the man was Aztoi, which Lono took to mean the name of his people, not his personal name.

Makani picked up a stick, scratched on the ground. He drew the island of the Aurwa, the island of the Maoli, and the Kanaka's island.

The Aztoi took the stick, drew a very long line eastward across the earthen map and squiggled a coast line. He did not draw a circular island. If his home was an island, it was a large one.

"They came from far," Ano said.

"Why?" Lono wondered. "A long voyage for what? This island is hardly worth raiding from so far away."

Lono kept shrugging, aping a confused face. He drew lines across the dirt ocean.

The Aztoi scribbled furiously. When he was finished, Lono and his companions were silent for a long moment. They all understood what the Aztoi had implied.

"The Kanaka attacked them first?" Holokai scarcely believed his own words.

"I have never heard of this great land to the east. How did the Kanaka even know of it?" Lono wondered.

The Aztoi uttered a word Lono did not know but inferred from the fear, respect and bile in the man's tone.

"Magic. Evil magic," Lono echoed.

Makani nodded.

"I didn't think the Kanaka had a ka-man among them," Ano said.

"This island is teeming with magic, not all of it good." Makani shrugged. "Some spirit here must have whispered dark words in someone's ear. Made a new ka-man. I feel sorcery at work."

The men shifted on their feet, nervous and wary. The benign folk magic of the ka-man was an ordinary element of their lives. Standing in the middle of an island crawling with the slowly dissipating energy of its magical creation brought superstitious fear and dread.

"Where are they now? Where are the Aztoi?" Lono asked. "Where are the Kanaka?"

The captured warrior understood the thrust of the questions. He drew a battle in the dirt. A battle the Aztoi had apparently lost. He drew a point on the Kanaka island's coast, further northeast. He drew multiple figures of men, then cut off their heads with a line in the dirt.

"Executions," Ano said.

"Sacrifices." Makani waved a hand. "I sense evil. I can nearly smell the blood."

"We know where to find the Kanaka now." Holokai said. "Let's collect the tribute and be done with them."

"What of their Aztoi prisoners?" Nohea asked.

"What of them? It's none of our concern," Ano's face was set and stern.

"We cannot let the Kanaka serve dark gods," Makani said.

"Not our concern," Ano said. "We're here to gather Kapua's tribute. Let Kapua decide what is to be done."

"We will go to the place. What we do when we get there," Lono shrugged. "That will depend on what we learn."

"And this one?" Ano indicated the Aztoi with a sideways jerk of his head.

Lono could not find fault with a desire for revenge. Loathe to kill in cold blood, Lono let the Aztoi live. They trussed the man with woven cord retrieved from one of the huts. Lono would cut him free when they were finished. If they failed to return, the Aztoi would die, too, unless he was very good at escaping.

***

Ahead, the beach halted where a jutting cliff stretched out into the water. Where the beach met the crook of cliff and forest, trees had been cleared. In the clearing, a large building had been constructed from carved blocks of black volcanic stone. The edifice was unlike any Lono had seen. The facade featured two flights of stairs reaching to the flat roof. Wooden doors to the interior sat between the staircases. A carved visage of a bloated toad face surrounded the frame. The surface of the door bulged like a tongue, making the entrance an exaggerated mouth.

"That should have taken years to build," Lono said.

"Sorcery." Makani spit on the ground.

"Not like yours?"

"Coconut oil in water. Floating, mixing but separate. Clinging and greasy, tainting anything it touches."

"What is it for?"

"A temple," Makani said. "A house for a god."

"What god?"

"A dark god. No friend to us, for certain." Makani bristled. He rubbed a nervous hand through his hair, rubbed his skin as though to push away the gooseflesh on his chest and arms. Whatever Makani sensed troubled the ka-man. He hadn't flinched an eye about the man-eaters but the temple made him as jumpy as Lono had ever seen him.

People lined the top of the square building. The colored plume headdresses, bracelets and anklets of the Aztoi stood out among their Kanaka captors.

The wind shifted and the stench of sulfur wafted through the air.

"Mud pits." Makani sneered. "I'd rather smell roasting boar."

"Stairs or the door?" Ano asked.

224

"Stairs." Nohea said.

Lono agreed. He didn't want to be an easy target for missile weapons.

"Talk or attack?" Makani asked.

"Observe." Lono chose the left staircase.

"Then attack?"

"Most likely."

The Kanakas watched them approach but they already had their hands full guarding their prisoners. Some undoubtedly wanted to attack but most recognized Lono and Makani. They knew Lono was a chief and deferred to his rank and to the laws of hospitality.

"Make way," Lono said. He gruffly shouldered people aside.

Reluctantly, the Kanakas parted for Lono's party to stand on the top of the wall. The center of the building had no roof. The open temple had been constructed around a natural phenomenon, a mud pit as large as a pond. The pit bubbled, hot moisture percolated the gray mud, steaming in a sulfurous reek. Lono had bathed in small mud pits. The stink had been an undercurrent and the mud had been pleasantly warm. The large pit of the temple stank and the heat came off it like fire.

On each of three of the four sides of the temple, a plank projected precariously over the boiling pit. The Kanakas poked and prodded the Aztoi into lines on each plank.

Oversized walkways from the front gate led around the edges of the pit. At the back wall another staircase ascended to a half-circle platform, set halfway up the wall. In a wedge formation, five Kanaka stood on the platform. Two women, lying prostrate; two men kneeling. At their head, a wizened Kanaka woman chanted and raised her arms over the gray pit.

She looked up at the people lining the wall and the Aztoi on the extended planks. She had not noticed Lono's arrival and her people had not dared to disrupt her proceedings.

"Punhaki! Now you will feel the burning flesh, the flowing blood of our enemies!" The woman's voice was rough and strong. "You will know it is I, Hopoe, of the Kanaka, who grants you this boon! Come forth, Punhaki! Come forth! We have mighty deeds for you to perform!"

"Hold, Hopoe!"

All fell silent and looked about in confusion for the source of the voice.

Hopoe glanced around, finally spotting Makani.

"Ka-man of the Maoli!" Hopoe cried. "You dare interrupt me?"

"He dares by my command." Lono raised his voice slightly but found he did not need to shout. The interior space of the temple amplified his words. "You know me."

"Aye, Lono chief of the Maoli." Hopoe's grin had no kindness. "We know you well."

Lono knew Hopoe, too. She was a wily woman who worked her way through men and position, even into her old age.

"I am not here as Maoli," Lono said. "King Kapua is displeased. Your tribute is lacking this year. Where is Matiu? Where is your chief?"

"There no chief here! Only Hopoe!"

The Kanakas murmured. They either liked their new queen or were terrified of her magic.

"What have you to say to Kapua, your king?" Lono asked.

"Say to Kapua - he no longer is our king and he will receive his due tribute soon." Hopoe raised her arms again. She gave a curt nod of her graying head.

The Kanaka guards shoved. Some Aztoi resisted but with tied hands they could not maneuver. They fell off the planks, screaming to their scalding, drowning deaths in the thick, boiling gray mud.

The ka-woman chanted frantically, unnaturally raising her voice over the screams, keeping her concentration focused.

"Come forth!" The woman cried. "With the blood of our enemies, I birth you from the pit to the earth!"

Then she spoke words Lono did not understand. The language tore at the fabric of the sky and the trees, men winced, women wailed. Only Makani failed to react, other than a grim determination appearing on his face and set jaw.

"What is she saying?"

"Abhorrent words." The ka-man instinctively signed a ward.

226

"Words not meant for man to speak. Yet she knows them."

"As do you."

Makani ignored the comment.

"She speaks now of water." Makani's eyes widened. "She speaks of wind over water. Lono! She seeks to grant it power of wind -- to travel over water! She will send it against the Maoli!"

"What? What does she mean to send?"

In the pit, mud churned. Bubbles rose to the surface in a sudden roil. The flat, boiling surface of gray disrupted into waves. Something broke the surface. When the mud dripped away, Lono saw an enormous head, with fiery eyes.

The thing waded from the mud pit, pulled itself up onto the walkway. It left charcoal footprints smoldering in the wood as it walked.

The demonic beast stood to the height of two and a half tall men. Its rotund toad torso stood on spindly legs. Four skinny arms sprouted from its body at random points. Each arm ended in an oversized hand with elongated fingers. Heat poured off the creature like lava.

"Kill the Maoli!" Hopoe shrieked. "Kill them!"

Both the demon and the Kanaka responded to the ka-woman's orders.

Nohea swung his patu, crushing a Kanaka face. Another Kanaka thrust his spear under the young warrior's chin and into his throat. Nohea grabbed the shaft and pulled the overeager Kanaka to both their deaths in the roiling mud.

Lono and his remaining companions fought their way to the stairs. As they descended, a spear transfixed Ano; his lifelessly body tumbled down the steps. They reached the bottom and the fiery mud demon smashed through the heavy wooden double-door which exploded in splinters. The creature took three great strides and blocked their path.

Lono ran swiftly, dodged a burning hand. His patu edge cracked against Punhaki's shin.

The demon did not notice the blow. Lono's hand ached as though he had struck stone or hardwood. He had expected shattered bone. The demon's thin limbs were not as frail as they appeared.

Makani was at his side, knocking away clutching fingers with his spear. Scorch marks burned into the wood where the weapon touched Punhaki.

They split in two directions as the demon stepped toward them. The thing twisted its torso back and forth, unsure which man to pursue.

The Kanakas bunched at the bottom of the temple stairs. From the top of the wall, Hopoe urged them to press the attack.

One of the Kanaka let out a battle cry and rushed at Makani. The demon saw easy prey, grabbed the man unawares. The man screamed in agony as the bony fingers seared his skin and the smell of burnt flesh and burnt hair filled the air.

The Kanakas hesitated to rush past the demon to attack Lono and his companions.

Makani pressed their mistrust.

"See!" The ka-man shouted, pointed up at Hopoe. "She can't control Punhaki. No one can! He will kill you as soon as kill us or the Aztoi!"

As if to demonstrate the ka-man's words, the demon swung a hand into the warriors bunched at the bottom of the stairs. The creature couldn't miss and men went sailing, some onto the sand, some cracking their skulls and bones hard against the stone wall.

Hopoe screamed at Punhaki in frustration, shouted commands, gestured signs with her hand in an attempt to direct the demon.

Lono did not know if she could take control of the demon and he wasn't going to take the risk.

"Enough of that witch!"

Lono grabbed a spear, ran under the demon, veered toward the less populated staircase. In a red fury of spraying blood and cracking bone, he bludgeoned through three opponents. His momentum faltered when he met a Kanaka twice his size. A jagged scar crossed over one of the man's eyes.

The man screamed at Lono. Rather than stabbing with his over-sized spear as Lono expected, the man swung the weapon overhead and down in a clubbing action. Lono, expecting a thrust, misstepped his dodge. The sharp edge of the spearhead sliced into the

228

skin of Lono's right shoulder but didn't penetrate into muscle.

Lono winced at the stinging pain and ignored the warm, red blood flowing along his arm.

The stairs gave the large man added height but left his legs vulnerable to leverage. Lono slid his spear sideways, and the shaft snaked across one shin and behind the other calf. Lono twisted the spear. The scarred man tumbled roughly down the stairs.

Lono ascended two-thirds of the staircase. He met Hopoe's gaze and the old woman feared for her life. She had no time to work magic to save herself.

Lono motioned to hurl the spear but hissed in pain at the slice in his shoulder. The old woman disappeared from his line of sight. He shifted the spear to his left hand and awkwardly tested throwing motions as he mounted the remaining stairs.

At the top of the wall, a cluster of Aztoi had freed their bonds. Even as Lono hurled the spear at Hopoe's fleeing back, an Aztoi grabbed the old woman. Lono's weak throw implanted the spear in the back of Hopoe's thigh even as the Aztoi threw her into the muddy pit.

Below, Punhaki roared and men screamed as he tore into their ranks in a bloody fury. Apparently, he had felt the ka-woman's death keenly but the severed bond had not proven fatal to the demon. The Kanaka warriors fled. The freed Aztois descended to the ground, grabbed weapons from fallen warriors and blocked their enemies from disappearing into the jungle.

The demon waded among the battling men, dealing burning death.

Lono fled down the stairs, found Makani crouched behind a rock outcropping. The ka-man tended Holokai, who had taken a wound in the side.

"The witch?" Makani asked.

"Dead."

"Good. Now we just kill the demon, eh?"

"You have an idea?"

"A good one." Makani winked.

Lono could scarcely believe the ka-man's audacity to enjoy the moment.

"How do we bring it down?"

"Water." Makani said. "Maybe."

"Maybe?"

"Hopoe tried to grant it the power of wind - to travel over water. We stopped her before she could call on the wind. Think what water would do to hot mud."

Lono looked over his shoulder. They were close to the shore but the sea felt miles away.

"Maybe we should just leave," Lono said. "If it can't cross water, let it stay here."

"Leave it here, some other ka-man might find it -- use it. Or it might find a way over water eventually. It will not take kindly to the people who left it in exile."

Lono knew his duty as chief. He had to protect his people. Even as he had suggested fleeing, he knew he couldn't. Besides, he was warrior and not one to run away from a fight.

"It's a demon but not a very clever one," Makani said.

"You think it will just follow us into the water?"

"Get it to the beach," Makani said. "That will be close enough."

"Close enough for what?"

Makani turned, ran along the strand toward the water.

Lono pulled his patu from his waistband. He knew the weapon was useless against the demon but it gave comfort. He approached the scene of battle, hollering to attract the demon's attention.

"Punhaki! Punhaki, you filth of stink!"

The demon ignored Lono's petitions.

"Hopoe!" Lono yelled. The name caught Punhaki's attention. He turned his head, red eyes glaring at Lono.

"Hopoe is dead!" Lono decided to embellish the truth. He thumped his chest. "I killed her! Me!"

The demon roared and stepped toward Lono. Using the distraction, the Kanakas rushed through the Aztois and into the rainforest. The Aztois hesitated, watching a lone madman scream and challenge a demon. Then vengeance overruled fascination and they gave chase into the forest.

"Just us now, Punhaki!" Lono yelled. "Surely the mighty demon of stinking mud can't be bested by two little men?"

The demon, if it did not completely understand Lono's words, understood the taunting tone. It growled a low rumbling thunder in its throat and lunged.

Lono leapt backward. He did not run, did not show his back to the damned creature. He continued to gaze into its baleful toad-face.

A few more taunts and deft leaps brought the demon onto the hard-packed wet sand of the beach. Punhaki stopped, glanced down at the damp sand, looked quizzically at Lono.

Makani waited, standing in the surf. The ka-man held his arms aloft. He chanted, calling to spirits of wind and water. Scudding white clouds slowed, hung in place over the beach and turned gray, heavy with rain. The wind blew hard over the water.

The ka-man's chant grew louder. Unlike the witch's grating words, Makani spoke of natural powers and the immense weight of the words formed dread in Lono's heart. Dread of storms too big for man to face, the power of cataclysm. Hopoe's magic had torn at the fabric of the world. Makani's magic called on the powers of the fabric of the world.

Punhaki sensed the power and the magic. Fear and uncertainty tinged the demon's screams and roars.

Rain poured in a localized torrent, drenching the demon, the temple, the rainforest where the remaining Aztoi warriors slaughtered the Kanaka. The demon surged forward toward Makani. As the demon stepped, it met resistance. Punhaki's gray, muddy skin steamed. The gushing rain cooled the creature and the wind dried and hardened its body.

The demon howled.

Behind Makani, a great wall of water rose from the sea. The ka-man's chant could still be heard, impossible over the noise of the wind and rain and demonic cries of fury. The demon saw the giant wave, poised to strike. Punhaki turned to flee inland but his brittle body seized.

Makani, face rictus with the effort of magic and controlling the elements, let his chanting voice carry one instruction.

"To the temple walls!"

Lono grabbed Holokai's arm, pulled the big man to his feet, pushed and dragged him along. Holokai screamed in agony as the wound in his side tore but he did not fall. They ran.

The wave crashed down. The surging water chased the two Maoli up the stairs. The water flooded into the jungle of the island. Screeches of terror replaced the battle cries of the remaining Kanaka and Aztoi.

When the water receded, they saw Makani standing in the exact spot where he had disappeared under the crashing wave. Before him on the sand, the body of Punhaki lay still.

"The demon is dead?" Lono called down.

Makani looked up. He appeared tired but unhurt. Lono did not understand how the ka-man survived the crashing wave. Then again, Lono did not understand magic and had no desire to.

"Yes." Makani wiped salt water from his eyes. "What of the man-eaters -- the Aztoi -- and the Kanaka?"

Lono listened for a moment. He heard no sounds from the rainforest.

"If any are left alive, they will probably kill each other to the last before they stop."

Makani nodded in agreement and walked toward the temple.

"What tribute do we bring Kapua now?" Holokai asked.

Lono stared at the demonic carcass for a few moments, then he borrowed Holokai's shark-toothed knife and descended the temple stairs.

***

The three men sailed the outrigger and arrived before the festival of tribute had ended. The feast was ready. Lono smelled roasting pig, the aroma of fresh cut fruit and cracked coconuts. They marched to their audience with the king.

Kapua leaned forward on his throne, looming like a buzzard.

"We waited to begin the feast," Kapua said. "What of Matiu, the Kanaka chief?"

"Dead before we arrived," Lono said. "I believe the woman Hopoe must have assassinated him."

"Hopoe?"

Lono shrugged. "She appeared to be their leader."

"Hopoe led the Kanaka?" Kapua was incredulous.

"The Kanaka woman gave herself to evil spirits," Makani said. "She became a ka-woman. Her people foolishly followed her. They paid the price. Dealing with demons is barter never won."

Kapua considered the information in silence while quiet whispers spread through the crowd like a fire across dry grass.

"You!" Kapua pointed at Holokai. "What of this?"

"They speak true, majesty. The Kanaka went mad. They sailed far and captured men called Aztoi, sacrificed them. The witch called forth a demon. Many died. They might all be dead now."

The whispers flew through the crowd again, then faded. Kapua again pondered with deliberation. A wry, toothy grin crossed his round face. His eyes beaded with mistrust and his nostrils flared with stoking anger. He stared hard at Lono.

"Then what tribute from the Kanaka could you bring to me?"

Lono placed a wrapped object in front of Kapua's throne. Makani pulled away the blanket. The odor of rotten meat and sulfur filled the air.

The demon's giant bony hand lay on the ground.

"What is this disgusting thing?" Kapua roared.

"The body of the demon was too large to bring back in our canoe," Lono explained.

The hand twitched. The crowd let out a collective gasp and some yelped in terror. Kapua's livid, angry face paled with fear.

"As you can see, your majesty, magic still resides in the hand." Makani grinned ruefully. "Fear not, it will dissipate. It was no easy demon to dispatch but Lono did so. He has killed many monsters in his time."

"A tribute to you, King Kapua," Lono said. "I believe the Kanaka have paid well."

Kapua considered the gift. Lono stood ready - for flight or fight, he did not know. There was a crafty readiness in Makani's eyes, too. If Kapua had grown tired of Lono's rising favor, it would be the moment for the king to strike. He could declare the gift an insult.

Men in Kapua's favor watched the scene, mindful, no doubt,

of where they had placed their weapons.

Kapua studied the hand, Lono, and Makani for long moments. Then the king laughed and eased his considerable bulk against the back of his throne.

"We accept the tribute of the Kanaka." Kapua clapped his large hands. "All tributes have been paid! Let the celebration begin!"

The night was memorable with tales told both old and new. Many compliments were paid to the bravery of the Maoli. The extravagant feast surpassed previous years' celebrations. And the roast boar was succulent.

Lono and Makani ate well.

Appendix One

Kharrn's Published Adventures.

"The Beautiful Lady Without Pity" *Widowmakers: an Anthology of Dark Fiction*. Bloodshot Books 2014.

"What Rough Beast" (With James A. Moore)_*White Noise Press* Chapbook 2015

"Black Tide" (With James A. Moore) *SNAFU: Black Ops.* Cohesion Press 2017

Bleeding Through: Clickers Forever: A Tribute to J.F. Gonzalez. Thunderstorm Books 2018

Appendix two

An Adrian Cole Bibliography

<u>NOVELS</u>

THE DREAM LORDS, volumes 1 – 3, published in USA by Kensington (Zebra paperbacks) 1975-77.
Reprinted.
New Dream Lords stories have been published in *Cirsova* magazine and these are "The Sealed City" (Issue #2), "A Death in Karkesh" (Issue #5), "Tear Down the Stars" (Issue #6) and the novella "In the Land of Hungry Shadows" (issue #7). Another novella, "The Blood Red Skies of Mars", will be in the forthcoming first issue of *Startling Stories.*

MADNESS EMERGING
PATHS IN DARKNESS
WARGODS OF LUDORBIS
THE LUCIFER EXPERIMENT
All published by Robert Hale (UK) in the late 1970s. (hardbacks)

MOORSTONES
THE SLEEP OF GIANTS
Published in the UK by Spindlewood Press early 1980s. (hardbacks)
Reprinted. (These are books for "young adults.")

THE OMARAN SAGA
Volume 1, **A PLACE AMONG THE FALLEN** Published in hardback in UK by Allen and Unwin and in the US by David Hartnell

All 4 volumes published in UK in paperback by Unwin (1990s) and in the US by Avon/Nova:
A PLACE AMONG THE FALLEN
THRONE OF FOOLS
KING OF LIGHT AND SHADOWS
THE GODS IN ANGER

STAR REQUIEM
All 4 volumes published in UK in paperback by Unwin and in the US by Avon/Nova (1990s):
MOTHER OF STORMS
THIEF OF DREAMS
WARLORD OF HEAVEN
LABYRINTH OF WORLDS

BLOOD RED ANGEL, published in paperback in the US by Avon/Nova (90s)
STORM OVER ATLANTIS, published in US by Wildside Press, 2001.

THE CRIMSON TALISMAN, published in the US by Wizards of the West Coast, 2001

THE VOIDAL Saga
Published in 3 volumes in the US by Wildside Press (vol 1 originally in 2001, vols 2 and 3 in 2011):

OBLIVION HAND
THE LONG REACH OF NIGHT
SWORD OF SHADOWS
These reprint all the stories that appeared in the 70s and early 80s in magazines and anthologies (Fantasy Crossroads etc) mainly in the US. Plus new material for the first time.

NIGHT OF THE HEROES, published by Wildside Press, US 2011.

YOUNG THONGOR
Short story anthology of stories by Lin Carter, edited by Adrian Cole

Short stories:

I have had about 50-100 short stories published, most notably:

In Lin Carter's **YEAR'S BEST FANTASY STORIES** series;
Eileen Datlow's **Year's Best Fantasy and Horror** series;
Hugh Lamb's horror anthologies (UK)
DARK VOICES 2 from Pan (UK) – ed Steve Jones/Dave Sutton
SHADOWS OVER INNSMOUTH – ed Steve Jones/Dave Sutton – various editions and reprints in UK and US
BOOK OF FRANKENSTEIN – ed Steve Jones
BOOK OF WEREWOLVES – ed Steve Jones – and reprints

My "**Treason in Zagadar**" REH pastiche of King Kull was published in 2 collections in UK, edited by Steve Jones. (**THE BOOK OF FANTASY AND THE SUPERNATURAL**)

My Elak of Atlantis pastiche, **BLOOD OF THE MOON GOD** was published in **Strange Tales** magazine, no 8, edited by Bob price (US) with a second Elak tale, "Witch Queen of Doom Island", published in *Worlds of the Unknown 1* and more new Elak tales to come from Skelos Press including the collection, **ELAK, KING OF ATLANTIS.**

NICK NIGHTMARE INVESTIGATES, Alchemy Press UK, 2014, collects the first arc of the occult detective stories and won the British Fantasy Award for Year's Best Collection. More Nick Nightmare stories have appeared in various publications (notably Weirdbook) and a second volume, **NIGHTMARE COCKTAIL**, is in preparation.

Quite a few of these stories and others have been translated into foreign language anthologies – in Italy, Holland, Belgium, Japan and Germany and there have been Russian editions of the Omaran Saga books.

APPENDIX THREE

Kharrn the Barbarian

The new anthology SNAFU: Black Ops dropped in Ebook form this Wednesday. It contains 'Black Tide', a story by James A. Moore and me, which features Jim's demon hunter/occult detective Jonathan Crowley teamed up with my character Kharrn. Kharrn is basically a 'Clonan' like Lin Carter's Thongor or Gardner Fox's Kothar. He's just still around.

I get a lot of questions about Kharrn. Mostly people want to know just how old he is. He and Crowley teamed up before in the WHITE NOISE PRESS Chapbook, 'What Rough Beast', which takes place in the Old West, and there were hints in the story that the two men had met before even earlier in the past. The answer to his age is really really old.

In his original conception, Kharrn was a time traveler. I wrote one short story 'The Silent History' which is unpublished, and now no longer canon, in which Kharrn was sent forth in time to the Victorian Age seeking vengeance. Later I wrote a second story, "Sailing to Darkness" which appeared at the late lamented MOORCOCK'S MISCELLANEY in which Kharrn took a trip on Moorcock's 'Ship that sails between worlds' (With Mike's kind permission). That one showed that Kharrn occasionally traveled in other dimensions.

When it came time to use the big warrior in another story, I decided that the time travel element was too hard to keep up with, so I changed Kharrn's origin to make him an immortal. His first published appearance was in Pete Kahle's anthology WIDOWMAKERS where Kharrn teamed up with Carnacki the Ghostfinder in a story called 'The Beautiful Lady Without Pity', a Christmas Country House Ghost Story with a Barbarian. Hey, I write what I like. (It also got me a mention in that year's Year's Best Horror collection.)

Later that year, Kharrn and Crowley ran into some werewolves in 'What Rough Beast'. Jim Moore and I have another crossover in the works called 'The Doll Maker' which sees the boys facing an Eldritch menace in Victorian London.

Oh, the reason Kharrn is spelled with two 'r's is that when I wanted to use the name Kharn for my Lord of the Rings Online avatar, the name was already taken. So I added a second 'r'. I got used to typing it that way and it stuck.

Anyway, 'Black Tide' reveals the most about Kharrn's past of any story so far, so if you're curious about the immortal Barbarian, give it a read.

79014611R00135

Made in the USA
Middletown, DE
06 July 2018